Praise for Mike Sager:

"I can recognize the truth in these Sager stories—demoralizing tales about the darkest possible side of wretched humanity."

—Hunter S. Thompson on *Scary Monsters and Super Freaks*

"Nobody alive today is writing better long magazine pieces than Mike Sager. If you want to find out what the gold standard looks like, or if you just want to read a breathtaking portrait of our motley nation, buy this book."

—Kurt Andersen on *Revenge of the Donut Boys*

"Sager writes in convincingly novelistic detail and supple pinpoint prose. Rating: A-" —*Entertainment Weekly* on *Revenge of the Donut Boys*

"Sager plays Virgil in the Modern American Inferno." —*Kirkus Reviews*

"Equally fearless and tenacious, Sager goes back to the gutter again and again to wrest art from the muck. His readers are lucky."

—*Austin American-Statesman*

"Now a writer at large for *Esquire,* Sager is a standard bearer for the type of new journalism that made that magazine famous. . . . From the rich and famous to the people you've never heard of, Sager makes them come alive in a way that few writers can." —*Baltimore City Paper*

"Mike Sager writes about places and events we seldom get a look at—and people from whom we avert our eyes. But with Sager in command of all the telling details, he shows us history, humanity, humor, sometimes even honor. He makes us glad to live with our eyes wide open."

—Richard Ben Cramer, Pulitzer Prize–winning author of *What It Takes* and *Joe Dimaggio: The Hero's Life*

"Mike Sager is the beat poet of American journalism. . . . Equal parts reporter, ethnographer, stylist, and cultural critic, Sager has for twenty years carried the tradition of Tom Wolfe on his broad shoulders, chronicling the American scene and psyche. Nobody does it sharper, smarter, or with more style."

—Walt Harrington, award-winning author of *The Everlasting Stream*

Also by Mike Sager

Scary Monsters and Super Freaks: Stories of Sex, Drugs, Rock 'n' Roll and Murder

Revenge of the Donut Boys: True Stories of Lust, Fame, Survival and Multiple Personality

Deviant Behavior

A Novel of Sex, Drugs, Fatherhood, and Crystal Skulls

Mike Sager

Black Cat
New York
a paperback original imprint of Grove/Atlantic, Inc.

Printed in the United States of America
Published simultaneously in Canada

FIRST EDITION

ISBN-10: 0-8021-7048-X
ISBN-13: 978-0-8021-7048-4

Black Cat
a paperback original imprint of Grove/Atlantic, Inc.
841 Broadway
New York, NY 10003

Distributed by Publishers Group West

www.groveatlantic.com

08 09 10 11 12 10 9 8 7 6 5 4 3 2 1

For Rebekah

One of my successes in life was that in spite of all the crazy things I had done, I was perfectly normal: I chose to do those things, they didn't choose me.

—Charles Bukowski, *Hollywood*

PART ONE

1

The door creaked open and Jonathan Seede peered out from the depths. There were dark circles beneath his glassy eyes; his lips appeared to be painfully chapped. He stepped into the vestibule of his narrow, turn-of-the-century row house, gripped with both hands the iron bars of the security gate—a twenty-nine-year-old urban pioneer wearing a hooded sweatshirt, black jeans, and a pair of fringed Indian moccasins he'd bought one weekend at a tourist trap in the mountains. "What's up?" he asked his visitor. The words turned to vapor in the frigid air.

"You look like you're in prison," said Jim Freeman, his tone mildly flirtatious. Thirty-five years old, with naturally curly hair and freckles, Freeman lived across the street. His pant legs were stuffed into calf-high, lace-up construction boots. A puffy down jacket and a fluorescent orange safety vest, the kind worn by crossing guards, completed his ensemble. In one hand, balanced expertly on his fingertips, was a turquoise Fiesta dinnerware plate, covered with aluminum foil.

"A prison of my own making," Seede said.

Freeman shifted the plate to his left hand. "How are Dulcy and Jake?"

"No clue."

"Ha, ha," Freeman deadpanned.

Seede looked past his friend, down the narrow, one-way street—cobblestone sidewalks, bay windows, Second Empire mansard roofs, everything faithfully restored. It was just after eleven P.M. on the third Tuesday of December 1992. From where they stood—on the elevated front landing of a brick Victorian, on the south side of Corcoran Street NW, in Washington, DC—the White House was ten blocks away. The traffic crawled eastward, bumper to bumper—engines revving, music blaring, the night abuzz with need and opportunity. Freeman took a half step to his left, into Seede's line of sight. They'd met seven years earlier, when Seede first arrived in town, fresh out of college, another in the legion of wing-tipped overachievers who'd come to the nation's capital to make his mark. Through the years, they'd grown close in the way that neighbors can: two men, rootless in a big city, joined by chance and proximity, their shared experience compounded over time, like interest. As Freeman liked to toast every Thanksgiving at his gathering of orphans and misfits: "To friends: because you get to pick them yourself."

"What do you mean *no clue*?" Freeman asked.

"I mean that I don't know how they are. They're gone."

"Gone, like, on a trip?"

"Just gone."

Freeman leveled him with his green-gray eyes. "What's up, Jonathan? *Spill*."

"What's with the outfit?" Seede searched his pockets for a cigarette, a lighter. "What is it—hard hat night at the Eagle?"

"Whore patrol—remember? You're still coming, right?"

"Tonight?"

"We could really use your expertise."

A deep drag; a voluminous exhalation. "Contrary to what anyone says, I have never in my life been a member of a whore patrol."

"But you know all the cops. You know all the hookers."

"Exactly."

"So you could be a great help."

"I could also lose my job. Newspaper reporters are supposed to be neutral. We can't take part in neighborhood protests — we're not even supposed to vote."

"It's not a protest. It's an action. You've heard of Take Back the Night? We're taking back our neighborhood. It's yours too, isn't it? Don't reporters get to be people sometimes? Come on Jonathan. *Please*. You don't have to wear the vest if you don't want to."

Seede looked at him. *Fucking Freeman*. About a month ago he'd announced his latest personal quest: a five-year plan to become the youngest-looking forty-year-old in Washington, DC. To this end, he'd taken up smoking and jogging—smoking to speed his metabolism and quell his appetite; jogging to counter the smoking.

"I like the hookers," Seede protested. "They're like landmarks in our little town-within-a-town. I use them to give directions: *Go north on Fourteenth Street, then turn east on Corcoran at the fat black hooker with the blonde Afro wig*."

"And I suppose you love the used condoms and the crack vials. I'll bet Jake has a super collection of syringes by now."

Seede's face fell. "I forgot—you lunch regularly with my wife."

"I've always said she has a good head on her shoulders."

"Not you too, Jim."

Freeman tilted back his own head appraisingly. At his suggestion, the Seedes had recently pointed and painted the facade of the house. It looked marvelous. "I could probably get you twice what you paid."

"And then I move where, exactly? To Fairfax County? I could take a van pool into work." He took another deep drag of his cigarette, exhaled the smoke thickly through his nose. The ash, two inches long, hung precariously.

Wisely, Freeman returned to the subject at hand. "What do you say, Jonathan? Will you come with us? You can just observe. If you're there, maybe people in the neighborhood will take us more seriously. *Pretty please?*" he crooned. "I even brought you a bribe."

Freeman held up the plate for Seede's inspection, raised the foil teasingly, like a skirt—revealing a thick, oozing slab of his famous blueberry-rhubarb pie.

For one brief instant, it appeared as if Seede was going to vomit. He reached out through the security bars with his hand, guided the plate away. He took another deep pull on his cigarette. "Did you get a permit? Did you call the Third District to let them know what you're up to? What if Wolfie gets into another altercation?"

"That was *not* his fault."

Seede smiled ruefully. "The woman was on her way to church, Jim."

"It was dark! She was wearing four-inch heels and a leopard-print jacket."

"Can't you guys focus on something else in the neighborhood? What ever happened to the food bank idea?"

"We even have a walkie-talkie," Freeman said. "It's Bob's from the war. He took it off a dead Vietcong."

"Bob was in the army?"

"Marines."

"What does he tell the fellas at reunions?"

"Are you kidding?" Freeman laughed out loud, a booming baritone rendition of a schoolgirl's nervous giggle. "You know what they say about marines: the few, the brave, the built. A whole contingent from the president's Honor Guard are regulars at Chaps. You should see the bodies on those guys."

"You mean that gay country-and-western bar?"

"Marching, two-stepping—it's all the same. Different music is all, different costumes. Plus you get to hold hands. Wolfie was a marine too."

"No way."

"*Waaay,*" Freeman sang. "Did I ever tell you that story? About the first time we met?"

Seede nestled his face between the newly painted, gleaming black enamel iron bars. His head ached, the right side especially, at the temple and the jaw. The cold metal felt bracing. "What kind of walkie-talkies do you have?"

"Well, actually, we only have one."

"*One?* What the hell do you think you're gonna do—"

Freeman waved him off with a limp wrist. "None of the hookers or johns will know. It's this big ole thing. You wear it on your back. We figured if we just walked around talking into the phone, we'd look more official."

"I'm sure you and Wolfie will strike fear into the golden heart of every hooker out there."

"So what's it gonna be? Will you come? Just do it for an hour. Please?"

A pained expression: "I don't know, Jim. "It's just so . . . suburban vigilante. Come in for a minute. It's fucking freezing out here."

2

Metropolitan Police Officer Perdue Hatfield leaned down into the half-open window of a burgundy Lincoln Mark IV. A previously owned model with a custom brougham top, it was parked at the curb outside Popeye's Chicken, on the southeast corner of Fourteenth and P streets, the heart of the Fourteenth Street Strip.

With his bulletproof vest and winter-weight uniform coat, his trapezius muscles bulging out of the banded neckline of his white thermal undershirt, Officer Hatfield looked a little like a cartoon superhero. His heavy leather utility belt was festooned with all the latest gear: Glock automatic sidearm, extra mags, stun gun, handcuffs, pepper spray, nightstick. A war on drugs was raging in the streets of Washington. It took a lot of neat stuff to fight it.

Unholstering his high output tactical halogen flashlight, Hatfield shined the concise blue-white beam around the inside of the car. His voice still carried the syrupy lilt of his native West Virginia. "I trust you're having a pleasant evening, Mr. Alfred?"

Ignoring the cop, Jamal DeWayne Alfred studied his manicured nails in the green glow of his dashboard. The engine was idling, the heater was blowing, smooth jazz played on the radio.

Through the windshield, Jamal could see the Central Union Mission, a landmark Victorian warehouse converted during the Depression into a shelter for men, part of a ministry founded after the Civil War to assist the homeless veterans who were living on the streets of Washington. Atop the five-story building—the tallest in the area, which was zoned for residential and light industrial use—was a ten-foot neon cross. Beneath the cross a row of pink and white neon letters spelled out the words of the Savior: COME UNTO ME.

Down below, at street level, the regulars worked the intersection—China Doll, Razor Sally, Titty Bitty, Crazy Michelle—their ranks swollen tonight by a contingent of part-timers, welfare cases, and struggling single moms looking to make some extra money for Christmas. They skittered like water bugs in and out of traffic, prancing and waving and flirting, flesh bubbling, ankles wobbling on four-inch heels, wearing hot pants and miniskirts and thong bikini bottoms, everything a size too small.

The police radio squawked and Hatfield straightened himself. He cocked his head, listened, spoke into the mouthpiece, which was clipped to the epaulet of his shiny blue weatherproof coat. With the coming of the holidays—and the attendant influx of tourists—the department had initiated its annual crackdown on the Strip. From the look of it, the area was being held by an occupying army. There were motorcycle officers in spit-shined, knee-high boots; bicycle cops in poncey padded riding tights; beat walkers like Hatfield, the grunts. Tech teams with infrared cameras and special microphones huddled together in third-story windows, gathering intelligence. A thirty-foot motor home, converted into a mobile Breathalyzer unit, was parked about a half block north of the Mission: a paddy wagon and three tow trucks idled nearby. Undeterred, customers continued to pour in from the suburbs—from Maryland to the north, Virginia to the south—and also from the bars around town. It was a wonderful centralized location, nothing more than ten minutes away: Capitol Hill, Georgetown, Foggy Bottom, Nineteenth Street, Adams Morgan. A sketchy sort of reckless urgency prevailed, a feeling like a cold drop of sweat rolling down a rib cage.

Jamal took a drumstick from the Styrofoam container in his lap. As he chewed, he set for himself the idle task of unmasking the undercover cops working the area. He identified a trio of pudgy crackheads by a pay phone; a hooker on the curb with opaque tights and an oversize handbag; a long-haired white guy and a cornrowed black guy driving together in a beat-up Chevy—a salt-and-pepper-team, always a giveaway.

Hatfield leaned back down to the passenger window, watched Jamal chew. "Can I ask you something?"

"Don't know if I'll be able to answer without my lawyer present."

Hatfield hesitated, not sure if he was serious.

Jamal's large head and round, dark face put one in mind of Smokey Bear—take away the ranger hat, add Jheri curls. He looked the cop in the eyes. "What do you want, Hatfield?"

"Don't take this wrong or nothin," he said earnestly. "It's just, well, how do I put this? It seems like black people are all the time complaining, you know, about being stereotyped and such. Am I correct?"

Jamal blotted his lips with a napkin. He had no idea where this was going; it couldn't be good.

"But if you really think about it," Hatfield continued, "you people are all the time doing stereotypical things. No offense, but here you are, sitting in a pimp mobile on the whore stroll, eating fried chicken. Every time I see you, you're out here in front of Popeye's, eating fried chicken."

"Where else you expect me to eat around here?"

"They have a pretty good cheeseburger sub over at Burger 7," Hatfield said thoughtfully, pointing his sausagelike index finger in a southwesterly direction. "You got the Post Pub on the other side of the circle—excellent daily specials, french fries smothered with melted cheese, amazing. The Silver Dollar Lounge has a buffet till midnight, but you have to watch out for foreign objects in the goulash, if you catch my drift. And up there on U Street there's all kinds of new places: State of the Union, Republic Gardens, Utopia. The Andalusian Dog has a very original tapas menu. You should try it."

"What are you, the new food critic for the *Herald*?"

Hatfield frowned, disappointed at the response. According to the department's new operating orders, foot patrolmen had been tasked with expanded community outreach. The feeling among the brass (and among their highly paid consultants) was that relationship-building with citizens would promote cooperation with the police, which in turn would aid police efforts in fighting crime and closing cases. On the other hand, according to a recent piece in the *Washington Herald*, 43 percent of all District residents had at least one blood relative who was either incarcerated or currently "in the system"—meaning arrested, awaiting trial, or on probation or parole. To this large percentage of city residents—a sampling that did not include juveniles under eighteen, 92 percent of whom knew someone in the system—the police were the enemy. And they would probably always remain so.

Hatfield knew this all too well. He experienced it every day. If one person ever said *please* or *thank you* to him, he'd probably stroke out in the middle of the street. The truth was, Hatfield felt the same way as the residents. He might have been sworn to protect and serve, but as far as he was concerned, he was protecting and serving the enemy. Back in high school—in the morning prayer circle, on the football and track teams—he'd had lots of black friends. Likewise in the marines, where they taught you to be color-blind. He'd even dated a couple of black women—DC was the mecca for fine black women, and they were forward too, not above telling you how they felt about you, what they wanted you to do. But after nearly five years as a beat cop in a city that was 70 percent black, well, put it this way: he didn't give a good goddamn if they liked him or not—it wasn't his job to be liked; his job was to follow orders. If that meant being friendly with the locals, taking the extra step, so be it. Like they used to say in the marines—shit flows downhill. He knew his place. He wasn't supposed to make or evaluate the policy, he was just supposed to follow it—always to the best of his ability, with no complaints. In the marines, where he'd risen to sergeant in only four years, you had three choices of direct response to a superior: *Yes, sir; No, sir; No excuses, sir*. He always wondered what the world would be like if everything ran on the same principle.

"Okay then," Hatfield said in a businesslike tone, satisfied now that he'd carried out his orders. "I just wanted to come over and let you know, you know, that I was on the job." He handed Jamal one of his new business cards. "Feel free to contact me at any time."

"You mean, like, Big Brother is watching?"

"Something like that. Your tax dollars at work—or wait a minute. You probably don't pay any taxes, do you?"

"The fuck I don't!" He used the officer's business card to pick something out of his teeth. "Quarterly payments, itemized deductions, the whole nine."

"You must have a gifted accountant: that's some suit."

Jamal picked a piece of lint from his sleeve. "Handmade. I have this great tailor in Chinatown. I could turn you on."

"What color is that anyway?" He clicked on his flashlight again, shined it into the car. "Kind of a light blue, ain't it?"

"In the swatch book, it's called robin's egg."

"*Whoo-wee,*" sang Hatfield, a tone of amazement indigenous to the thick forests of the Appalachian Mountains, where he grew up, the son of a lumber mill worker and his pious wife. The cop played the light beam slyly around the interior of the car. "Hey!" he exclaimed. "What have we here?"

The beam was trained on the aftermarket drink caddy that was straddling the hump beneath the dash—a cheap-looking, molded plastic thing with sandbags on either side for balance. In it was a large Popeye's Coke with a straw, a package of tissues, a nail file, a pack of Juicy Fruit gum, some spare change . . . and a rolled-up dollar bill.

"I was using it to clean my ears," Jamal protested, half-amused, half-indignant. A search of the Lincoln at that moment could have proved disastrous.

"Then you won't mind reaching down, real slow, and handing it to me." Hatfield's voice had an edge now, a deeper pitch, what they called "command tone." It was the first thing you learned when you got off the bus at boot camp—how a voice can have the power to knock you to your knees.

Hatfield examined the bill under his flashlight. The end was caked with crust and goo. He raised it to his mouth.

"I wouldn't do that if I were you."

"Obviously you ain't me," Hatfield said disdainfully. He dabbed the crusty edge of the bill on the tip of his tongue . . . and then his face imploded—a look of foul disgust, like he'd just eaten a spoiled oyster.

"I tried to warn you," Jamal laughed.

Sputtering and spitting, Hatfield tossed the bill back through the window, stepped away from the vehicle. He pointed his thick finger, rosy from the cold, at Jamal's face, the message unspoken but very clear. Then he headed south on the Strip.

Jamal took a pull from his soda. The clock on the dash said 11:07. Razor Sally was on the far corner, her wig slightly askew, bargaining in sign language with four Salvadorian busboys who were seeking a group discount on blow jobs. Sana, a beauty from Saudi Arabia, was leaning into the back window of a stretch limousine; by day, it was said, she was a George Washington University student. Across the street, in front of a used car lot, colorful streamers flapped in the variable breeze. Two of the younger pimps paced the sidewalk, blowing on their hands for warmth, looking expectant. They'd smoked up all their money in a nearby crack house that catered to players. Now they needed to collect from their hos. On the street they called this "checkin the traps." The only problem: these traps were constantly on the move. In the economy of the Strip, the johns paid the hookers for sex, the hookers paid the pimps for love and protection, the pimps paid the pipe—they called it "suckin on the glass dick." Jamal had had his time with rock—in the days before crack, he used to cook it himself, using a Bic lighter, baking soda, and a glass cigar tube. But he hadn't touched the stuff in years—since the night he'd hit bottom and made his return to the Strip, to the family business. And that's exactly how he approached it—as a business. He needed to keep his head on straight. He needed to save his receipts. He needed to pay his accountant—who had him laundering his money through a shelter corporation, an erstwhile home cleaning service. Often he passed his idle time reading the dog-eared Webster's dictionary that he kept in the glove box. He tried to learn a new word every day. His game with himself was to try and work the word naturally into a conversation. Like they used to teach at St. Michael's Academy—where he'd gone from first through eleventh grade before quitting to join the army—*Scientia est Potentia*.

Jamal took a bite of his biscuit. The taste of butter was strong; it tickled the back of his tongue. A brand-new Volvo station wagon, the tags still temporary, pulled to the curb in front of him. The passenger window slid down. The streetwalker with the opaque tights and large leather handbag stuck her head partially inside. After a brief discussion, she opened the door and got in.

The Volvo merged into traffic. The beat-up Chevy with the salt-and-pepper undercover team pulled in behind; the counterfeit crackheads by the pay phone began to move. At the intersection, a patrol car rolled slowly into the Volvo's path and stopped, causing the Volvo driver to slam on his brakes. Two uniforms jumped out of the patrol car, guns drawn. The hooker pulled her .38 service revolver out of her oversize handbag; the crackheads pulled the driver out of the car—a balding, fortyish man wearing a Patagonia fleece jacket.

They spread the suspect on the hood of his safe and sensible Swedish import and searched his pockets. His gold wedding band glinted in the amber light from the reproduction, turn-of-the-century streetlamps that had recently been installed, along with planters and concrete benches, as part of a residential initiative to reclaim the neighborhood.

In an hour or so, Jamal knew, the Volvo guy would be inside a holding cell at the DC Central Jail, on the phone to his wife, trying to explain his predicament. Jamal thought about the time when he was fifteen, hanging out one night on the Strip with his dad. He'd asked, "Why do they call them tricks?"

His father had laughed heartily. "What else do you call a man who pays forty dollars to put on a rubber and come all over hisself?"

3

The Pope of Pot sucked a last long drag from a joint and stubbed it out. He was a great doughnut of a man, sweet and puffy, lightly glazed, wearing Coke-bottle glasses and an oxford-cloth shirt, ink-blotched and frayed, a wardrobe remnant from his days as a federal bureaucrat. Cradled to his ear was a heavy Bakelite receiver from an old rotary telephone, one of eight lined up neatly before him on his government surplus desk, the nerve center of this storefront, which was located just across Fourteenth Street from Popeye's. A large sign on the wall identified the place as the Church of Realized Fantasies.

"Gotta go now, toots," the Pope rasped, smoke leaking from his chipmunk grin. He threw back his head and laughed, *Ah ha ha ha HA!,* his rusty trademark cackle, a series of four exuberant chuckles followed by a trumpeting guffaw, strung together in sets like waves, crashing upon the jagged shoreline of his crooked yellow teeth, spraying mirth and spittle and tar-tinged phlegm, *Ah ha ha ha HA! . . .*

Whereupon he was seized suddenly by a fit of coughing that jounced the phone from his hand. He clutched the arms of his swivel chair, riding the deep black hacks, a rag doll on a Brahman bull.

"You okay, Pope?"

Waylon Weidenfeld was tall and gaunt, bar certified—Ichabod Crane in a Burberry raincoat and a Brooks Brothers suit, a silk print tie by Armani, everything purchased at a Salvation Army store on Capitol Hill. He was sitting in a stackable plastic lawn chair, one of a dozen or so scattered about the room. Occupying the remaining chairs was the ragtag assortment of humanity comprising the Pope's inner circle—his minions, his messengers, his ongoing projects—all of them seated at a respectful distance from the spray of his possibly infectious laugh.

Waylon walked over to the shiny industrial refrigerator and poured the Pope a cup of cold water. The Pope had found him six years earlier, broken and bleeding, in a Dumpster behind a nearby Chinese carryout—a once promising DC city attorney whose fondness for gambling had led him afoul of the wrong elements. Waylon's face registered deep concern. There'd been tests recently; the Pope was not well. Thirty-six hours on a concrete bench in a holding cell at the DC Central Jail hadn't helped any, either. The DA's office had apologized formally, profusely, pleading mix-up, lost paperwork. But everyone knew the score—fifty-nine-year-old white guy "misplaced" for thirty-six hours in a ten-by-twelve-foot holding cell. It was a mystery that explained itself.

The room was cold; the furnace was on the fritz. Cracked plaster walls, scarred concrete floor, steel-reinforced front door—an odd choice by the former tenant, considering that the rest of the frontage was constructed entirely of glass, painted black in lieu of curtains. A large pot of water was boiling on a hot plate, the only source of heat. A bare bulb in the ceiling provided the only light. Everything in the place had been purchased at government auctions—the gunmetal gray desk, the olive drab sleeping bags piled in the corner, the eight black telephones with their snakes' nest of tangled wires—all of it for pennies on the dollar.

Prior to founding the Church of Realized Fantasies, the Pope—under the name Michael David Rubin—had toiled for nearly twenty years in the bowels of the Office of Management and Budget. He still had friends in government; he knew where the deals were buried.

Waylon handed the Pope his cup of water, retrieved the phone from the floor, hung it up. He took a seat on the edge of the desk. "So what are we gonna do about product?"

"How much did they get?" asked Beta Max. He'd shown up at the Pope's doorstep one humid night the previous summer. His hair was long on top and shaved at the temples. A spindly goatee hung down to the middle of his chest. His rippling arms were tattooed with sleeves of snakes and skulls and medieval weapons. As always, his face was hidden behind his video camera, which itself was dwarfed by his beefy paws. Waylon had been the one who dubbed him Beta Max, after his soon-to-be-obsolete choice of equipment. The Pope had named him official church videographer.

"They took seven pounds," the Pope said.

"Was that everything we had?" Waylon asked.

"But they only *charged* me with possession of *four* pounds."

"What a surprise," Waylon said sourly. "*Cops steal drugs! Film at eleven*."

"Fret not, my child," the Pope said. "The balance is to be returned. I have set the wheels in motion."

Beta Max zoomed in for a close-up. "A lot of people say that your interview with *Capitol City* magazine was the reason the cops decided to target you," he said to the Pope. "Do you think you could explain why you gave that interview in the first place?"

"He called and I answered: *Howdy, honey, howdy!* That's why we got the toll-free number, right? 1-555-WANT-POT. You call. You get the Pope. I send out a messenger with your order. Guaranteed service in one hour or less. How was I supposed to know that we were delivering a quarter ounce of sacrament to a freelance writer at *Capitol City* magazine? I might be the Pope of Pot, but I'm not a mind reader. And anyway—it's over now. Think of the free publicity. I know *I* do. I think about it all the time. All the time. That and sex, toots. Because right now, what's critical to us is mass. *Critical mass,* don't you see? Not until we reach our goal of one million members will the tide begin to turn. The voice of the people is the voice of God in a democracy. I have to convert the world to a more sane policy. It's the cross I have to bear. It's the burden of being the Pope, *Ah ha ha ha HA!*"

Feeling celebratory, the Pope spun around in his high-backed leather office chair like a kid in his daddy's office, one full revolution, then another, then a half . . . then stopped himself with his back to Waylon and the rest, facing his credenza. A beautiful walnut piece from the General Services Administration's executive line of furnishings, it had seen service in Al Haig's West Wing office during the final days of the Nixon administration. Inside the credenza, the Pope stored his office supplies: Post-its, pens, highlighters, binder clips, steno pads, staple refills, paper clips—he was passionate about office supplies. Like he always said: "You need the right tools to do the job." Displayed across the top of the credenza was the Pope's dusty collection of robot toys, Ken dolls, and rubber cartoon figurines, and also a life-size skull fashioned from a large piece of translucent crystal rock. Perched atop the skull was the Pope's papal miter—a high, white, John Paul number with a nine-inch green velvet marijuana leaf sewn onto the front. He picked it up with both hands, placed it atop his head.

"May I have your attention, your holiness?" Waylon pleaded, obviously annoyed.

The Pope of Pot spun around in his chair again, one revolution, then another . . . then caught himself on the desktop, facing front. "My attention is yours, *consigliore.*"

"Okay, this is the story," Waylon said, recounting. "We've got no product. We've got no money. We haven't eaten in nearly twenty-four hours. We've got two hundred thousand dollars cash in a suitcase in a locker at Dulles Airport because nim-nod over there"—pointing now to Louie, sitting in one of the plastic chairs, a rain-thin albino in a rabbit fur hat—"lost the key somewhere and can't remember the number of the locker. We've got to face facts. We've got to do something. We're totally screwed."

"Screwed?" A radiant smile broke across the Pope's face. "When? Where? Don't be a tease, now!" He batted his eyelashes coquettishly.

Waylon put both of his hands on the Pope's shoulders. "I know you don't like bad news," he said quietly, "but there's no way around it. We've got to start dealing with stuff. This could *really* be bad."

Sadness emanated from the Pope's watery blue eyes, which looked huge and alien behind his thick corrective lenses. "Have faith, my son. God has given us the sacrament to cure our ills, to set our minds free. He has given us credit to sustain us in times of need. He has given us telephones to help us communicate across vast distances. Get Colombia on the line immediately! Ask for Don Diego. Tell him the Pope desires a private audience."

"The *charges*!" Waylon said, exasperated. "I'm talking about the charges! It's one thing to be cited for handing out a few joints to the people waiting in line for the White House tour. But this is a major possession charge, Pope. Possession with *intent*. Seven pounds. You're on the chopping block. They finally have you where they want you. Jesus H. Christ! They brought the press *with* them to the bust! Are you starting to get the picture here? They want to put you away for a long, long time."

"Four pounds," the Pope said.

"What?"

"They only charged me with possession of *four* pounds."

"Four, seven. It doesn't matter. Mandatory minimums, remember? We marched against them in the NORML demonstration."

"The Popemobile. What a hoot! We need to do that again!"

"You're looking at twenty-five to life—with no judicial discretion. That means no intervening circumstances. With your string of misdemeanors, they could try to make this into a three-strikes case. You could get life in prison without possibility of parole. You could end up—"

A knock on the door—three percussive blows, fist meat against reinforced steel. The windows rattled and shook.

The Pope of Pot clapped his hands with childlike glee. "We have visitors, kids!" he trilled.

4

Four men in dark suits around a large, round mahogany table, overhung with a crystal chandelier. An immense stone fireplace, flames dancing and crackling, flanked on either side by a suit of medieval armor. A butler in white gloves cleared the dishes.

The host was a diminutive billionaire named Bert Metcalfe. He sat atop a silk pillow in a saber-legged chair, his shiny tassel loafers, size six, swinging idly above the Persian rug. Though the setting was intimate—a wood-paneled dining salon on the second floor of his Georgetown mansion—he spoke in a formal manner, referring to index cards.

"Every night, after I turn off my reading light, I lie awake in my bed for a span of time, reviewing my day. I think about the things I've done, the contributions I've made, the mistakes I've made, the things I could do better tomorrow. I think about where I've been and where I'm going—how far along the path another day has brought me. Invariably I am visited by the same eternal questions: Why am I here? What is my purpose? What is *our* purpose?" He opened his arms to include his guests and all of humankind.

"I think about the way consumerism has become a form of religion in our country—the new opiate of the masses," Metcalfe continued. "I think about the woman's movement—the way all the rules have changed over the last twenty years, the way men and women have been at each other's throats: hell hath no fury, indeed. I think about God—I wonder why mankind fights so many wars in the name of religion. I wonder what happens when we die. I wonder: Are we alone in the universe? What about Inner Earth—does it exist? What about Atlantis—did *it* ever exist? What happened to the Mayans? How does someone like Hitler get as far as he did without anyone stopping him? Why does it always seem like the leaders of this great country—men and women educated in the best institutions we have to offer—don't seem to have the slightest understanding about the way the leaders of other countries think, especially when those leaders are nonwhite or non-Christian? Why can't we find an alternative to fossil fuels? Why are our schoolchildren falling behind the children in the rest of the world? What are we going to do about AIDS? Why can't we all get along?"

The three guests at the table sat frozen in poses of weighty consideration. One nodded his head sagely. Another worried the bristles of his neatly pruned mustache. The third stared raptly at the frescoed ceiling, absently fellating a thick Macanudo cigar. All three earned their livings as pundits—paid handsomely to auger the bones of current events, to shape the tenor of public debate, to add their own two cents. Here in the early years of twenty-four-hour-a-day news, content was at a premium. These men were the new stars, able to fill large blocks of airtime with the slimmest of budgets.

For the past several weeks, Metcalfe had put much of his energy into these evenings of intellectual exchange, inviting Washington's brightest minds and sharpest tongues into his house for dinner, followed by a hearty round of debate. While the reason for these powwows—the actual goal, what he was trying to achieve—wasn't clear to anyone, that in itself was not unusual when it came to Bert Metcalfe. In fact, little about him was actually known. It was said that he'd spent his youth being shuffled between foster homes, that he'd come into his fortune quite by surprise when he turned twenty-one. It was said that he owned a castle in Scotland and an island off the coast of West Africa. It was said that he funded scientific and humanitarian projects across the globe. It was said that he had recently, by secret arrangement with the government of Egypt, purchased one of the pyramids at Giza. But all of this remained speculation—nothing had been pinned down. In a town of endless investigations, where information trumped money the way paper trumped rock, Metcalfe had somehow managed to stay beneath the radar—obviously he hadn't pissed off anyone important. He was a private citizen, albeit a fabulously wealthy one. He owed explanations to no one.

As could be expected—for Washington was first and foremost a town of endless gossip—these evenings at Metcalfe Mansion had become a hot topic, the flames fanned by the lack of other action in the city. Ten days before Christmas, the place was emptying out; most of the people who worked in government had roots somewhere else. In one month's time, a new administration would be sworn in. Twelve years of Reagan/Bush Republican rule—*Voodoo economics . . . Just say no . . . I can't recall . . . Read my lips*—had come to an end. The first baby-boomer president, a hip young saxophone-playing dude from Arkansas, was waiting in the wings with his piano-legged first partner, wearing the halo of the untried. A rare calm had descended on the most powerful city in the world, the deep cleansing breath of political transition.

And so it was, as word spread, bored pundits from all across town, print and broadcast alike, waited jealously for their personal invitations to Metcalfe Mansion. They might have called him Bertie the Hedgehog behind his back, but when Bertram Hedgewick Metcalfe III snapped his stubby fingers, you came. The honorarium didn't hurt either: it was rumored to be twenty-five thousand dollars in cash.

Metcalfe hopped down abruptly from his perch at the table, his tiny tassled loafers landing on the floor with a resounding thud—though small, he was no lightweight. He commenced pacing, moving around the room distractedly, like a professor in front of a class. "Now, I realize that these questions beg the question, so to speak. I know that there are scientific or academic answers to many of these, and plenty of intelligent speculation about the rest. Among my possessions is the largest private library in the world. I spend at least five hours speed-reading every day; I employ a dozen young scholars to read and summarize. Huge amounts of knowledge are available to me. Any resource known to man, really, and I take full advantage. I'm well versed on topics as diverse as molecular theory and Dianetics; I've read extensively on mathematics, existentialism, pragmatism, humanism, romanticism, world history, and Tex Winter's triangle offense. I've studied the Talmud, the Bible, Mao's Little Red Book, *Mein Kampf,* the *Rigveda,* the entire catalog of Spiderman comics. I had the good fortune to be able to hire my own team of scholars to create an alternative translation of the Dead Sea Scrolls—you would be amazed at the difference a few words can make. Even one word. Take the Koran. In one translation, a martyr to Islam is blessed, upon his arrival in heaven, with an unlimited supply of plump, ripe virgins for all of eternity. In another, the same word is translated as *olives*—plump, ripe *olives* for all of eternity."

Metcalfe paused by the fireplace to warm his hands. "You see, gentlemen, this is the point: Our libraries are filled with opinions, theorems, hypotheses, and ideologies. We have old saws and wives' tales and common wisdom aplenty. But what do we really know? What are we *sure* of? We are so smug, we humans. We think we're so smart. We think we're so advanced. We think we have all the answers. We think that we can manipulate our environment and our destinies to our own ends. Who else but man could come upon a pristine, snow-covered mountain and envision a ski resort?

"I ask you, gentlemen. What if we're just deluded?" He pulled out his silk handkerchief, rubbed off a stray blotch of red sauce that had somehow come to rest upon the breastplate of one of the suits of fourteenth-century armor. "What if we're just shitting ourselves? Who says pi equals 3.1417? And what the hell is pi, anyway? A man-made construct, something we invented. Something that just happens to fit, that happens to explain the unexplainable. That is man's greatest talent. We rationalize. We make things fit. We explain the world around us with such confidence, such élan. Have you ever spoken at length to a college senior? They think they have it all figured out too. That's humanity for you, the perfect metaphor: Joe College Graduate, diploma in hand, ready to take on the world. The Aztecs believed that human sacrifice had a direct impact on corn crop yields. As recently as twenty years ago, surgeons were performing frontal lobotomies as treatment for mental illness. Look at the science on dieting. Every few years it's a total one-eighty. High carbs or low fat? High protein or high fiber? If man is so smart, if we're so advanced, if we're so darn clever . . . why can't we figure out how to lose a few pounds and keep them off?

"And what about this," he said, continuing his circuit around the table. "I'm sure you've all heard of Einstein's theory of relativity?"

The visiting pundits appeared to be bored. Usually they were the ones who got to talk. They nodded in unison.

"How about quantum theory?"

More nods.

"Einstein's theory describes the large-scale universe to an astonishing degree of precision, or so they say. Quantum theory describes the small-scale universe with the same astonishing exactness. Much of our understanding of the world is based on these two hypotheses.

"But the problem is," Metcalfe said, pausing to make eye contact with each of his three guests in turn, "Einstein's theory is *not* compatible with quantum theory. The two theories are incompatible, gentlemen. *Incompatible.*

"To correct this little glitch, scientists came up with something called string theory, which marries the concepts of Einstein's theory with those of quantum theory. I won't bore you with the details, but string theory has to do with the existence of tiny strings vibrating in ten-dimensional space. Scientists say it would take a particle accelerator larger than the entire solar system to create the energy needed to actually see one of these strings. Which means, essentially, that strings will never be seen, or even detected, by humans. Which means, essentially, that we must take on faith the fact that these strings exist—in the very same way that we must take on faith the fact that God exists."

"Excuse me, Mr. Metcalfe." This was the one with the neatly trimmed mustache, the Washington bureau chief of the *New York Tribune*. "I think I'm missing something, sir. What's the so-what graph here? What's your point?"

"And, more specifically, what does it have to do with *us*?" added the cigar guy, the moderator of a popular Sunday morning political chat show. He looked left and right to his fellows, enlisting support.

"My point," Metcalfe said archly, "is that these theories—both of which are important building blocks in the foundation of the way we profess to understand our *entire physical universe*—could well be meaningless. Somewhere out in the cosmos, a highly advanced race is laughing its collective ass off."

The three pundits eyed one another dubiously.

"Interesting idea," said the guy with the mustache.

"An excellent point," said the guy with the cigar.

"Definitely something to make some calls about," said the third, nodding his head sagely.

5

Jonathan Seede pulled the door shut behind him, making a mental note for the umpteenth time to oil the squeaky hinges. He selected a key from an oversize ring and locked the doorknob, selected another, locked the dead bolt. Turning to his right, he punched a four-digit code into a security keypad, then stepped outside, closed and locked the iron security gate—two more keys.

Twirling the key ring on his middle finger like a cowboy gunslinger, he joined Freeman at the rail. The landing was about eight feet above the sidewalk, the crowning platform of an ornate iron staircase that Seede had recently spent a bundle to restore. Per Freeman's referral, the work had been done by the same craftsman who'd restored the statue atop the U.S. Capitol dome. Seede had lived in Washington since the summer after college. He'd driven or walked past the Capitol dome countless times. But it was only after they'd hired the man—who promptly removed the staircase, leaving them to their back alley entrance for the next three months—that Seede had learned for the first time that the greenish oxidized figure atop the dome was actually a likeness of Persephone—the mythical daughter of the Greek god Zeus, kidnapped by Hades, who made her his queen consort of the Underworld. Why she was chosen to reign atop the world's ultimate symbol of representative democracy remained a lively debate in some quarters. Seede himself wondered if it didn't have something to do with the deal Persephone had struck with her captor husband, whereby she was allowed to leave hell for part of every year and return home—the same arrangement enjoyed by the nation's elected representatives.

Freeman was still wearing his whore patrol getup, complete with orange crossing-guard vest. He gestured like a game show hostess in the direction of the street—a graceful sweeping motion, palm up, indicating the scene below: a single line of cars, inching bumper-to-bumper along the narrow one-way street. Kids on bicycles darted in and out of traffic. The sidewalk was crowded with homeboys and hangers-on, hustlers and homeless, crackheads and undercovers—and down the way an actual resident, dragging his recycling bin to the curb. Acrid blue exhaust hung in the air at the level of the amber streetlamps, mingling with fireplace woodsmoke and the booming subsonic vibrations of gangsta rap. Freeman shook his head sadly. "It's like Grand Central Station out here."

"More like *Night of the Living Dead*," Seede said. He watched with interest as three hookers click-clacked past on stiletto heels, joking and cussing, headed in the same direction as the traffic, east toward Thirteenth Street, a dark and leafy corridor that served as a sort of employee lounge for Strip denizens, featuring trick pads, crack houses, and shooting galleries sprinkled among the SROs and renovations.

Hunkered on the southwestern corner of Corcoran and Fourteenth, like an anchor store in a mall, was a monolithic AME church. Built of red brick, listed in the National Register of Historic Places, visited over the years by several U.S. presidents—but only during election years—it was attended on

Sundays by members of the black upper crust, most of whom now lived in suburbs outside the city. Across the street, on the northwest corner, was a self-service gas station with a bullet-proof cashier's kiosk. The east side of the block dead-ended into Thirteenth Street—it was this terminus that gave the neighborhood its intimate feel, at least during daylight hours. At that junction another historic church, Baptist and built of stone, catered to a more local congregation. Its two-story stained-glass rendering of a praying Jesus glowed softly against the night.

When Freeman first took possession of his house in the Fall of 1979, many of the properties on the street were boarded up or burned out. It had been eleven years since the King assassination riots, ten years since Marion Barry and Stokely Carmichael marched down U Street wearing dashikis in an effort to reclaim the peace. A family of eleven lived in the basement of Freeman's house. They couldn't afford coal for heat. They cut up scavenged railroad ties and tried to burn them in the furnace. An extension cord, plugged illicitly into a basement outlet in the house next door, kept their thirty-inch color console TV in service. Everyone told Freeman and his partner, Tom, that they were crazy to buy here. Freeman's parents even refused to visit—though that was probably more about Tom then the neighborhood. Not only was their son gay; he was sleeping with a *black* man. It was something that well-bred boys from Newport News just didn't do.

"So what's up?" Freeman asked Seede, employing a no-nonsense tone. "Where's your little family?"

"What do you call a grouping of hookers?" Seede asked.

Caught off guard: "Huh?"

"A gaggle of hookers. A pride of pimps. A covey of crackheads. A den of dealers," Seede said, gesturing here and there, pointing in turn to each of the different groups. "It's like one of those Discovery Channel documentaries out here. You ever see the one about the watering hole in the Kalahari? 'Corcoran Street: Crossroads of the Animal Kingdom.' "

Freeman grimaced. "That sounds racist, Seede."

"Why is it that you can call a white person anything you want—a bear of a man, pig nose, storklike, skeletal, built like a brick shithouse—but if you use an animal term to describe a black person you're racist? Remember that kid at University of Virginia? He got into trouble for calling that girl a water buffalo? But if you ever saw her picture . . ."

Freeman refused to bite. "What about Dulcy and Jake?" he pressed. "What's going on, Jonathan?"

Seede shrugged.

"What do you mean, *shrug*?"

"I honestly don't know," Seede said. "I woke up yesterday afternoon and they were gone."

Freeman stared a hole through Seede. He'd been the best man at their wedding—a gathering of fifty that he'd hosted in his own showcase living room and grand foyer. The joke among the threesome was that Freeman had been miscast as best man—he *should* have been maid of honor. In fact, Freeman had been with the Seedes on every step of their marital journey—from their first meeting (at a Freeman dinner party), through the chase (an obstacle course of dating rules and modern complications), to the eventual surrender and ceremony (leading to the perilous first year of marriage, when all the grim baggage was unpacked). He'd overseen every detail of the wedding himself, down to the draping of Dulcy's satin and lace train on the stairwell, a marvelous cascading effect that *made* the photos. And while he'd politely declined Dulcy's invitation to be present at the birth of their son, Freeman *was* the one who'd suggested calling the La Leche League in those early days when breastfeeding had been problematic. Suffice it to say: Freeman had every right to ask personal questions. "Did she leave a note?"

Seede looked out toward the street. He watched a kid on a too-big ten-speed bicycle—he lived down the way, eleven or twelve years old—coast up to the window of one of the cars in the line. A dance of hands; the kid rode off. Down at the stop sign, meanwhile, the lead car made its right-hand turn, south on Thirteenth Street, headed for another lap of the Strip. The line of cars moved ten feet forward.

Freeman put a consoling hand on Seede's shoulder. "Are you alright?"

"I'm not sure how I feel," Seede said. "Like somebody punched me, I guess. But also kind of liberated. Kind of free. Like this huge weight of regret has been lifted.

"This whole marriage thing, the baby . . . It hasn't been working out that well. They make it seem like having children is the ultimate human act—the joy of parenthood, watching them grow, all that crap. But I don't see it. I just don't see it. I haven't reaped one single benefit that I can think of. What was wrong with the way things were, anyway? I liked the way things were. We were this great couple. She was smart and beautiful. She loved me. She understood my work. We had a great life. I felt so fuckin lucky. I had my career, she had her classes and her working out—she was decorating the place real nice. We had sex all the time. Things were perfect. Why did we need to change anything? What did we need a baby for?

"Now I come home from work and she hands me the kid and goes off to aerobics. If I complain, I'm not being *supportive*. This baby was her idea, right? I work all day—I do my job. Why can't she do hers? Clearly she doesn't need a husband. And she doesn't need a helper, because I'm paying for a part-time nanny, twenty hours a week. What she obviously thinks she needs is a slave. To carry shit. To pick shit up. I swear to you: I do not exist except in the context of *What can you do for me now*. And I'm supposed to be alright with that. I'm supposed to be *supporrrrrtive—*" a drawn-out mocking tone. "How I loathe that word. Support *this,* you know what I'm sayin? As far as I'm concerned, it's all a total rip-off. Fatherhood: what's in it for me?"

Seede pulled his cigarettes from his coat, his lighter from the front pocket his button-fly jeans. "It's like the other day," he said, lighting up. "I was in the deli on Seventeenth Street. That Indonesian chick was at the cash register. The one with the ass? She smiles at me—this huge, friendly, inviting smile—and she says: 'I know you. You're *Jake's* dad!'" Seede's eyes bugged.

"You *are* Jake's dad, aren't you?" Freeman said, not comprehending.

"Yeah, but it was the *way* she said it—*Jake's Dad*. Like that's my fuckin name. Like that's my whole purpose in life. I'm no longer Jonathan Seede, the guy who's been working and sacrificing for years to make a name for himself. That guy is gone. That guy is toast. When she said it, it just floored me—it hit me like a ton of bricks."

"What?"

"What about *my* needs, you know what I'm saying? What about *my motherfuckin needs*? There's no *me* anymore. I have ceased to exist in my own house. Nine months of pregnancy. Eighteen months of worshipping at the altar of this squirming, shitting, crying machine and his overwrought mother. You'd think she's the first woman who ever had a child."

Seede took a deep drag. There were big things going on within the confines of his household, things much larger and more important than his feelings or his career ambitions, his wanton needs, the state of his marriage. Monumental things. Primordial things. The biggest thing: reproduction. And he was there for specific purposes: To serve. To accommodate. To support in every sense of the word. To pay the mortgage, the taxes, the auto and house and life insurance. To deal with the investments, the retirement plan, the leaky roof, the hinky furnace, the steaming pile of human excrement left in the alley behind their garage, crowned as it was with a soiled wad of the *Washington Herald*. To stay out of the way—unless called upon. To carry stuff. To drive somewhere in the middle of the night and purchase essential items. To do all the food shopping, cook half the meals, wash half the dishes and all of his own laundry. To take out the trash. (Why is it again that women can't take out trash?) To clean the diaper genie: the long, tubular, plastic bag inside reminded him of a giant snake—a wretched, shit-and-powder-smelling python or anaconda dragged up from the depths of hell, the evidence of its swallowed prey bulging at even intervals along its considerable length. To pick up anything that was left on the floor. Waist down: that was his domain. Dulcy had not bent down to pick up one single thing—besides Jake, of course, whose every movement she tracked with the vigilance of an NSA satellite—since her fourth month of pregnancy. Seeing for the first time the swell of new life growing in her tummy, a swell she'd shown off so proudly, had literally brought him to his knees with love for her. How could he have predicted the rest to follow?

"And check this out," Seede said, "we've got two more *years* before the kid is even out of diapers."

"When's the last time you had sex?"

Seede looked at him.

"I can't ask?"

"I'm embarrassed to say."

"How bad can it be?"

"Nine weeks. The first weekend in October, a Saturday night. We got a room at the Hotel Washington."

"Did you go to the roof bar?" Freeman enthused. "I *adore* the view from there."

"Yes, yes. We went to the fuckin roof bar. And to the restaurant. To the tune of a hundred bucks."

"You got off cheap."

"No shit. She still isn't drinking. She's still breastfeeding—a topic, I might add, that we spent most of the evening discussing: her problems doing it, the advantages of doing it, when she should stop doing it. Have you ever noticed how women are obsessed with breastfeeding? It's like they carry these cumbersome flesh sacks around with them their whole lives, and then, when they finally get a chance to use them for something, they can't seem to put them down."

"The breast is an amazing organ," Freeman said wistfully.

"The point is: why the fuck do I have to drive six blocks and pay for a hotel room—*and* for parking—so I can have sex with my own wife? It's not enough that I pay the mortgage and all the bills?"

In the light of the streetlamp, Freeman could see tears welling in Seede's brown and bloodshot eyes. "Good Lord, Jonathan. I had *no* idea."

Seede took another drag. "Well, that's how it goes in Breederland, my friend. You serve at the pleasure of the queen. Then she eats you."

"Yo, Seede."

Below them, on the sidewalk, a homeboy named Kwan. He was eighteen years old, almost too pretty for a male, with fawn-colored eyes and long lashes, wearing a knee-length, overstuffed down parka. In the style of the day, the merchandise tags were still dangling from the eyelets of his brand-new Timberland work boots.

"What up?" Seede asked, slipping into the local dialect.

Kwan spread his arms, offering himself as his response.

"Impressive as always," Seede said.

"You holdin any dat sinse?"

"What—so you can roll it up in one of them stanky blunts?"

Kwan raised his chin, playing at being hard. "You holdin or you ain't?"

"Come by tomorrow."

"Tomorrow? *Shit.* Don't know if there *be* no tomorrow."

Seede came down the stairs, followed by Freeman. He put his arm fondly around the teenager's shoulder. Beneath his puffy coat, Kwan felt small and insubstantial, bringing to Seede's mind a toy poodle. "So what are you doing right now, homey?" Seede asked. "You wanna join us for whore patrol? You live in the neighborhood. It's your civic duty to volunteer."

Kwan wriggled out of Seede's embrace. "Ho patro? What dat?"

"Come on," Seede cajoled. "We'll have a few laughs."

Kwan backed away from them slowly, his hand held out in front of him with the thumb and first two fingers extended—a make-believe handgun. He held the gun high and sideways, his elbow winged out, like all the gangstas in the movies. The previous year, the murder rate in Washington was number one in the nation. There was no telling what it would have been if the gang bangers ever learned how to aim properly.

"*Tomorrow,*" Kwan insisted.

"Ring the basement door," Seede said. "And bring me something large. None of that pebble shit this time, okay?"

6

Jamal sat in the driver's seat of his Lincoln with a steno pad and a pencil nub, doing a little figuring.

Twelve days earlier, his bottom wife, his main woman, had been arrested and charged with solicitation. Debbie was currently incarcerated in the DC Women's Jail, awaiting trial, facing a mandatory minimum sentence of ninety days. Every night, when he dropped her off on the Strip, he always said the same thing. *Pay attention out there.* Five years together, he must have said it roughly fifteen hundred times by now. *Pay attention out there. Don't get popped.* Debbie would be turning twenty-eight in April. She'd been working the streets—in LA, Vegas, Atlantic City, and now DC—for more than a decade. She'd been talking a lot lately about squaring up with Jamal, getting married, leaving "the life" behind. Deep down, Jamal couldn't help but wonder if she'd gotten herself busted on purpose. There was no other good explanation. He'd been sitting across the street watching—he could see it coming, like a train wreck in slow motion. The trick was sandy-haired, wearing earmuffs and a trench coat, a muffler tied jauntily around his throat like a K Street lawyer. The giveaway: he'd approached Debbie on foot. Most of the white tricks were afraid to leave their cars. No matter how drunk or puffed up they were, you could always sense it, you could see it in their eyes: terror. He's in a dicey neighborhood, cops everywhere, looking to do something illegal and immoral, something his wife would divorce him for in a heartbeat. He's pulling over his car, he's dealing with a woman, possibly on drugs, who is desperate enough to parade around in a bathing suit in subfreezing weather in order to sell her pussy. The law of supply and demand is in effect: she has what he needs. What he obviously can't get anywhere else.

Undercover cops are not afraid. You can see it in their eyes too: the agitated gleam of a true believer who is mucking about in sin.

Roughly calculated, Jamal figured Debbie's arrest and conviction were going to end up costing him more than fifteen thousand dollars in lost earnings and expenses. Subtracting her customary days off—every Sunday, the first three days of her menstrual periods—she would be missing about seventy-five nights of work, an average of two hundred dollars a night. He'd already laid out $550 as a retainer for the lawyer; more would be due after the trial, which was really just a formality anyway, given her prior arrests and the mandatory sentence. Not to mention the thirty dollars a week he was putting in her jail canteen account for snacks and sundries, and the cost of stamps so she could write him every day in her rounded, backhand, little girl cursive, the envelopes sealed with SWAKs and hearts and ILYs. Before mailing the stamps Jamal spritzed them with his Drakkar Noir cologne, as he had the photo she requested—Jamal in his younger days, shirtless at Virginia Beach. She'd be showing it off to the other hos in the joint, he figured. Maybe one of them would want to get with him too.

Shaking his head over the figures like a shopkeeper come upon lean times, Jamal dropped the pencil into one of the compartments of the drink caddy, stashed the steno pad in the glove box with his Webster's. *You've been down before*, he reminded himself.

A little more than five years ago, Jamal Alfred had been living in the suburbs with his wife and daughter, employed full time as a day-shift security guard at the Naval Ordnance Station at Indian Head, Maryland. He'd gotten the job through his military connections—he'd done two tours in Vietnam, army infantry, down and dirty. He shipped out in June 1970, assigned to a forward base. His first day in-country, hooked up with his unit, he was standing around smoking a cig when one of the corporals asked him for a light. Jamal dug into his pocket, clicked open the Zippo his brother had given him before he left, rolled the flint wheel . . . *CRACK!* A sniper's bullet split the air. Jamal felt it sizzle past his ear. The corporal crumpled to the ground at his feet, the back of his head a mess of bloody pulp.

Shaken, Jamal was removed to a tent, given a joint for his nerves. Life went on. Weeks passed. He became accustomed to the routine—the night patrols, the C rats, the trips to the whore house in the village, the bodies, the gore. No matter what they were doing, morning till night, he and the fellas were always smoking joints. Drugs were cheap and plentiful in the Nam, guys were generous—never once was Jamal asked to buy.

Then came the monsoons. The enemy launched an offensive. Cloud cover was thick; there was no air support. The entire base was pinned under fire. Nobody was sharing any drugs. Jamal became ill with flulike symptoms—runny nose, chills, a deep soreness in his joints. He asked one of the older guys should he go see the doc. Dude laughed. There was heroin sprinkled in those joints.

Dope sick and enraged, embarrassed by his own guileless stupidity—he had, after all, grown up on DC's notorious Fourteenth Street Strip, the son of an old-school pimp—Jamal demanded the name and location of the dealer. He went to his hooch, grabbed a pillowcase and his .45 sidearm, breached the barbed wire perimeter of the base, low-crawled into the jungle, through enemy lines. As directed, he followed a meandering stream for five clicks, came upon a village. At the fourth hut he gave the *mama-san* the pillowcase and a wad of cash. He gestured with the gun: fill it up.

Jamal stayed high for the rest of his tour. Then he re-upped for a second tour, with a special dispensation that he didn't have to return stateside in between, as GIs were normally required. Given the cost and purity of the junk in Vietnam, the elephantine size of his habit, he knew he couldn't afford to go home.

After the second tour Uncle Sam wouldn't let him stay any longer. He thought for a while about moving to Thailand as some of the guys were doing—back in America the antiwar movement was coming to a crescendo; there were stories about hippies spitting on returning vets. Compared with a cheap and bottomless supply of heroin and pussy in Bangkok, the decision seemed pretty much a no-brainer. But then he got the news of his brother's death. His father was already gone. Things at home required his attention. He flew back with a six-month supply of the purest Golden Triangle heroin he could find, imported specially from Bhutan. When his stash was nearly spent, he had a little going away party for his habit. Then he locked himself in a motel room in southeast DC and kicked cold turkey, the most brutal week of his life.

Discounting his intermittent insomnia and frequent nightmares—and his curious need to keep at hand an envelope containing old photos of his long-time drug dealer, his buddies from the squad, two of his favorite bar girls, and his collection of enemy ears, arrayed on top of a desk, that he had acquired in combat over the course of his two tours, three dozen or so unmatched curls of desiccated human flesh—the next six or seven years of Jamal's life passed in relative calm. He met a fine, light-skinned sister at a disco in Georgetown. They married, bought a house, brought a daughter into the world. Then one night Jamal was having a few drinks at the local tavern with some of his fellow security guards. All of them were vets. All of them, like Jamal, saw a VA shrink at least once a week. When you go to war, something innocent inside of you breaks. Like your cherry, you can never get it back. Toward the shank of the evening, one of the guys took him outside to the parking lot and gave him his first hit of freebase cocaine.

By the time he hit bottom, Jamal had lost eighty pounds and his job. The bank was foreclosing on his house. His wife's Toyota had been repossessed. His checking and savings accounts were empty. His gas tank was empty. His daughter needed three hundred dollars for a school trip to New York. He had four dollars in his pocket.

And so it was, on that fateful day in 1987, that Jamal took one last heroic hit of rock cocaine and jacked off to a porno. Afterward he flushed his crack pipe down the toilet, swallowed a few Valium, went to the closet, dug out his best suit—a gray worsted-wool pinstripe from Men's Fashion Depot. He put his last four bucks into the gas tank of his aging Ford Bronco and drove toward DC, heading for the Fourteenth Street Strip, a place to which he'd promised himself he'd never return.

He drove around the Strip a few times—a few laps around the track, as they used to say. Things had changed some, but not so much. The What's Happenin' Now had become the Moulin Rouge; the Blue Mirror was a pizza joint. The Strip itself had expanded somewhat both north and south. The residential part was a lot nicer; some of it had been expensively renovated. To his surprise, he saw that Cornbread and Killer Joe—contemporaries of his father—were still working, as was his old buddy the Donut Man, who sold crullers, condoms, and other sundries out of his station wagon near the all-night People's Drugs.

Jamal parked his Bronco on a dark corner beneath a ginkgo tree. He crossed the street, walking tall and casual through the gridlock, rolling his shoulders as he moved, hitching his step just the slightest, like his father used to do. He made a beeline for a tall white girl. She was apple-pie pretty, a little on the plump side. As his father liked to say: *Get you one with a lil meat on her bones. The skinny ones is mean.*

By dawn the next morning, when he dropped Debbie off at the Capitol City Motor Lodge and paid her first night's rent, Jamal had enough money in his pocket for his daughter's school trip and several new outfits to go with. By the end of the month his house was safe; he went shopping for his first previously owned Lincoln. For a time he even had his wife convinced that he'd gotten his old job back, albeit on the night shift.

Now, on this cold December night in 1992, he was comfortably ensconced in the creamy leather interior of his third Lincoln vehicle, a burgundy Mark IV, nearly new, only twenty thousand miles on the odometer. Out of the corner of his eye he detected a familiar movement.

If anything was signature about Salem, it was her walk—a graceful, long-legged gait that put one in mind of a giraffe running in slow motion. She crossed the street about a half block south of the Lincoln, her pace a step faster than usual, her head of spiky blonde hair held averted, as if she believed that not looking was nine-tenths of not being seen.

Opening his door, Jamal unfolded his six-foot frame, turned to face Salem over the roof of the car. She was sporting the new outfit he'd bought her that afternoon at the Prince George's County Mall—white leather miniskirt, black fishnet stockings, and a black-and-white ruffled blouse, hitched down off her shoulders like a punk rock Daisy May. He put his fingers to his mouth and whistled a distinctive blast, high-low, two sharp tones.

Busted, Salem turned and waved in his direction, unabashed, her manner that of a country matron who'd just spotted an old friend at a steeplechase.

Jamal frowned and pointed emphatically to the passenger side of his car. Salem had been with him for ten days. She was a strange girl, not at all the kind of ho he was used to. Sometimes it seemed like she was doing nothing but running game. But then he'd check her trap and find two or three hundred dollars. Something was different about this one. He just hadn't figured out yet what it was. And he probably never would—right now, he had enough on his plate. All these girls were twisted in some way or another or they wouldn't be hos, a lesson he'd learned pretty thoroughly a couple of years back, when he and Debbie had tried to expand the business, taking in four additional wife-in-laws at one time. Now, with Debbie in jail and the others long gone, his life in the suburbs just a memory, Jamal knew he was lucky to have come across Salem when he did—a fine lookin white girl with low mileage who was willing to pay five hundred dollars up front to get with him.

Salem jerked open the back door and climbed inside the Lincoln.

"I thought you were going on an all-night date," Jamal admonished.

"Dude never come back around the corner to pick me up." Though her skin was a milky shade of bluish white, Salem talked like she was black—a tall, white-blonde, peaches-and-cream type, overdubbed with Queen Latifah. She nestled into the plush leather, brought her knees to her chest, revealing a hint of white panty. "It cold, Jamal. Can we please go home?"

"Where's your coat?"

"I lef it at the bar. Ella say Pam took it home wit her."

"Girl, I paid good money for that coat. What do I have to do, sew name tags in your shit?"

"May I get a cigarette, please?"

"You already smoked that whole pack?"

"I got friends, you know. They smoke too. You got any condoms in the car?"

"Tell me you don't have any condoms."

"I'm *out.*"

"Then take five dollars and go get you some from the Donut Man down there by the drugstore. Tell him I said what up."

"You got five dollars?"

"Now I *know* you fuckin with me." Jamal cracked a smile. "Why don't you just go on now and be a good ho and make me some money."

She looked out the window. "Leave me alone, Jamal. My tummy hurts."

"You said it ain't your time for another week."

"This skirt too tight."

"The skirt I just bought? Why you insist on buying a size two if you don't wear no two?"

"I *do* wear two."

"I tole you to try it on. I tole you: *Try that shit on.* All clothes ain't made exactly the same. Different manufacturers use different measurements. Don't you—"

She leaned up over the front seat. "Can't you just carry me back to the hotel and I'll change real quick?" She batted her long lashes. "Please?"

Jamal addressed her with a level voice, a teaching tone, like a parent to a child: "Listen good now, baby. I got a way to solve all your problems, you hear? I got just the solution you need."

Annoyed: "Can't I jus go back and change?"

He gave her a look: *Don't even try that shit on me.* "This is what you need to do. You need to go to that corner over there and pull over a trick. You get into his nice warm car. And when he asks you for a blow job, you bat those big blue eyes at him, just like you did to me. You give him your real nice smile and you tell him, 'Please mister, it's cold outside.' Tell him that your skirt is killin you, that you'd really appreciate it if he'd take you back to your motel room so you could change. Tell him for three hundred dollars, you'll show him a *really* good time."

Salem put her hand to her mouth, playing mock horror. "Oh my God, Jamal!"

Alarmed: "What?"

"That's an indecent sexual proposition!" she giggled. "I could get in *trouble* for that."

7

The Pope of Pot sat behind his desk in his storefront church, wearing his marijuana bonnet. He clapped his hands with childish glee. "Start the music! Serve the canapés! Do we have any of those lapel pins left? Hop to it, people. We have visitors!"

Waylon rolled his eyes heavenward. *Canapés?* "Pope, please," he implored. "We have no money. We have no product. We have no food. Even if I represent us on all the charges, I still need to hire cocounsel and private investigators. There are filing fees, messenger fees, copy charges, transcripts . . . We need to come up with a plan." He pointed toward the door. "What we don't need right now are any more freeloaders."

"As you well know," the Pope declared zealously, "we turn no one away."

"But *Pope—*"

"You're becoming a real pooh-pooh, toots. Get a shot of him, Beta Max. Tight close-up: Waylon the Pooh."

A new round of pounding at the door. The blacked-out windows rattled and shook. Everyone looked to the Pope. "Who wants to answer?" he asked.

Louie the albino rose from his chair and shambled across the scarred linoleum toward the door, his rabbit fur hat slightly askew. He slid open the service window, a foot-square panel cut into the reinforced steel.

A beefy face, florid, with a black pompadour and a monumental nose. "Police. Open up!"

Panicked, Louie slid the window shut, just missing the nose. He had a wild, frightened look in his eyes, like a dog that knows what's coming next. The last bust had been Louie's first. His first time in jail too. He was hungry the whole time. Scared. He felt like an animal in a cage. He still awoke some mornings in a panic sweat, thinking he was back inside. He didn't want to go there again—ever. "What do we do?" he asked.

The Pope of Pot threw his hands up jubilantly. "Open the door," he said. "The police have come at my request."

Waylon stared at his leader, totally flummoxed. It had been two years since the Pope had rescued him from the Dumpster—the Pope liked to joke that if it wasn't for five pounds of spoiled chicken he was desperate to discard, they never would have met. The Pope had paid Waylon's medical bills, nursed him back to health, settled his six-figure gambling debt with the mob. By way of squaring the balance sheet, Waylon had taken upon himself the job of in-house counsel. Given the Pope's brand of cockeyed idealism, it was a Sisyphean task. Like the time the Pope had conspired to collect two dozen used syringes from Lafayette Park and turn them in to the police. Waylon had warned him that possession of syringes was illegal, that he could be arrested. Couldn't he have thrown them away somewhere quietly? Wouldn't that have achieved the same purpose? Couldn't he have called a news conference and just pointed out the syringes *in situ*? Or like Halloween, when the Pope had insisted on passing joints out at the parade in Georgetown—not really the greatest idea when your main source of income is an ongoing criminal enterprise. He'd also advised against the free matchbooks, with the Pope's name and a big marijuana leaf on the cover, listing the name and phone number of the DC police chief, urging residents to report all instances of police misconduct in the city.

Walyon held one finger up to Louie, indicating that he should wait a moment before opening the door. He scanned the room, looking for any incriminating items. His attention settled upon a teenage girl sitting lotus style on one end of Al Haig's credenza.

Her name was Sojourner Yeong Cohen-Lawrence—Sojii for short. She was sixteen years old, a runaway the Pope had met some months ago at the Greyhound bus terminal. An exquisite creature of indeterminate race—long chestnut hair, full lips, olive skin, emerald eyes—she was dressed in a fuzzy pink angora midriff sweater and antique bell-bottom jeans. As was the case with Waylon, Louie, Beta Max, and the others, Sojii subsisted solely by the Pope's good graces—she slept in his storefront, ate his food, picked up spare cash delivering the sacrament across the city on a twenty-one-speed mountain bike provided by the church. No doubt her presence in the storefront opened the Pope to myriad charges.

"Sojii," Waylon said in a stage whisper, "we've got to get you out of here."

The girl appeared to be in a trance. Her almond-shaped eyes were fixed upon the object in her lap—an uncannily lifelike representation of a human skull, rendered from a giant piece of crystal rock. The skull had been in the Pope's possession for as long as anyone could remember, the official resting place for his papal miter. Sitting there in Sojii's lap, it appeared to be giving off a greenish glow.

"*Sojii,*" Waylon repeated, louder this time, annoyed. He went quickly to the west side of the room, reached into the crevice beside the industrial refrigerator, flipped a latch. The massive appliance pivoted easily outward from the wall, exposing a passageway. A ladder led upward.

Blinking away the cobwebs, Sojii shoved the skull into her backpack and hustled across the room. She stepped into the passageway, looked back once at Waylon. Then she began to climb.

8

Thornton Desmond untied his apron and folded it away in a drawer. With a heavy sigh, he studied his reflection in the glass-doored cupboard—full head of snow-white hair, aristocratic cheekbones, patrician nose spiderwebbed with broken capillaries. In a few weeks, he would be turning sixty-eight, a time when most men should be resting on their laurels. Like a child on a motor holiday, he couldn't help but wonder, *Are we there yet?*

He gripped the edge of the granite counter, crouched down painfully on arthritic knees, retrieving from the nether regions beneath the sink an expensive bottle of single malt scotch. Born in Swords, north of Dublin, Thornton was the last living descendant of an illustrious Anglo-Irish family that could be traced back ten centuries. His ancestor, Geoffrey Desmond, had been a close confidant of Uther Pendragon. Arnold Desmond had shared a fence line with Geoffrey Chaucer. Sir Ferdinand Desmond helped found the Plymouth Colony—the third man off the first longboat from the *Mayflower*. Samuel Desmond's historical novel *The Gateway to Rome*, first published in 1788, has been read by English schoolboys for more than two centuries. And then there was Dickie Desmond, infamous for his bungled attempt at stealing the Scottish crown jewels at the turn of the twentieth century.

In his own salad days, Thornton Desmond had been one of the original jet set, part of the international fraternity of swells and bon vivants who made the fifties glamorous. A sometime freelance photographer and Hollywood PR man, he counted Sean Connery, Nigel Dempster, and the Earl of Lichfield among his closest confederates. When he was in his early forties, he stood by impotently as his mother sold off the ancestral estate—as it was, only the barn and several outbuildings remained; the manor house had been razed because of termites some years earlier. At the urging of her third husband, she used what remained of the Desmond family fortune to buy a hotel in Tangiers. Two years later, upon her death, her only child inherited her controlling interest in the place. Moroccan law made it impossible for Thornton to sell—or rather, impossible for him to take the proceeds of any sale out of the country. Thornton had no choice but to exile himself to the Tangiers Gibraltar Hotel, a clean but middling accommodation that catered, as the name would suggest, to British tourists from across the straits. That he lasted in Morocco for nearly twenty years was a miracle which could be attributed only to inertia—and, perhaps, to the ready availability of vice of every flavor in a city known for its so-called "sympathetic" system of law, which allowed all manner of victimless crime to flourish. Right about the time he could take it no longer, for reasons of both health and sanity, an old chum from Eaton turned up, another blue blood similarly dispossessed by time and modernity, hoping to cadge a free room at the hotel. One boozy night he shared with Thornton his idea of moving to America and hiring himself out as a butler, the latest rage among early-eighties parvenus and Wall Street masters of the universe. "Your accent alone should fetch at least eighty K a year," the friend suggested.

Now, in the roomy first floor kitchen of Bert Metcalfe's Georgetown mansion, Thornton Desmond, gentleman's gentleman, filled a Baccarat juice glass with three fingers of the rich, caramel-colored liquid and knocked it back. At least he was still living in the style to which he'd been born—Jamaican Blue Mountain coffee, fresh cut flowers in every room, Egyptian cotton pillowcases, a case of Macallan 25 in the larder. Replacing the glass on the counter, he loosened his Turnbull & Asser tie, unfastened the top button of his hand-sewn shirt. On his right ring finger he wore his father's signet, the Desmond family crest—a golden whirlpool on a platinum shield. He often wondered about the whirlpool, what it actually symbolized, how it had come to be. Ten centuries of recorded Desmond family history was strangely bereft of any mention of the origin of the very graphic by which it was identified. Throughout the years, as he'd felt himself being pulled farther from the comforts of his privileged upbringing, into the vortex of dark adventures and calamities that had characterized his life, he'd sometimes wondered what the arc of his story line would have looked like if his family had been represented symbolically by something a little more, well, awe inspiring—a lion perhaps, or maybe a hawk or an eagle. Had he believed in such things, he might have speculated that the Desmond family had long ago been cursed, that the whirlpool was a graphic harbinger of fortunes to come—everything down the loo.

He poured himself another shot and drank it off, rinsed the glass, placed it in the dish rack. After returning the bottle to its hiding place beneath the sink, he exited the kitchen, made his way down the dark hallway, the leather soles of his Gucci slip-ons clicking roundly against the marble floor. He took the elevator to the roof.

The doors opened onto a metal catwalk. On his first day of service at Metcalfe's, unaccustomed to modern appliances after twenty years in North Africa, Thornton had neglected to properly shut off the gas in the Viking stove, causing a minor explosion. He was found unconscious on the kitchen floor by his new employer, who helped him to his feet. Ten guests were expected for dinner that night. "Will you be okay to cook the *pullet*?" Metcalfe inquired.

Gathering his wits, Thornton had risen from the floor and excused himself to his sumptuous basement apartment, where he changed his shirt and shaved off what remained of his mustache. Then he returned to the kitchen and cooked and served a lovely dinner, roundly complimented by all in attendance. Metcalfe had gone so far as to introduce him to the company. Of course he told the story of finding his new manservant on the floor. It got him a big laugh.

Later that evening, Thornton's work in the kitchen at last complete—the dishes washed and put away, the leftovers wrapped as prescribed in the three-inch-thick loose-leaf binder that listed the preferences and procedures of the household—he had come up here to the roof, as he had tonight, summoned to bring coffee to Metcalfe in his gallery. Drawn by the view, by his feelings of hopelessness, he stood at the very edge of the slippery slate, four stories above the ground. To the southeast, he could see the majesty of the city's lights—the phallic glory of the Washington Monument, the pleasing mammarian swell of the Capitol dome, crowned by the erect nipple of Persephone. He challenged himself: *Name one last thing you have left to lose*.

For several long minutes, very long minutes, Thornton Desmond wracked his brain for an answer, a reason to go on, a reason not to jump. He'd been struggling now for so long. He felt so tired. What was the use?

And then it came to him. One last thing he had to lose.

"My nerve," he said out loud, the dulcet tones of his Etonian boyhood still evident in the creases of his ragged tenor. Deep into the third act, you never knew: a plot twist was always possible.

The catwalk led across the roof to another door, this one thick and armor-plated, like a bank vault. Thornton placed his palm on a light box. The door opened with an electric whoosh.

He stepped into a large circular room. The ceiling was retracted to reveal a girder-and-glass roof, through which could be seen the inky night sky, a sprinkling of stars.

Around the room, at each of the four cardinal directions, stood a granite pedestal, three feet high, four feet in diameter. On each of the pedestals sat a likeness of a human skull. Lit from beneath, the eye sockets glowed.

The skull at the north was made of amethyst. Dark purple in color, rich and translucent, it had been purchased from a Mayan priest near Oaxaca, Mexico. To the east was a skull of jade, excavated by Chinese archaeologists from beneath the site of an ancient Buddhist monastery on the Tibetan border. To the south was the Zulu Skull, made of lapis, used by African shamans for centuries as a weapon of war. The western skull was crafted of rose quartz. Purchased at great expense from a secret society based in London, it was known as the Templar Skull. Some scholars argued that the true objective of the Crusades was the liberation of the Templar Skull from its Moorish captors.

At the center of the room was a fifth round pedestal, identical to the others. Upon this one sat Bert Metcalfe, his tiny loafers swinging idly, heels knocking against the granite. Scattered around him on the floor were a dozen cardboard document boxes, all of them overflowing with old diaries, moth-eaten books, yellowed newspaper clippings, and musty letters.

Metcalfe looked up from the fragile pages of an old leather-bound journal. The cover was embossed with his name: Bertram Hedgewick Metcalfe. "They found my grandfather's diary!" he exclaimed.

9

Exhausted and bereft after another unrequited day of an eventful but generally unsatisfying life, I was sitting on the pristine, sandy beach—or rather, at a table on the beach at the hotel bar. Like the chair, the table was fashioned entirely from the wood and woven fronds of a coconut tree, another example of the ingenuity of the native population. The hotel was called La Casita del Mar. For the past six months it had been our base of operations: inexpensive but clean, it was set within a palm forest at the western end of the island of Guanaja, one of a chain of tiny islands off the northern coast of British Honduras.

The date, I shall never forget, was April 21, 1911. I was fifty years old. Time had weathered my face as it had the sheer limestone cliff rising from the mangrove swamp to the south. As I watched the orange wrath of the Caribbean sun melt into the silent and reproachful sea, I was at a low point. After years of searching, years of hoping, years of belief against all odds, I had begun to lose faith. Where was all of this getting me? What good was it to think against the grain? Perhaps I was wrong about my beliefs—maybe all of the others were correct. I poured another glass of rum. The tide of my personal fortitude was fast approaching its ebb.

Just then, from the direction of the shoreline, I heard a shout. It was Bobbie, my ward. She was thirteen years old at the time, just beginning to blossom into her estimable womanhood. She ran toward me at an exaggerated pace, her firm, muscular, suntanned legs at full gallop; her mane of dark hair flying like a prize filly's. Standing knee-deep in the surf behind her was a grizzled islander. He appeared to be wearing nothing but a loincloth. From the distance, given my lifelong myopia, I could not discern his intentions. I figured they couldn't be well—the haste with which Bobbie was moving toward me caused my blood to run cold.

I rose quickly from the table and took off in her direction—mine was a hobbled gait, an old warhorse still in the race; the splinter of a Winchester bullet, a remnant of my days with Pancho Villa, was still embedded in my hip bone. As we drew close, as Bobbie's countenance entered my field of focus, I could see that it was not alarm that was registered on her face, but rather the utmost delight. She smiled largely—her teeth were as white and brilliant as coral. "Look, Father! Look what the man gave me!"

I reached out and carefully took the object from her hand. It appeared to be a human jaw, constructed from a wondrous, glasslike substance—instinctively, I knew it was crystal quartz. It was an exquisite piece, clearly ancient, perfectly preserved, without so much as a dent or scratch—obviously it had been broken away from a larger piece, presumably a skull of crystal. From the moment I set my eyes upon it, I knew it was like nothing ever seen before by modern man. As I believed that day, without question or doubt, I believe still, twenty-one years later, despite the widespread condemnation by my many and vocal critics: I was holding in my hand an important relic from the long lost continent of Atlantis.

Immediately, I looked down to the shoreline for the Carib in the loincloth.

But he was gone without a trace.

In that instant, my path became clear; my life's purpose was finally revealed. Guided by unknown forces, lured down through the years and across thousands of miles, I was, I now saw, a mere pawn in a greater plan—how could it be otherwise? Surely everything had happened for a reason. Why else would the son of a banker give up the secure and comfortable life of his kin and class to go live with the Canadian Eskimos. Had I not lived with the Eskimos, I would never have suffered from frostbite. Had I not suffered from frostbite, I would never have gone to the Sonoran Desert to bathe in the healing waters of the Jamacha Spa. Had I not gone to Jamacha, I would never have met Pancho and his gang. Had I not met Pancho, I would never have been able to afford the expeditions—first to Guanaja, and later to the treacherous interior of British Honduras. Had I not pushed on, past the point of reasonable personal endurance, Tumbaatum would have remained buried in the overgrown jungle. For that matter, had I not taken upon myself the added burden, despite my peripatetic bachelor lifestyle, of caring for a female orphan in the first place (one, I might add, with a stubborn fondness for following her own wiles despite my wishes), I would never have found the object of which we now must speak—a relic so powerful that it defies all of the so-called Wisdom of the Ages.

10

Metropolitan Police Officer Perdue Hatfield emerged from the alley carrying a brown paper sack. He moved quickly on the balls of his feet, practicing the stealth tactics he'd learned at the academy, keeping to the shadows, taking cover behind a Dumpster. His target was ten meters east, in a puddle of light beneath the streetlamp. He cupped a hand beside his mouth: "Psssst."

Spooked, Salem spun around. "*What the—*"

Realizing his folly, Hatfield stepped out of the darkness. "Easy now," he said, palm out, a tone he might have used back home, trying to calm a skittish colt in his uncle's barn. "It's just *me*."

"You! Mother*fuck*! Don't you *never* sneak up on me like that again!"

"I didn't mean . . . I mean . . . *shoot*. I was just tryin to be friendly is all."

Shrill: "What I need to be friendly wit you fo?"

"Because we're linked by our common humanity?"

She let out a little snort. "Some of us is humans and some of us is cops."

He didn't know what to say to that.

She stretched a pink strand of bubble gum out from her teeth, wrapped it around her index finger. "What you want? Ain't no law against standin here, is they?"

"Actually, there is. It's called loitering. And there's a law against walking up to cars and offering sex. It's called solicitation."

"Dude lost!" she said, indignant. She ate the strands of gum off her fingertip. "He axe for directions."

"I didn't realize you'd opened a franchise of triple A."

Hugging herself for warmth, she looked up and then down the street. No sign of the burgundy Lincoln.

"Don't you have any family?" Hatfield asked. He took a step closer. "There must be someplace else you could go. Maybe I could put you in touch with—"

"Whatta you—Officer Save-a-Ho?"

Caught off guard by her humor—not the usual weapon of choice among the streetwalkers he knew—he stared at her for a few seconds, trying to size her up. When he'd first seen her on the Strip, he could tell right away that there was something different about this one, though not necessarily a bad kind of different—just unexpected, like when you fingertip a few grains of something white from the kitchen table and lick it, expecting salt, and get sugar instead. Back in Capon Springs, his family lived in a large depression on the down side of a mountain slope, known in geologic terms as a hollow, pronounced *holler* by the locals. A sort of backwoods cul-de-sac, it was home to an eclectic collection of buildings and ruins, all of them occupied by Hatfields—a ramshackle barn; an A-frame house; a log cabin; a tarpaper shack, smoke curling from its crooked chimney; a suburban-grade ranch with whitewashed siding, a green sofa out front beneath an oak tree. Until she turned twelve, Hatfield and his sister, Maybell, had shared a room. At night, by the glow of the hall light—she was afraid of the dark—Perdue could see her collection of dolls, dozens of pairs of eyes staring out dumbly from their shelves. Now, standing in the cold on the northwest corner of Fourteenth Street and Thomas Circle, Hatfield had an overwhelming urge to cradle this tall, pale-as-plastic creature in his arms, to tip her backward, to see if her lids would shut.

"You want some hot chocolate?" He opened the brown paper sack, removed a cup.

Waving him off: "No free pussy tonight, officer. It too cold. You ain't even have no car."

"Go on, take it." He took a step closer, offered the cup. "It has marshmallows. The little ones you like."

"How *you* know what I like?"

"I seen you get it that way at 7-Eleven."

She checked up and down the street again. Like a squirrel taking a nut, she snatched the cup from his hand.

"That wasn't so hard, was it?"

"Could we move outta the fuckin light?"

He gestured with mock formality, imitating a maître d'. "May I suggest that shadowy spot over there?"

They moved closer to a brick wall. It was defaced with colorful graffiti, an urban sort of veterans' memorial, carrying the tags of many from the neighborhood who were no longer living. Hatfield ripped open the drinking tab of his cup lid. He could feel the warm liquid sluicing through his anatomy. "Say what you want about 7-Eleven, they have great hot chocolate."

Salem ripped the tab off her cup and let it fall; it propellered slowly to the ground like a seedpod from a sycamore. Hatfield almost said something about littering but he caught himself. She took a sip. He took a sip and smiled, looked at her thoughtfully. She studied the skuffed toe of her black leather pump.

"I like your name," he said at last. "It's unusual—menthol fresh. Is it your real name or just a street name?"

"My real name is Jennifer," she recited. "I was molested by my uncle when I was seven . . . Is that what you want to know?"

"Well, I—"

"When I was ten I was sent to an orphanage. The nun would call me into her office every night before bed. She'd make me kneel between her legs and recite my Hail Marys."

Horrified: "Is that true?"

She winked at him lasciviously. "It is if you want it to be, baby."

Hatfield's face fell. He'd never been very good with women. Or at least he hadn't had much chance to get good, which pretty much explained the sorry state of his social life. Growing up, he'd attended church with his family three times a week; some of the congregants spoke in tongues. His parents wouldn't allow him to go to dances or to movies; he'd taken his cousin to the prom. He finally lost his virginity in Singapore, but only after the guys in his squad had shamed him into a whorehouse. He told the girl he'd pay her but she didn't have to do it. Amused, she insisted. Even as he was being trained by the U.S. government to kill people for a living, Hatfield had a strong sense of what was right and what was wrong—premarital sex was one of the wrongs. He felt like sex should be something special, done with someone you love. As he saw it, in life there is a line in the sand: on one side is Right; on the other side is Wrong. This is the way he tried to live. Sometimes it proved to be difficult.

Salem was a little bit moved by his vulnerability. He reminded her of someone. She couldn't put her finger on it. She imagined him as a child, a beefy boy with a cowlick, playing cops and robbers. *Maybe he isn't such a dick after all.* He was kind of cute in a rube-ish sort of way. But he was obviously after something—what cop wasn't? She looked up soberly into his large moon face. "I shouldn't be talking to you. I'll get in trouble."

It occurred to Hatfield that Salem had momentarily dropped her ghetto accent—a small bit of peripheral information left unprocessed for now. "You mean get in trouble with Jamal?" he asked. "No way. Me and him go way back."

"Ain't you the one locked him up?"

"Yeah, but—"

"I don't think he likes you very much."

"I've always been fair to him."

"I don't think he see it like dat."

"Say what you want," Hatfield said, turning cold. "I just happen to believe that a piece of shit like him, if you pardon my French, shouldn't be exploiting vulnerable young women like yourself."

Salem's lazuline baby doll eyes flared with anger. "You ain't know shit," she said.

"I know that it's not safe for you to be out here. And I know that a smart young woman like yourself should be doing something more dignified, if you don't mind me sayin so."

"You don't know nothing about me, *bitch*." She walked over to the Dumpster and made a little ceremony of pouring out his hot chocolate.

Then she turned on her four-inch heels and headed off in a northerly direction, hips working overtime.

11

Two cops in plain clothes barged past the steel-reinforced door of the Church of Realized Fantasies, knocking Louie the albino against the wall, *oooff,* dislodging his rabbit fur hat.

The one with the nose wore a trench coat. His blue-black hair was combed up into a thick, oily pompadour. His partner wore a suede jacket, displayed a gold badge. "Internal Affairs," he announced.

"Howdy, honey, howdy!" trilled the Pope. He was sitting behind his government surplus desk, wearing his papal miter. He raised his hands to shoulder height and rubbed little circles in the air—the official papal greeting. "We're so pleased you could come," he gushed. "Would you like your shoes shined?" He clapped his hands. "Bring the polish at once!"

The cops exchanged glances. The Pope's reputation had, of course, preceded him.

Waylon stood beside his beloved client and pontiff, coolly adjusting the knot of his silk tie. His résumé listed Exeter, Princeton, Harvard Law, a clerkship with a federal judge, a coveted spot in the DC city attorney's office—until he'd discovered the horses, his life had been very different. Though gambling is legal, in one form or another, in just about every state of the Union, it is a powerful drug, easily available, hard to kick. In Waylon's case, the horses were the gateway, discovered innocently enough on an outing with some colleagues to Baltimore's Pimlico Race Course. Within a year Waylon was wagering on anything, just to get that high. Prep school basketball, women's college field hockey, curling. How many times a judge would call recess on the morning after attending a Mexican-theme charity ball. Whether or not the city attorney's hot paralegal would be wearing a bra to court. Who could get the most phone numbers on a Friday night at Rumors, the popular Nineteenth Street disco that catered to the legal set.

"What can we do for you, gentlemen?" Waylon asked, motioning to the several stackable plastic chairs that were lined up in front of the Pope's desk. Like any reformed addict, he still had the urge. He fought it every single day. His higher power was the Pope.

The pompadour sat down first. His name was Massimo Bandini. "As I understand it," he said, addressing Waylon, "Mr. Rubin here wanted to lodge a complaint."

"That is correct," said the Pope. "I wish to report a theft."

The other cop took a seat by his partner. His name was John O'Rourke, known as Jack. He removed a notepad from the inside pocket of his mustard-colored suede jacket, licked the tip of his pencil. "What was the date of this theft?"

"It was the night the church was raided," the Pope said. "What date was that, Waylon?"

"Last Wednesday."

"December ninth?" asked O'Rourke.

"Stipulated," Waylon said.

Bandini: "What specifically was taken?"

"The sacrament," said the Pope.

"You mean, like, wafers?" asked O'Rourke.

"The pot. The herb. The weed," the Pope said. "The merry-gee-wanna."

O'Rourke: "Can you describe the suspects?"

"They were wearing blue uniforms," the Pope said.

"What sort of uniforms?"

"*Police* uniforms, toots. DC police uniforms."

Bandini leaned forward in his chair. "You're saying that officers from the Metropolitan Police Department stole marijuana from you?"

"What, specifically, are your allegations?" asked O'Rourke, his pencil poised above his pad.

"Wednesday night, after the church was raided by the police, John J. Hill said that a search of my premises had yielded seven pounds of pot," the Pope explained. "But I was only charged with possession of *four* pounds."

"John Hill?"

"John J. Hill. He's one of your assistant chiefs."

"Chief Hill?"

"The very same."

"And he said there were seven pounds? When did he say this? In a conversation you had with him?"

Exasperated: "He said it at the news conference. The one they held in front of the church. After the bust. Where all those members of the press just happened to be assembled—at 5:30 P.M. on a weekday evening, just in time to go live on the local TV newscasts. The Lord works in mysterious ways, detective. The Lord is my shepherd, I shall not want. The Lord helps those who help themselves. I believe we have Chief Hill's statement on video. Beta Max, bring us the tape."

Beta Max crossed the room toward a shelf full of books, videotapes, and sale items—marijuana-leaf lapel pins, roach-clip key chains, poker chips with the Pope's likeness embossed in gold on one side.

"So you're admitting at this time that you were in possession of seven pounds of marijuana," Bandini reiterated.

"We're admitting nothing," Waylon said. "What we're doing is lodging a formal complaint."

"It was seven pounds," the Pope said, sick to death of all the bullshit mumbo jumbo—why do you think he'd founded his own church? He accepted the videotape from Beta Max and placed it on his desktop, within reach of the two detectives. "I have a pretty good idea of our supply. It's *my* sacrament, after all. I'm a member of the clergy. I have tax exempt status. I have souls in my charge, troubled people, people who depend upon myself and my minions to keep this town running, to keep this nation running—if you must know the truth. I could give you names. We're talking international figures. I could tell you things, believe you me. I'm the Pope, you see. I am on a mission to divert the world onto a more sane path."

O'Rourke drummed on his pad with the eraser of his pencil. "Was anything else taken?"

"I wasn't going to mention it, but since you've asked, there was a watch taken," the Pope said. "A gold Hamilton watch given to me by my sister. She teaches third grade. She throws beautiful clay pots. I don't know what relevance that watch has to the case or why the police would need to take it. And also there was a kitchen knife, a brand-new kitchen knife that I bought recently at the restaurant supply store down the street."

"Was the knife for cooking or was the knife for chopping marijuana?"

The Pope removed his Coke-bottle glasses, proceeded to clean the lenses with his shirttail. The whites of his eyes were an unhealthy shade of yellow. "You don't *chop* pot, detective. You take it and you crumble it. You do it with your fingers, or sometimes you use scissors. Or you can use a strainer if it's real seedy, but we don't like seeds, that's the headache weed, we use only the finest seedless strains of scientifically engineered sacrament in our ceremonies, green and sparkling with resin, buds as fat as your thumb. Only the best, detective. Producing a high high: clear and happy, penetrating and original. As opposed to the sleepy, lethargic head of the—"

"Anything else?" interrupted Bandini.

The Pope of Pot returned his glasses to the bridge of his nose. He struck a conciliatory tone. "You know, detective, I don't have any problem with cops smoking pot. The good Lord gave us the sacrament to use as we see fit. When I lived in Amsterdam, some of my best customers were police—and, I must add, they received a generous professional discount, which I am prepared to offer you as well. But what I do have a problem with is cops *stealing* pot. The knife, the watch, the sacrament . . . I see a disturbing trend here. This drug war of yours: it's Frankenstein's monster. A police officer cannot go around picking up things that are nice and putting them in his pockets just because he likes them. This is not Nazi Germany. This is not Soviet Russia. A warrant to search is not a warrant to steal."

As the Pope was speaking, Bandini rose from his seat, made a show of stretching his back, rotating his neck, de-kinking himself. He began to wander about the room in a casual manner, idly picking up a pamphlet here, a coffee cup there, peering into the trash can . . .

"Don't get me wrong," the Pope continued, "I'm not anti-police. I just want to see justice done." He placed his elbows upon the desk, leaned his face across the expanse of gunmetal gray toward O'Rourke. "The police stole my sacrament, detective. If you're not going to charge me with those other three pounds, I want them back." He issued a beatific smile. "If the cops want pot, they can darn well pay for it like everyone else."

By now, Detective Bandini's casual stroll around the room had taken him to the bookshelf on the back wall, near the refrigerator, behind which was concealed the trap door and the ladder. Bandini idled there for a moment before the shiny industrial shelving, which stretched from floor to high tin ceiling, inspecting the Pope's collection of videocassettes. He picked up *Bikini Houseboys,* studied the cover, replaced it. He picked up *Reefer Madness* and did the same.

And then, suddenly, his florid face twisted itself into an antic expression of surprise and amazement. "What have we here?" he asked rhetorically. "Right in *plain sight*?"

Bandini reached into the shelf and appeared to retrieve a small, clear plastic bag. Turning around to face the assembled—his partner, O'Rourke; the Pope and Waylon; Beta Max, Louie the albino, and the rest of the messengers seated in the plastic chairs —Bandini held the bag up in the air before him and let it unfurl, revealing a substantial quantity of white crystalline powder. He opened the ziplock seal, dipped a finger, took a little taste.

Now O'Rourke issued a beatific smile of his own. "Everyone down on the floor," he ordered.

12

Jonathan Seede and Jim Freeman marched eastward on Corcoran Street, hoping to link up with the main element of the whore patrol. Side by side on the narrow cobblestone path, they shared an easy closeness, Freeman slew-footing in his calf-high, lace-up construction boots and fluorescent orange vest, Seede wearing his navy surplus peacoat, the hood of his sweat-shirt pulled up over his head for warmth and anonymity.

"I can't wait till you see the bumper stickers," Freeman enthused.

"Bumper stickers?"

"We're putting them on the back of every car that makes the turn onto Thirteenth Street. They're *faaaaaabulous*. Black and white, high contrast—a silhouette of a hooker leaning against a lamppost. It says: THIS CAR HAS BEEN PROWLING THE STRIP."

"I wouldn't want to be in that garage," Seede said. The thought brought a smile to his face, his first of the evening.

"Drama in suburbia!" Freeman intoned, the voice of a radio announcer. Since he'd divorced his high school sweetheart and quit his job as the youngest schools superintendent in the history of Newport News, Virginia—bound for Washington and the love of a good man—Freeman had worked tirelessly to make Corcoran

Street and its surrounds into an island of gay gentility: a Georgetown for Marys, as he liked to say. He was a fixture at city council meetings, a member of every local development board that would have him. The streetlights and planters? His idea. Likewise inviting Liz Taylor to the clinic fund-raiser and countless other brainstorms. A perennial member of his real estate firm's Million Dollar Sales Club, who'd moved properties all over town, Freeman considered the thirteen hundred block of Corcoran his own personal fiefdom—over the last decade, he'd sold thirty-two of the forty houses, some of them more than once. As was befitting, Freeman's own house was the jewel of the street—the centerpiece of an ornate Second Empire terrace that occupied the entire north side of the street, a post–Civil War take on what would be called, in more modern times, a townhouse development, built during the heyday of the neighborhood, when nearby Logan Circle was the most fashionable address in Ulysses S. Grant's bustling capital reserve. A highlight every winter on the Logan Circle Tour of Homes, Freeman's place still had its original carved wooden cornices, isinglass windows, and dumb waiter—large and sturdy enough to raise a man from the ground floor kitchen to the third floor master bedroom, as they'd discovered last Halloween.

Seede and Freeman continued along the sidewalk, easily outpacing the line of cars to their left. "Who gave you the idea to target the johns?" Seede asked.

"I was at this property I manage—1505 T. The tenants were GW students, the little shits—these rich kids from Bahrain, spoiled rotten. They couldn't afford a maid? They moved out a month early without giving notice and left all this food behind. There were roaches *everywhere.*" He shuddered involuntarily.

"What does that have to do with the johns?"

"Well, I had the exterminator come to give me an estimate, and he was talking about roaches and how it was all a matter of the food supply—if you eliminate the food supply, the roaches go away, because they don't want to be in a place where there's nothing to eat. And right then, it hit me—hookers are like roaches! If you want to get them out of the neighborhood, you have to eliminate the food supply, also known as *johns*. I thought to myself: If we get rid of the customers, won't the hookers go somewhere else?"

"Apparently the city council agrees with you. There's a bill before them that would give the cops authority to impound any vehicle from which a driver or passenger is soliciting a prostitute."

Freeman grimaced. "That'll never get passed; those do-nothings will debate it until the Second Coming, like everything else. We've got the stickers. We're taking down license numbers. We're buying an ad in the *Herald*. We're going to publish names. We're going to make it very embarrassing for someone to be seen in this neighborhood trying to get a blow job."

"Excluding anyone you might be dating, I presume."

"Ha, ha, ha."

"By the way," Seede said. "The cops don't just give out that kind of data, you know. License plate registration is not public information."

Freeman twirled the waxed end of an imaginary mustache. "Ve have vays," he said.

"You're starting to really scare me now," Seede said, only half kidding. He looked out absently over the line of cars to his left—and caught sight of a familiar head of spiky, white-blonde hair.

Salem was sitting in the passenger seat of a mud-streaked Chevy pickup truck, a wheelbarrow in the bed. The driver wore a ponytail, a backward baseball cap. His jaw was grinding side to side; his eyes were glazed and fixed on the car ahead. The truck rolled forward a few feet.

"We have to do *something*," Freeman said. "It's getting worse. Last night I found one in my fucking garage."

"One what?"

"A hooker. She was passed out. She still had the syringe in her arm!"

"Are you kidding? How'd she get in?"

"Crawled beneath the door. It had gotten stuck about a foot off the ground; the repair people had to order a part. She didn't weigh ninety pounds. She probably could have crawled through the mail slot. I had to call 911. I couldn't believe how long they—"

"Well, well, *well*! Look who's finally decided to grace us with their presence!"

Wolfie was standing on the southwest corner of Corcoran and Thirteenth, a wisp of a man with moist, rubbery lips, dressed in camouflage fatigues and a pair of midseventies-vintage platform heels. His circa-Vietnam walkie-talkie—an ancient piece of military hardware the size of a dorm-room refrigerator—sat by the lamppost, abandoned. With Wolfie on the corner was the rest of the whore patrol—longtime partners Sam and Dave. Midforties and affable, Sam and Dave looked and dressed alike, as many couples of long standing tend to do. The problem was, no one was sure which was Sam and which was Dave. Not even Freeman, who'd sold them their house. Everyone on the street just addressed them collectively, as in "Hey, SamDave, what's the gossip?" Since they were always together, it worked out fine. At the moment, one of them was standing beneath the streetlamp, holding a spiral notebook and a pen, taking down license numbers. The other was stationed near the stop sign, in the shadows behind a parked van. He had a stack of bumper stickers. As each vehicle in the line came to a halt, preparing to make the turn south, he'd reach out stealthily and slap a bumper sticker on the rear end.

Wolfie assumed the toe-forward pose of a fashion model, one hand on his hip. "I was beginning to think you needed an engraved invitation."

Freeman jerked his thumb at Seede. "This one over here took a little convincing."

"It's nice to have the fourth estate behind us, so to speak," Wolfie said, his vampish manner reminiscent of a forties film star, with the addition of a pronounced liquid lisp. Every aspect of Wolfie's persona seemed to radiate the sentiment of his favorite activist cheer: *We're here! We're queer! Get used to it!* The rhinestone tiara didn't hurt either.

"I'm here strictly as an observer," Seede insisted, playing along.

"What's *that* for?" Freeman asked, pointing to the elaborate leather sling-type device that was affixed to Wolfie's chest like a baby harness. Instead of a baby it held a very old, very large, Hasselblad camera. Affixed to the side of the camera, with the help of some bailing wire and duct tape, was a huge industrial-grade flash attachment.

"It's one of Bob's toys," Wolfie explained. "It's magnesium or something. Check this out."

He popped open the viewfinder, aimed the camera toward the intersection, closed his eyes, depressed the shutter.

For one brief moment, the entire intersection was bathed in blinding silver light.

And then: a sickening crunch of metal against metal, a tinkle of glass, the outraged squeal of hastily applied brakes . . .

Seede rubbed his eyes. Slowly, patches of his sight returned. He was able to make out the image of a fat man getting out of his car, cursing, mad as a hornet. Planted into the rear end of his vehicle was the front bumper of the mud-spattered pickup truck, the suspension of which had been tinkered to a higher than normal height, resulting in greater than normal damage to the fat man's car. Salem was still in the passenger seat of the pickup. She was struggling with the ponytail guy, trying to open her door, trying to get out. The ponytail guy was amped and hollering. He had Salem by the meat of her arm.

Without hesitation Wolfie moved toward the muddy pickup. He grabbed the passenger door handle and yanked . . .

. . . and Salem tumbled out, knocking Wolfie into the gutter, landing on top of him.

The ponytail guy came out after them. He had a blue-steel revolver in his hand. He stood unsteadily over the tangle of writhing limbs that was Wolfie and Salem. "Get back in the truck, ho," he slurred. He raised the gun, pointed it at Salem's face.

Wolfie depressed the shutter.

Blinding silver light.

Followed by a distinct hollow crack—a sound like a hammer splitting a coconut.

And then a heavy thud—like a side of beef hitting the floor.

As his sight returned, Seede was able to make out the image of a large black man, wearing wraparound sunglasses and a three-piece suit, holding what appeared to be an athletic sock full of quarters.

Jamal stepped over the unconscious figure of the ponytail guy. "What up, Seede?" he said, reaching down to help Salem to her feet, a Cheshire cat grin on his face. "Can I be of some assistance to you and your friends?"

13

Sojii swam languidly upward from the depths of sleep, bits and scraps of dreams and memories floating past her mind's eye . . . A blue party dress. A salt-and-pepper Afro. The lonesome *scree* of a bird. A Greyhound bus pulling away from the terminal, spewing oily fumes. A hot pretzel, crusty and chewy at once, yellow mustard on her fingers.

Breaching the surface of wakefulness, she rolled over and stretched luxuriantly. Sleeping every night in a moldy old sleeping bag on the cement floor of the Pope's church was hard even on a teenager; she felt more rested than she had in months. She inhaled deeply through her button nose—the dorsum slightly concave like her Korean grandmother's—and then exhaled slowly through pursed lips—full and spongy like her dad's, a Louisiana Creole. At last, she opened her eyes—twin emeralds inherited from her great-grandfather, born in a shtetl in Lithuania.

And found herself on a beach.

In a patch of shade beneath a coconut palm.

The fronds clattered in the breeze—a faint, percussive melody, like a marimba.

She sat up and looked around. The fine ivory sand was guarded on three sides by a lush tangle of vegetation. A line of red ants marched over a miniature dune; a hermit crab in a colorful shell motored sideways, probing with an outsized claw; a gecko darted into the brush. The lagoon lapped gently at the shoreline. Fish of all kinds fed in bands and swirls of shimmering amethyst and aquamarine. The sky was the blue of a storybook; frigate birds and herons and pelicans wheeled gloriously overhead. A half mile distant, ocean waves crashed upon a protective coral reef.

The last thing she remembered, Sojii had been sitting in a beanbag chair in the cluttered disarray of the Pope's attic hideaway. For most girls her age—for most people of any age, for that matter—this radical change of scenery would have no doubt caused a panic. But Sojii was no ordinary girl. As it was, she owed her very existence to a series of cosmic hiccups.

Her grandmother had been born in a small village in South Korea, a farmer's daughter forced by the circumstances of war into a life of prostitution in Panmunjom. Her grandfather was an American GI, a troubled Jewish premed student from Chicago who'd left school, over his parents' vociferous objections, to enlist in the army. The two met in a comfort bar at the beginning of a ten-day furlough. Within a week they were engaged to be married. Despite the language barrier, he wrote his brother, "I have found my soul mate." One month later, the Jeep he was driving blew a tire on a mountain road. He was killed.

Sojii's mother, Ruth Yeong Cohen, was thus born by special arrangement in a Red Cross field hospital in the heady days preceding the signing of the Korean armistice in July 1953. She was raised by the brother and sister-in-law of the dead GI in a Craftsman house in Evanston, Illinois. Following the adoption, the heretofore barren couple (a city planner and his wife—a wonderful cook, doting mother, and popular past president of the sisterhood at Temple Oheb Shalom) went on to conceive two daughters and a son. Ruth grew into a spirited young woman with high cheekbones, wavy chestnut hair, and the pronounced nose of her eastern European forebears, which lent to her face an asymmetrical, Picasso-esque quality—more than a few likened her to an Asian Barbra Streisand. While the family atmosphere was certainly loving, Ruth lived a mercurial life, given to elaborate flights of fancy and deep bouts of depression. She could never shake the notion that she didn't really belong—on the playground with her younger siblings, she was often mistaken for the nanny. So it would be for a lifetime. Neither this nor that, she was always searching.

By 1974, twenty-one and divorced, Ruth found herself employed as a receptionist in the biology department at UCLA, serving a group of scientists that included a handsome, light-skinned Creole microbiologist named Robert Lawrence. Born in the tiny backwater of Morrow, Louisiana, population 242, Lawrence was one of ten children—a rainbow assortment of recombinant features and hues, a gene pool comprising African-American, French, and Native American DNA. At sixteen, seeking a better life, Lawrence had run away from the bayou and joined the navy. With the help of the GI Bill, he worked his way through college and graduate school. Ten years older than Ruth, he sported a large, prematurely gray Afro. The colorful dashikis he favored offered a comfortable alternative to the department-mandated shirt and tie—during those early days of affirmative action, no one was brave enough to tell him to put on regular clothes. The couple was married in a civil ceremony at the Beverly Hills city hall, then flew immediately to Paris, where Lawrence was slotted for a fellowship at the Pasteur Institute.

Two years later, the marriage in tatters, the spouses already encamped in separate domiciles in Washington, DC—where Lawrence was now employed at the National Institutes of Health

—a daughter was born. In honor of her serendipitous heritage, they named her Sojourner Yeong Cohen-Lawrence.

Two months after that, Ruth appeared unexpectedly one night at the door of her estranged husband's apartment. There was a wild, defeated look on her oddly beautiful face. She thrust the colicky bundle of their daughter across the threshold. "I just can't handle it anymore," she said. And then she slung her backpack over her shoulder and was gone, never to be seen again.

So began Sojii's nomadic youth—a Korean-Lithuanian-African-American-French-Native Indian Jew with no mother, a workaholic father, and no particular place to call home. As you could imagine, from an early age, identity was a big issue for Sojii. Her dad preached the "one drop rule"—one drop of African-American blood makes you black, no matter what other kind of blood you might also have. Sojii's experience didn't prove quite so cut and dried. As a first grader in Manhattan Beach, California, she'd been the darkest in her class. One day a kid told her that her skin was the color of poop. When Sojii's father called the boy's house—the teachers at the school knew the child as Horrible Harry—the mother was nonplussed. "We're not racist," she insisted. "We have *season tickets* to the Lakers." During middle school, Sojii and her dad moved to Richmond, Virginia—where she was tormented by a clique of dark-skinned girls who called her Chinky. *Who am I REALLY??????* she'd doodled in her sketchbook/journal. Absent unequivocal answers, she had learned over the years to operate without them. She had become accustomed to going where life led, each new day neither a mystery nor an adventure, simply another day to survive.

Rising from her place beneath the palm tree, Sojii walked toward the water. The sand was hot between her toes. She couldn't help but notice that she was now dressed in a beautiful batik lavalava, a large rectangular cloth native to the South Seas, arranged ingeniously into a halter-top minidress, secured behind her neck with a bow.

She kind of figured she was dreaming, yet everything seemed so real. She swam around for a time in the warm and gentle water; it was hard for her to relax. Something was about to happen—why else was she here? She wished to herself that it would just go ahead and happen.

Sure enough, the next thing occurred. She heard this weird fluty music emanating from the jungle.

She waded out of the water, scanned the tree line, trying to locate the source. The scale was strange, but the tones were pure—haunting round notes floating on the air like a sweet aroma.

A well-worn path led into the sun-dappled jungle, all vines and ferns and razor grass, presided over by tall coconut palms, curved and vain, ripe with green nuts. The underbrush chattered and rustled with the presence of lizards and small mammals. Insects sang; birds twittered and fussed. Sojii was charmed.

At length, the music ceased. She came upon a large circular clearing, the ruins of an ancient place, a meeting or prayer spot, most of it reclaimed by the jungle. At the center was a stone slab, three feet high, four feet in diameter. Atop the slab was the Pope's crystal skull.

Instinctively she picked it up, heavy as a bowling ball, and cradled it in her arms. It was a marvelous object—flawless, transparent, anatomically correct.

As she held it, the skull began to darken. Inside the cranium, an image began to form, a hologram—what appeared to be clouds. Three-dimensional, well resolved, rendered in full color, the clouds became thicker and more dense, like a time-lapse video of a gathering thunderstorm. After a few moments, a dark spot became visible at the center of the storm. The spot grew slowly larger, until the central mass of the skull was entirely dissolved, leaving a black void. It was as if the fabric of daily life had been eaten away, revealing a small patch of limitless space.

Presently, an image appeared.

She was asleep in a beanbag chair in the littered disarray of the Pope's attic hideaway, wearing her pink angora sweater and vintage bell-bottom jeans. A copy of *High Times* magazine was open in her lap. Next to her, on a low table, was the Pope's crystal skull.

A door in the floor swung open. A man emerged. He was wearing a peacoat and a hooded sweatshirt.

And then someone was touching her shoulder. She could feel the breath, hot and urgent on her ear: "*Wake up*. Hurry. We gotta go."

PART TWO

14

Jonathan Seede backed his motorcycle to the curb, levered down the kickstand with his heel. It was Wednesday morning, just after dawn. Dulcy and Jake had been gone since Monday afternoon. The air was raw, the light was tenuous and grainy. Pigeons cooed in the eaves of the ruined townhouses that lined both sides of the street; starlings chattered in the spindly bare limbs of the forlorn, planted-by-the-city ginkgo trees. Also called maidenhairs, identified by scientists as the oldest species of tree on Earth, ginkgos were prized for their fall foliage, a dazzling yellow. By some curious bureaucratic decision, all of the ginkgos in the city, roughly one per residence, were female. Each fall, along with their beautiful leaves, the trees produced an abundant crop of gooey, malodorous fruit, with mildly toxic skin, that stuck underfoot like doggie diarrhea. It seemed a perfect metaphor for life in the nation's capital.

Seede dismounted the bike, an eleven-year-old Honda, a vehicle choice that was more about parking than anarchy, though that was part of it too, the feeling of primacy that came as he drove unfettered through the middle of a rush hour traffic jam. In a way, Seede's motorcycle—neither big nor showy; purposeful in an offbeat but well-considered fashion—seemed a perfect metaphor for Seede himself, a nobody from nowhere whose stubborn desire to type for a living had taken him further than anyone could have imagined. The Honda also figured prominently in his courtship of Dulcy—another stubborn quest. Of course, they hadn't been on the bike together since she got pregnant. The larger her belly swelled, it seemed, the more insulated from him she became. Eighteen months into child rearing he felt more like an administrative assistant than a husband. He was always on call, there was no room for dissension. The boss was a ballbreaker: she who must be obeyed.

He locked the helmet on the frame of the bike, retrieved a woolen watch cap from his coat pocket, fit it onto his prematurely balding head. Patting his pockets, he ran a checklist of his paraphernalia. At twenty-nine he was considered by now a seasoned professional. He worked for an esteemed institution, the *Washington Herald*. He wrote front-page stories read by millions, some of them the most powerful people in the world. Yet, deep down, he felt like he never knew exactly what he was doing. Each time he started a new story it was like starting over from scratch. He wondered if everyone felt that way. *When do you begin to know? Do you ever?*

Crossing the street, he assumed a slight hitch in his step. In the ghetto a man's walk is his vehicle; it places him on the scale between player and mark. Though the block seemed deserted, he knew he was being watched. He was short, dark, and bearded, with a hoop earring in his left lobe. Cops took him for a criminal. Criminals took him for a cop. It could be a hindrance or an asset. He could never predict which.

A burgundy Lincoln was parked down the way. Seede approached the driver's side. The tinted window slid down with the usual electric hum.

"Your little buddies all tucked in for the night?" Jamal snickered.

Seede smiled ironically. He liked to say that he could spend an hour eating dinner with anyone on the planet. There was no harm in being open, but it was sometimes hard to explain; most people preferred the company of their own kind. Heat eddied from the window of the car, warming Seede's face, radiating a potpourri of scents—the leather interior, Jamal's cologne, his Newport cigarettes, the Christmas tree air freshener hanging from the rearview mirror. Despite their apparent ease, the two men had only recently met. Long story short: Jamal stomps into the office of Debbie's lawyer, mad as a hornet for losing her case, a slam dunk due to mandatory minimums. Lawyer, thinking fast, offers up the telephone number of a newspaper reporter he knows—Jonathan Seede. "Try it in the press," he advises.

While Seede knew that getting the story assigned was a long shot—it was, after all, a family newspaper—he ran it by his editor anyway, partially because he owed the lawyer a favor, partially because he promised Jamal that he would, partially because a story idea rejected still counts as a story idea proposed (he had an unwritten quota), and partially because, in a newsroom peopled with the likes of FDR's granddaughter and James Dickey's son, having a real live pimp as a source counted for tons of street cred. As expected, the editor wasn't interested, though he did urge Seede to maintain contact. Which was good enough to make it kosher for Seede, as a courtesy, to go ahead and phone the public information officer at the women's jail and ask a few suspiciously innocuous questions. Mysteriously, right after Seede's call, Debbie was moved to the protective custody wing. It wasn't something Jamal was going to forget anytime soon. As he often said, "You do fo Jamal, and Jamal *will* do fo you."

"So . . ." Seede said elliptically, moving to the matter at hand. "He's in there?" He looked furtively over the roof of the car, indicating with his eyes the row house in front of which they were loitering. It was set back from the street on a little hill, one in a line of identical neighbors in various states of repair, conjoined like Siamese twins, sharing here a common roofline and there a common eave, distinguished as individuals only by abrupt changes of paint color as the eye moved across the property lines. A small yard in front of this particular house was encircled by a rusty iron fence; the grass was worn to mud, littered with broken bottles, food wrappers, and postage-stamp-size ziplock bags. A Big Wheel trike lay on its side. A staircase led to a wide porch. The front door was painted a festive shade of red.

"I don't think he ever leaves," Jamal said.

"And you're sure he's cool about doing an interview?"

"I let him know."

"A'ight," Seede said, his use of the slang sounding a note of false bravado. *Let him know? What the fuck does that mean?*

The sky was growing lighter. The streetlamps shut off with an audible click. Jamal detected Seede's hesitation. "You need me to come with?"

Seede rapped the rooftop of the Lincoln two times with his knuckle. "I'll call you later and tell you how it went."

15

A pair of immense armored gates swung slowly inward, admitting a black paddy wagon into the basement sally port of the District of Columbia Central Jail.

Eight stories high, built of diarrhea-colored brick, the DCCJ loomed over a hazy landscape of empty lots, low-slung housing projects, storefront churches, and liquor stores in the far southeastern sector of the city, separated from the rest of Washington by the Anacostia River. The river and the area around it were named in 1608 by Captain John Smith for the Anacostian Indians, who hunted the abundant hardwood forests and fished the once sparkling tributary. After the Civil War, Anacostia was developed as one of the city's first suburbs, a bedroom community for blue-collar workers employed across the river at the Washington Navy Yard, a source of the sewage and industrial waste that had, by modern times, rendered the river virtually lifeless. The first subdivision had restrictive covenants prohibiting sale or rental of property to Negros, mulattoes, Indians, Irish, and Jews. One hundred forty years later, 93 percent of Anacostia residents were African-American. A similar percentage could be found among the inmates housed within the eight-foot-thick walls of the DCCJ. Less than three years old, it was already overcrowded.

The paddy wagon pulled to a stop in front of the intake center. Officer Perdue Hatfield exited the passenger door, sauntered toward the back of the wagon, juggling his nightstick on its leather leash like the old-timers used to do, making it dip and twirl and dance. His three-to-midnight shift had been nearly over when the call came—officers requesting backup, an arrest at the Pope's church. While it struck him odd that detectives from Internal Affairs had made a drug bust on the Strip, he did what he always did—followed orders unquestioningly and to the best of his ability, even if it meant putting in overtime to shepherd the hapless Pope and his merry men through interrogation, booking, and transport. As it happened, he had nowhere else in particular to go—his spider plant seemed to be perfectly okay at home without him. Plus he could use the overtime. He was thinking about buying a BMW direct from Germany. Back when he was in the marines, he'd spent a month in Bamberg, attending an antiterrorist course, something you had to take if you chauffeured a colonel or above. The highlight of the training was "evasion skills"—students were put through their paces on a high-speed track in specially tricked-out BMWs. Since then, owning a Bimmer had been one of Hatfield's utmost goals. You could fly to Germany, go to the plant in Munich, pick up your car, drive it anywhere you wanted—a friend had suggested touring the wine country in France, but the thought of all those drunk tourists on the road gave him pause. When you finished, they'd ship the car to America, all for about the same price you'd pay at the local Mile of Cars. Just thinking about being behind the wheel of a machine like that made Hatfield feel alive. Like his grandma used to tell him: *Life is full of suffering, Perdue: You need something to look forward to*.

Now, at the DCCJ, twenty-six hours since he'd last slept, Hatfield's eyes felt twitchy—everything was moving slow, as if he was under water. Reaching the back of the paddy wagon, he unlocked the rear doors. Out spilled the Pope of Pot, hands and ankles chained. He was followed by Waylon, Louie, and Beta Max.

They shuffled through an electric sliding door and queued up as directed, noses against a cinder block wall. Across the room, the intake cage was built of steel bars and bulletproof glass, with a pass-through for paperwork. It housed a large woman in a tight white nurse's uniform. She was sitting on a high stool before a computer terminal. Her white shoes were on the floor beneath her. The heels had been crushed, making them slip-ons.

"You first, your holiness," Hatfield said, choosing to address his prisoner in respectful terms. The church was on his foot beat. On cold nights he sometimes stopped in for a cup of herbal tea.

The Pope of Pot stepped up to the counter, taking care to place his feet precisely in the red footprints painted on the floor. "Howdy, honey, howdy," he sang. Though his manner was upbeat, his voice was thready and strained. His head was flushed an alarming pinkish red. Hatfield put the booking slip in the pass-through.

With the languid, economical motion of a city employee, the intake nurse retrieved the slip, returned her attention to the computer screen. Her three-inch nails click-clacked, clawlike, across the keyboard, glue-on jewels sparkling beneath the harsh fluorescent lights.

After some time, she looked up. "Michael David Rubin," she recited. "You are now in custody of the District of Columbia Central Jail. I am going to axe you a series of questions."

"Axe away, toots!" the Pope enthused. "Cut me up like Lizzie Borden!"

She shot him a withering look. "Are you injured or have you been in an accident in the last seventy-two hours?"

"Certainly my civil rights have been injured. I have been deprived of my liberty, but I'm fairly sure it was no accident. This whole thing is obviously a setup. It's ridiculous! A huge misunderstanding. I am the Pope, you see? I speak with the voice and authority of God."

"No injuries, no accidents," Hatfield said.

"Any major medical problems?" she asked.

"I guess that depends upon your definition of *major,*" the Pope answered thoughtfully, "and upon your definition of *medical.* And of *problem,* for that matter. Problems are relative, I'd say. On the one hand, given the *ooooof—*"

Hatfield poked him in the ribs with his nightstick. Not hard, just a little jab, like someone knocking a stuck CD back onto track.

Waylon's nose, as previously ordered, was still against the wall, which was painted industrial gray and smelled of vomit and ammonia. He craned his neck, trying to see what was happening to the Pope. "Harm him in any way and I will have your badge!" he bellowed.

"Fuckin A!" Louie yelled.

"Damn straight!" called Beta Max.

"Nose against the wall!" Hatfield reiterated, assuming now a command tone lest things deteriorate further—he was, after all, outnumbered. He turned back to the nurse, a bit agitated, a bit adrenalized by the notion of possible threat. "He's healthy as a horse, ma'am," he confirmed.

She pushed the form back out the window and Hatfield signed it, ripped off the top two copies, returned the rest to the nurse. He stuffed one of the copies—the goldenrod—into the Pope's front pants pocket, a rather intimate gesture given the circumstances. The pink copy went into his own pocket. Then he guided his prisoner across the cement floor, toward a heavy steel gate, behind which stood a deputy.

An alarm sounded: a short metallic burst.

The gate slid open.

Hatfield reached for the ponderous key ring hanging from a retractable hook on his utility belt. He unlocked the Pope's cuffs, replaced them in the holster on his belt, then gave the Pope a little shove, propelling him, like a toy sailboat across a pond, in the direction of the deputy. "Be careful in there," he said to the Pope's back.

The gate slid shut with a resounding clank.

16

Thornton Desmond made his way down the long, dim hallway carrying a silver tray, knocked at the door of Bert Metcalfe's bedroom suite. Hearing no response, he let himself in, as he did every morning. He never knew what he'd find.

This morning, curiously, he found nothing. The room remained as he left it the night before, the curtains drawn, the Frankart lamp on the night table lit—its two slender nymphs rendered fetchingly in bronze, holding aloft a glass orb. The king-size canopy bed was unrumpled; the custom-tailored silk pajamas and matching brocaded robe that Thornton had laid out were untouched, as were the cookies and milk.

At the far end of the room was a door. Light filtered from beneath.

Bert Metcalfe was sitting at a library table in the private study off the bedroom. The walls around him were lined with shelves, crammed to the ceiling with leather-bound volumes. He was still wearing his pin-striped suit and loafers from the night before. A reading lamp cast a solitary ring of light.

"Coffee, sir?"

Startled, Metcalfe looked up from the journal before him. "Must you be so damn quiet, Thornton?"

"May I serve?"

Metcalfe rubbed his face; his stubble made a scratchy sound. The table was covered with dog-eared manuscripts, brittle maps, dusty letters, yellowed photos, antique newspaper clippings—the accumulated writings and personal effects of his grandfather, the original Bertram Hedgewick Metcalfe. He gestured toward an empty spot.

Thornton set down the tray, off-loaded the cup and saucer, the cream and sugar, a silver bud vase containing a red Sweetheart rose. "Is it everything you hoped for, sir?"

Like an archaeologist who had finally unearthed his long sought prize, the diminutive billionaire's eyes sparkled with exhausted delight. "His family was middle class—from Manchester, England," Metcalfe said. "They wanted him to follow in his father's footsteps. I think he realized at some point that he'd be trapped forever if he didn't do something decisive. At seventeen he took a boat to Canada—he went steerage—and ended up just beneath the Arctic Circle, living with a family of Eskimos."

Metcalfe sifted through a pile on the table, came up with a faded photograph. "This is an eight-hundred-pound catfish. He landed it from a dugout canoe in the Caribbean. Do you believe the size of that thing? It looks prehistoric. And this is him later"—he picked up another photo—"in the Honduran jungle, when he was searching for the Master Skull." A tall, thin, serious man squinting against the tropical sun, wearing a floppy hat, woolen jodhpurs, and knee-high boots. An extra-long-stemmed meerschaum pipe angled obliquely from his mouth.

"He sounds like a real-life Indiana Jones."

"I know," Metcalfe said, disappointment in his tone. "Everything anymore seems already done, doesn't it? But think about it. In his time, in his era—the early 1900s, before flight—this guy was the real deal. He was a true adventurer, a man who followed his gut instinct to the ends of the Earth and back."

"And you never had the opportunity to meet him, sir?" Desmond poured the coffee with flair, raising the carafe higher and higher as the cup filled—a dark, rich, stream issuing from the swan-neck of the silver spout.

"My father never even mentioned him. Like he didn't exist. For years I had the impression my father was an orphan. He didn't talk about either of his parents. Now I'm beginning to understand why."

"We all have our sad stories, don't we, sir?"

"That we do, Thornton."

The butler placed the serving tray under his arm. "Will there be anything else then?"

Metcalfe looked up affectionately at his manservant. "How are the bunions, Thornton? Has Dr. Woo's treatment helped you at all?"

He smiled gratuitously. "Fair to middling, sir."

"Why don't you have a seat?" Metcalfe gestured to a chair across the table. "You've *got* to hear some more of this."

"If you insist, sir."

"I do insist, Thornton." Metcalfe reached to a shelf, pulled down a dusty souvenir coffee mug, set it on the library table. "You know how it is with rich folk," he said, shoving the just-poured cup with saucer toward Thornton, "we have to employ people to be our friends."

17

On a fine, sunny April morning in 1914, loaded with a veritable king's ransom in kit and perishable supplies —enough to see a crew of fifteen through a three-month expedition—the Ninita pulled into the splintered but picturesque docks at Punta Gorda, 120 miles south of Belize, the capital of British Honduras.

Accompanying Bobbie and myself were Dr. Stephan Ambrose, medical doctor and leading authority on Mayan civilization, and also H. R. Stuke, a somewhat known Cornish watercolorist who had become fascinated by the region we proposed to explore and begged us to bring him along. As a lifelong devotee of the higher pursuits of fine art and personal expression, I succumbed to his requests—hoping, perhaps, that he could initiate my young ward into the secrets of his craft. It was a decision I would regret for a lifetime.

In Punta Gorda, as I had hoped, amid the thatched adobe dwellings of the soporific Caribs—small in stature with brownish red skin, thick lips, and fuzzy negroid hair, hailing originally from the territories surrounding the mighty Amazon River—we picked up further information about the existence of what I hoped was the Lost City of Tumbaatum.

The ruins, we were told, did indeed exist—deep within a treacherous and nearly impassable jungle. To reach the place, we were advised, our best route would be along a muddy river, which met the sea at a point four miles north of Punta Gorda. Exactly how far upriver we needed to travel was of some dispute. The Carib concept of time and space was difficult to fathom. Some measured the distance in days. Some said weeks or months. In the area around the ruins, it was further alleged, lived a small but fierce tribe of hunter-gatherers, said to be direct descendants of the mighty Mayan race which had built the Lost City. We could get nothing definite; the stories had the gossamer quality of legend.

As we know from archaeological studies, the Mayans developed a culture and civilization that flourished for more than a millennium, beginning around 850 b.c. Looking at the historical record they left behind, we find a curious and contradictory picture. Developmentally speaking, archaeologists of all stripes consider the Mayans a Stone Age people. They subsisted mostly by primitive methods of agriculture and had a limited diet. They had few tools that we know about—few material possessions beyond the rudimentary have been found in archaeological digs. And yet, as we well know, the Mayans were—oddly and concurrently—experts in theoretical science and mathematics. They developed complex systems of hieroglyphic writing and numbering, a well-ordered system of government. Their vast network of independent city-states was linked by roads; each magnificent city was itself a distinctive work of art, expertly designed and executed—breathtaking pyramids, soaring temples, exquisite palaces, beautiful shrines.

Their religion was based on the rhythms of the natural world; they worshipped a pantheon of gods and superheroes who demanded regular tribute. In one such rite, the priest would remove with surgical precision and hold aloft the still-beating heart of a sacrificial victim, a young man or woman who had been pampered and groomed since birth for this divine service to his kind. The Mayans, we also know, were adept in the arts of clairvoyance and divination. They were avid astronomers who placed great emphasis on prophecy and prediction; they had a well-defined understanding of the annual calendar and the workings of the stars and were able to accurately predict eclipses. Imagine the power of a shaman who could predict the very day that the moon would blot out the sun.

After nearly a thousand years of growth and refinement, however, the story of the Mayans abruptly ends. Left behind was no evidence of famine, drought, disease, or war. They simply disappeared, as if into thin air, sometime around a.d. 830.

It was this grand mystery that brought me in quest of the Lost City of Tumbaatum. There, I hoped, were answers to these and other questions: From whence had the Mayans come? Who were their ancestors? How had a people—who hadn't yet developed the wheel—gained the advanced knowledge necessary to build a great and complex civilization in such a short space of time? What secrets did they possess? Where did they go? And most importantly: What role did crystal skulls play in this mysterious and timeless drama?

Anxious to move onward, I engaged a small motor launch —the only one available in the village—and two ancient dugout canoes, fashioned from cedar logs. As to our crew, the word "pitiful" would not be inaccurate: no one in the village seemed interested in undertaking an expedition. The best we could come up with were three smallish orphan boys and a couple of village drunkards whose fears and superstitions were overshadowed by their need for rum.

At dawn on the sixth day, we departed from the docks at Punta Gorda, our faithful Ninita bravely towing behind her the motor launch and the two dugouts. We were bound for the mouth of a river called Rio Pulgas—rough translation: River of Small Biting Insects. A more apt name could not be imagined, as we would learn soon enough.

As we stood on the deck, watching the village recede, Bobbie, my young ward, looked far from elated.

"What is troubling you, daughter?" I asked.

She looked at me dolefully. "I have a premonition of trouble, Father."

Upon hearing this, I did not laugh. With me now since the first days of the new century, Bobbie had been a blessing in so many ways. Sixteen years old, she was an expert with both rifle and handgun, a savvy hunter, a patient and crafty fisherwoman; at the card table she was always a difficult adversary. A beautiful young maiden, an able comrade, a passable cook—she had been a loyal partner in my quixotic quest for the answers to some of life's more compelling riddles. On more than a few occasions, I must faithfully report, I had found her hunches correct.

But the time for questioning was behind us. The mysteries of the Mayan civilization, I was convinced, were connected to the mythical island of Atlantis, which had been located, according to ancient maps and writings, in the Caribbean Sea due east of British Honduras. Surely evidence of this connection—one or more crystal skulls—could be found in Tumbaatum. To think otherwise was impossible to consider. We had come too far.

I pulled Bobbie close and gave her a reassuring hug. "Have courage, my daughter," I told her. "We must press on."

18

Behind the red door of the ruined townhouse Seede found an alcove, and behind that another door, most of the glass panes broken or missing. The foyer was expansive, with a filthy marble floor and dark wainscoting, the wood scarred and gouged. The rooms immediately to the left and right—in Victorian times the library and the parlor—had been put into service as separate accommodations; tattered blankets hung in the doorways in lieu of doors. The smell was a pungent mélange of fried food, dirty diapers, mildew, garbage, and decay.

A little girl appeared. She sported a full head of pickaninny braids, each one anchored fastidiously with a pink bow. Seede followed her up the central staircase to a room on the third floor. The door was partially open.

He stood for a few seconds, working up his courage. From an early age he had wanted to express himself, to be noticed, to be heard. After false starts in high school with rock guitar and photography, he figured out he was good with words—a good bullshitter, his mother liked to say. A couple of creative writing seminars in college led to the next lightbulb: he loved to write but had nothing to say. Hence the newspaper career—another stubborn quest. Next key realization: He was not outgoing. He did not like to meet people. He did not like to ask questions. Owing to an incident when he was ten years old—intending to send him to his grandparents for the summer, his parents had inadvertently put him on the wrong interstate bus—he had a fear of being lost. Every time he had an interview he'd arrive fifteen minutes early, just to make sure he found the place, which was usually not very hard, given that the city encompassed barely twenty-two square miles, a good portion of which was parkland and federal memorials. With the site of his appointment clearly in view, he'd sit there on the Honda or in the car, psyching himself up, making himself ready to take off his helmet or open the car door, to walk up to the house, to knock, to introduce himself, Jonathan Seede from the *Washington Herald,* to commence asking deeply personal questions of strangers—all of which, supposedly, served the public's right to know but really served his own need to have something to write about, his own need to be read and recognized and loved.

He poked his head in the door, meanwhile *rap-rapping* with his knuckle, a dribbling series of tentative knocks. The room was dim, the only light a Tiffany table lamp, a diffuse ruby and amber glow. The lamp sat upon a round, leather-topped table, which itself sat inside the semirotunda of the bay window. Next to that, in a bent-arm morris chair, sat a substantial man wearing an Arab djellaba and a black wool cardigan. His salt-and-pepper hair was plaited into cornrows; his stocking-clad feet rested on an ottoman.

Seede took a hesitant step into the room. The air smelled of sandalwood and freesia. "Bo Franklin?" he inquired.

"Who askin?" He had the gravelly phlegm-tinged voice of a bluesman or country preacher.

"Jamal sent me."

"What'd you bring?"

Seede knelt and reached into his sock, came out with a lightweight plastic sandwich bag, knotted at the top.

Franklin tore the bag with his teeth, poured into his large, leathery palm a piece of freebase cocaine, white and crystalline like an aquarium stone, a perfect sphere. He nicked it with the edge of his manicured thumbnail. "Where you get *this* at?"

"Cooked it," Seede said.

"You cooked this?"

He shook his head, affirmative.

Franklin's eyes narrowed. "Bull*shit*."

Seede froze—not the reaction he expected.

Franklin looked him up and down. "What do you want?"

"An interview."

"About what?"

"I thought Jamal was supposed to—"

"Run it past me again."

"I'm doing this, well—it's sort of a long-range project."

"Sort of?"

"A book. About the war on drugs—that's part of it. I trace it back nine years to Nancy Reagan."

A blank expression.

"See, when Ronald Reagan first got into office, Nancy needed an official cause. All first ladies have them—ever since Eleanor Roosevelt. Usually it's something warm and fuzzy like literacy, hunger, poverty. Lady Bird Johnson's was highway beautification. Remember? *Keep America Beautiful.* When Reagan was elected, Nancy decided—or her advisers, whoever was pulling the strings decided—that her cause should be kids and drugs, you know, stopping children from abusing drugs—which, by the way, was not a term in common use at the time. Back then it wasn't called drug *abuse,* it was called drug *use,* which is subtle, I know, but that's what we're looking at here, the subtle way language can change societal attitudes, or the way it reflects changes, or both—it's a chicken-or-egg kind of question. And not only that: if you ever met Nancy up close, as I have, you could tell she was totally blitzed—tranquilizers, sedatives, antipsychotics, *something.* Once, during an appearance she made at this camp for underprivileged kids, I was the designated pool reporter; I followed her around for the entire day. She was wearing this pleated skirt and pink espadrilles. And she never blinked her eyes. Not once. She was like a fuckin zombie, I shit you not. Toward the end of the day, she was in the arts and crafts shack. It was Nancy, her handler, the camp counselor, a dozen of these little black kids, and me. They wanted Nancy to help them make a silk-screen T-shirt commemorating her visit. Somebody squeezes the paint onto the screen, you know, out of the tube, and they give Nancy this squeegee thing that you use, the wand or what have you, and she starts drawing it across the screen. And then, like, halfway across, she drops the squeegee, just lets it fall. She's gotten paint on herself—this forest green paint, a few dabs on her knuckles. And she looks stricken. *Horrified.* This look of pure panic, you know, like she's been dosed with radiation or something. So her handler rushes over. And Nancy looks up with her big, round, unblinking eyes and asks, 'Will it . . . come off?' "

"Just say no," Franklin laughed.

"You know what I'm sayin? Crazy, right?" Seede continued. "I bet you didn't know this: they kicked off Nancy's campaign with an appearance on a TV sitcom. Remember the show *Diff'rent Strokes?*"

"With that little guy."

"Gary Coleman."

"I think I partied with him once at Studio 54."

"The show aired in March 1983. A rainbow-colored assortment of children and teens gathered around the first lady. They all shouted into the camera: 'Just say no to drugs!' In retrospect, it was probably the defining coinage of the late twentieth century: *Just Say No*. Bush spent eighteen billion dollars last year on the drug war. The ranks of law enforcement agencies across the country are swollen to all-time levels. The court system is gridlocked with drug cases. New laws dictating mandatory minimum sentences leave judges with no discretion; they hand out prison time with the help of little charts—this much drug equals this many decades behind bars. Meanwhile, according to NIH statistics, among high school seniors, the use of cocaine and marijuana was up by 10 percent last year."

Franklin dropped his chin to his chest. He pretended to snore.

"It's more than that," Seede said, struggling to explain. Granted, there wasn't actually a proposal. He was still fleshing out the idea. But in his heart, in his *soul,* he knew what he wanted to say. "I want to write a book about the whole notion of prohibition. I mean, what happens when we follow Nancy's advice? What happens when we Just Say No? Think about it. It's the basis of Judeo-Christian ethics: abstinence, control, denial of the human urge. Idle hands are the devil's playground. All that shit. But I wonder: Maybe too much self-control is bad for us? What happens when people are wrapped *too* tight? What are the ramifications of living in a world where everything pleasurable is evil? No fat, no sugar, no cigarettes, no sex. Everything will kill you. Everything is bad. Where does that leave us? What does that *do* to people? Doesn't that fuck them up even more?

"Denying your natural urges makes you pent up inside. When something natural is withheld, it becomes idealized, fetishized. It festers and mutates, turns malignant. Like Catholic priests. They can't have sex. They can't even masturbate. And look what happens: The pressure builds. People explode. All sorts of aberrations ensue. This is how our culture teaches us to deal with normal desires and emotions. We're taught to suppress our instincts, our human needs, lest we end up consigned to hell. But doesn't that end up leading us to a whole other kind of hell? What if we were allowed to have our fantasies and secret desires? What if it was all okay? Would the world come off its axis? Or would it be a better place?"

Franklin reached over to the table next to him and retrieved a hammered-copper ashtray, transferred it to the wide arm of his chair. He placed Seede's rock in the tray, sawed into it with his thumbnail, extracted a wedge. "Sounds like you got plenty of theories. What do you need me for?"

"Because you're right," Seede said. "Theories *are* boring. But you . . . you're the living *antithesis* of prohibition. You're the poster boy for Just Say *Yes*. You've defied every convention, you've broken every rule, you've taken every drug. Like you said in your last *Rolling Stone* interview: 'I never met a pussy I didn't wanna eat.' You're the living, breathing embodiment of *Frankenfunk*—which, by the way, has always been one of my favorite albums."

"And I got three years hard time at Folsom to show for it."

"Everybody knows you got screwed. It was early in the drug war. They needed to make an example of someone, and you were it. That woman returned to your house on her own volition. She said as much. It was in her testimony. I read every word of it. I've read the transcripts to the entire trial. You put her up in your guest room. You gave her a clock radio, for chrissakes. Who gives a clock radio to someone they're imprisoning?"

Franklin reached to the table again, retrieved a small glass water pipe. He placed the chunk of freebase into the shallow bowl, atop a multilayered filo dough of metal mesh screens. He looked up at Seede. "What's your name again?"

"Jonathan Seede."

A whimsical grin creased the big man's face. "You mean like that storybook character—what the fuck his name?"

He'd heard it his whole life.

"Johnny Appleseed!" Franklin exclaimed. "That's it, right?"

Seede raised a hand in resignation.

"You ever plant any apple trees?" Franklin laughed. He slapped his thigh with his free hand.

"I like to say that I plant seeds of a different sort."

"That's deep, bro."

Seede felt himself blush. He removed his watch cap. "Mind if I take off my coat?"

Bo Franklin motioned with his pipe toward the empty chair opposite, a twin of his own. "Make yourself comfortable, Appleseed."

19

At the eastern edge of town, just inside the District line, the Capitol City Motor Lodge occupied a small plot of land between a busy thoroughfare and a vast Amtrak railroad yard.

A dreamer's notion of a can't-miss roadside attraction, it was built in the 1950s in the shape of a horseshoe. A later owner added the red tile roof in an effort to evoke association with a well-known national chain. Given its location, the building's design served well. The base of the horseshoe fronted New York Avenue, a congested six-lane ribbon of rutted asphalt favored by truckers and commuters. Shrouded in fumes, permanently under repair, it functioned as a service entrance into official Washington—a back route through the ass end of town. Sharing the boulevard was an assortment of old warehouses and light industries, a plumbing concern, an office furniture outlet, a burger franchise, a couple of gas stations, and a miniature golf course, now closed, the entrance of which was guarded by a gigantic fiberglass likeness of King Kong climbing the Washington Monument, a putter clutched in one fist. A school bus abandoned on the premises served as a trick pad and transient residence.

Guest rooms at the Cap City were set around back of the building, tucked safely along the inner contour of the horseshoe, giving the place the protected feel of a natural harbor. The Amtrak acreage was visible from nearly every room—an elephant's graveyard of old railroad cars, rusty components, barrels of solvent and other toxic stuff, obscured by a thick tangle of weed trees and wild grasses and shrubs, all of it surrounded by a high cyclone fence crowned with concertina wire.

At the center of the horseshoe was the parking lot. Moored there on this overcast morning was a remarkable collection of American-made land yachts—Rivieras and Electra 225s, Eldorados, Coupe deVilles, and Lincolns—their conditions ranging from brand-new to up-on-blocks, testament to the varying fortunes of the residents of the CAP OL CIT M T R LO GE, as read the rooftop sign with its requisite burnt-out letters. Above the sign was a brightly lit billboard featuring a bas-relief likeness of the Capitol. On a clear night, if you took a ladder to the roof, you could actually see the dome, rounded and familiar, upon its little hill, the geographical center of Washington, the highest point in town. In its literature, motel management touted this view, intimating proximity. Great was the disappointment of many an unsuspecting tourist who'd booked by phone or by Web site.

Salem stood before the sink in the bathroom of room 215, wearing comfortable jeans and an oversize Miami Dolphins sweatshirt. The door was locked; the exhaust fan rattled and squeaked. Leaning closer to the mirror, she applied a coat of lilac lipstick, a pleasant compliment to the blue-white tones of her skin. In the car the other day, as she was freshening her lips, Jamal had shared with her the fact that whenever he saw a lipstick tube, he thought of a dog's erection. Now, every time she went to reapply . . . She smiled clownishly at herself in the mirror, crossed her eyes. Then she put her hands on her hips, gave herself a leveling stare: *What have you got me into this time, bitch?*

Salem had been in residence at the Cap City for almost two weeks, since the night she met Jamal and decided to "get wit him," as he'd put it, a privilege for which she had paid the customary five hundred dollars cash. When he mentioned the fee, she was incredulous. "You asking *me* for money?" There they were, in Georgetown, at Club Gemini—upscale, members only, catering to Arabs and other wealthy internationals. Salem was in her best dress; she'd left Miami with only a small roller bag. Jamal was wearing one of his Chinatown custom three-piece suits, the chocolate brown. Of course, both of them had scammed their way into the joint. They would laugh about it later, how both were running game—and how Jamal was obviously the more accomplished. That night at Gemini, he'd explained the whole deal with a good bit of charm: how the tricks paid the hos and the hos paid the pimps, the price for protection and love. Salem wasn't much interested in the love part; as things stood, she'd had enough of love for the time being. But given her situation, the possibility that she was being followed, the possibility that her life was in imminent danger, she went ahead and paid Jamal the money. Protection was exactly what she needed. She couldn't go to the cops. What else could she do? Who would ever think of looking for her here?

As was his custom, at the conclusion of their first night together—a night of drinking and dancing—Jamal took his new girl to Denny's, paid for her breakfast with some of the money she'd just given him. Then he brought her here, to the Cap City. As he had with breakfast, he paid for her first night's lodgings, thirty-five dollars, with her money. Hereafter, he explained, she'd be responsible for her own motel tab. Though she was frugal by nature (and shrewd too, given to stashing at least 20 percent of her earnings, all of which were supposed to go to Jamal) she declined to take advantage of the weekly rate offered by the motel, even if it would have saved her five dollars a night—thirty-five dollars a week, almost the cost of a blow job. A week in advance, at this stage of her life, seemed exceedingly long range.

It was only three years ago, after all, that Salem had been working at a popular nightspot in South Beach, rubbing shoulders with movie stars and fashion industry royalty, serving cocktails in a gold lamé bikini. Along the way she'd gathered around herself a number of gentleman suitors. They'd take her to dinner, buy her expensive things, give her gifts of cash from time to time. One of the men, a married dentist with real estate interests, set her up in a condo. Another, the owner of a large GMC dealership, gave her a Corvette. Eventually she dropped the waitressing entirely. It was an easy life, not at all unsatisfying, built around the trade of a commodity she possessed in ample supply. As she saw it, what she was doing wasn't much different than other women she knew. Everyone said that marriage was a barter system. Why couldn't dating be the same? When she was younger, living with her mom in a mobile home park in the shadow of Cape Kennedy, a bookish girl who kept scrapbooks on her favorite astronauts and never missed a space launch, there was an old redneck who lived in the trailer next door. A disgusting man with a deeply wrinkled neck, he was always saying that women had an unfair advantage in life. "They own half of the money and *all* of the pussy in the world," he'd complain. Now that she was older, she could see his point. Maybe it *was* God's little gift to women—an inexhaustable commodity that held its value for many years, a small bonus to offset the awesome responsibilities.

About a week after she'd gotten with Jamal, he'd announced that he was moving into her room at the Cap City. With Debbie in jail awaiting trial, looking at ninety days, Jamal had gone ahead and sublet her apartment, where he usually stayed, a two-bedroom in a high-rise in Crystal City, Virginia, just across the Fourteenth Street Bridge, convenient to both the Metro and the Pentagon

City Mall. Still very new in town and feeling vulnerable, Salem didn't think she was in much of a position to argue. In truth, she missed her old life—her friends, her car, her condo, her beloved collection of designer shoes. She felt relieved when Jamal moved in. For the first time in years, she realized, she was going to sleep at night feeling totally safe. Jamal wasn't so bad. She was even kind of starting to feel close to him in a friendly, brother/sister sort of way—if that's possible when you're having sex with someone. That was the other thing. After a steady diet of middle-aged dentists and car lot owners, Jamal was a treat—strong and trim and good-looking, all the silly pimp talk notwithstanding.

As far as her deeper feelings—that was another subject. She tried not to deal too much with those. She knew she had some issues to work out. Clearly this was not a lasting career choice. She was biding her time, lying low, living this way out of necessity. She tried to see it as an enrichment experience, like an X-rated version of Outward Bound—a total immersion deal, fraught with personal hardships and yucky hygienic challenges, yet also full of valuable and clarifying life lessons. She was making money; the conditions were not the best but the work was not hard—all in all, her customers were a tame lot who presented themselves as shy and rather pitiful, like so many grown-up Oliver Twists: *Please, miss, may I have a blow job?* She just needed to stick it out a few more weeks, then she'd be off to the next chapter.

Marginally satisfied with her appearance, Salem shut off the bathroom light, killing the annoying rattle of the fan. The tussle the night before with the ponytail guy had looked much worse than it actually was—she'd sustained only a scraped elbow and a bruise on her rear end. Even so Jamal had given her the rest of the night off; she'd actually gotten a good long sleep. Now she was due to meet her new friend Brenda for breakfast at the diner downstairs off the lobby.

There was only one problem: since Jamal moved in, he'd become extremely possessive. He wanted to know what she was doing every minute; he wouldn't let her come and go as she pleased—a request to perform a simple errand, like going across the street for cigarettes, could turn into a huge debate. Jamal had just returned to the room after being out all night and part of the morning. If she tried to sneak out, he'd wake up and start an inquisition. If she woke him to ask permission, he'd say no. This one called for a little finesse.

She opened the bathroom door slowly and peeked out. Jamal's large and well-formed ebony body, as dark as she was light, was sprawled across the king-size bed, his face buried in the pillow. He was wearing a plastic shower cap, protection for his hairdo and his pillow, each from the other.

Salem sat down next to him. The room was soupy and overheated; the blanket was low around his waist, exposing the swelling foothills of his gluteal mass. She whispered into his ear, the same white-girl-talkin-black patois she'd been affecting ever since she'd met him, in all his glory, at Club Gemini—an accent she'd picked up from a fellow waitress back in South Beach, a girl from Liberty City. The whole accent thing seemed right at the time she'd met him. It gave her the feeling she was playing a role, starring in a movie that wasn't really her life. Now she was stuck with it. "Jamal? Baby? Wake up."

A few seconds passed. She caressed his shoulder, tickled his ear. "Come on, baby," she cooed. "I need to *axe* you somethin. *Pleaaaase?*"

No response.

Shaking him now: "*Jamal.* Wake *uuupp.*"

"I'm sleepin," he groaned into the pillow.

"Why was you talkin to that ho last night?"

His eyes popped open. "What you talkin about?"

"*Why was you talkin to that ho last night?*"

Rolling over: "What ho?"

"That ho outside Burger 7."

"Who?"

"Flower."

"Flower?"

"Big ass *Flower*! The Flower who you always say gotta make two trips to haul ass."

He propped himself against the headboard, adjusted the pillow behind him, half a smirk on his face. "What about her?"

"Why was you talkin to her?"

"We was just talkin."

"You was runnin game."

"That was *not* game."

"Then why you tell her you ain't ate in three days?"

Jamal looked at her like she was nuts. "When's the last time you seen me eat?"

"Remember when you bought me that steak and cheese sub? You bought *you* a breakfast."

"That was three days ago."

"That was *not*."

"Was *so*."

"Was *not* and you know it."

Jamal grinned again, abashed. "*Flower* didn't know it."

"But I knowed it."

"You gonna tell her?"

She crossed her arms dismissively. "You wasn't doing *nothing* but runnin game."

As if to shield himself from the charges, he pulled the lightweight polyester blanket up to his chin. "Why does you *care*, anyway?"

"What woman ain't fed her man in three days? You make me look like a nonpayin ho."

"How can I make you look like something when your actions speak for theyselves?"

Irate: "My actions do speak for theyselves, and you eat *every* motherfuckin day. If my man go tellin some *bitch* that I ain't fed him in three *motherfuckin* days—"

"Then that makes me out a liar because they know my actions speak for theyselves too," he said, laying it out for her. "They know that, hey, this girl Salem is about her business. If this man ain't ate in three days, it's cause he done doped up the money or smoked it up or shot it up or somethin." He snapped his fingers, elementary. "You know what I'm sayin?"

She stuck out her bottom lip, a droopy lilac petal. "I'm hungry, Jamal. I wanna go git somethin to eat."

"Call room service."

"I don't *want* no room service. I'm sicka room service."

"Well I ain't going *nowhere*. I just got in the bed"—he checked the clock radio—"two hours ago."

"I'll jus go down to the diner."

He shook his head, definitely not.

"It's only in the lobby. What could happen?"

"You know I don't like you goin down there by yourself. It's a bad neighborhood."

"Awww, *baby*," she cooed seductively. "That's so sweet you care about me so much. Is there somewhere else you'd rather have me go down to?"

With that, she grabbed a handful of his blanket, began pulling it slowly toward her.

He offered no resistance.

20

The Pope of Pot was slumped on a concrete bench in a holding cell at the DC Central Jail, his eyelids at half-mast. His breathing was labored, his skin was an unhealthy reddish pink. There was a dark patch on his trouser leg where he'd wet himself—lately he was peeing all the time; it seemed to happen without warning. If he wasn't so sick he might have felt sorry for himself, for the passage of time and youth and health. But he was the Pope. Somebody had to believe.

The cell was humid and oppressively small, ten by twelve feet with a low ceiling. Three of the walls were constructed of cinder block, painted industrial gray. The fourth wall featured a glass viewing window and a sliding metal door, bright blue. There were dozens of similar holding cells of various sizes on the first two floors of the DCCJ. Known as the tanks, they brought to mind a science-fiction movie—a series of secure enclosures in which to display human specimens.

The concrete floor inside the cell sloped downward to a large central drain, allowing for easy hose-down. Littered about were remnants of jail-issue bag lunches—wadded balls of coarse brown paper, deconstructed baloney sandwiches, stunted yellow oranges that looked as if they'd been picked from someone's backyard tree. In one corner was an aluminum sink and toilet combo, the commode lacking a proper seat, standard now in all modern prisons, another tidy fortune secured by a private contractor, trickle-down from the drug war. Over the last five years, the war on drugs had become a kind of drug itself—a powerful economic stimulant that had everyone hooked, from the politicians standing smugly upon their can't-miss law-and-order platforms to the jail guards in their baseball-style caps with gold-embossed bills, the most expensive head covering offered in the prison supply catalog, chosen by the warden's second wife as she soaked in a heart-shaped tub in a Catskills resort on a five-day seminar for law enforcement officials, all expenses paid by federal grants.

Across from the Pope's bench was an identical bench. Hanging above it were two telephones—a blue one for free local calls, a black one for collect long distance. The steel cords that connected the handsets to the bases were only eight inches long—an experiment by prison officials, who were hoping to diminish the efficacy of using the handsets as weapons or instruments of suicide. As you would imagine, this modification made phone use somewhat awkward. At the moment, a young black man was using the blue handset. To talk comfortably, he was squatting on his haunches atop the bench, a rather simian-looking position familiar to prisons and most of the Third World, owing to a lack of proper chairs. He was wearing a pair of Timberland boots with the merchandise tags still dangling from the eyelets; per jail procedure, the laces had been confiscated by the guards.

The Pope had been in the cell with him now for almost fifteen minutes, but Kwan had so far pretended he didn't exist —a social strategy that generally worked well during incarceration. Rule number one: keep your eyeballs to yourself. But Kwan was generally a sociable person; he wasn't used to being alone— over the course of his life he'd never had much of a chance to be alone. He'd grown up in his grandma's crowded household, people coming and going at all hours—he still stayed there most of the time. Likewise, he never rolled without a partner. Out in the streets there was a war in progress, a war against the police, a war against rival gangs. It wasn't prudent to venture out alone. Until the Pope was brought in, Kwan had been in this holding cell by himself for nearly six hours. He'd spent most of that time on the blue phone, talking to his baby momma. Now he let his fawn-colored eyes drift upward, ventured a look at his cell mate.

Kwan's face lit with recognition. "You dat marijuana mothafucka!"

The Pope raised his hands weakly, an attempt at the official papal greeting. "The Pope of Pot at your service, toots."

"You the dude gave out dem blunts at Halloween."

"The sacrament, my son."

"That shit primo. You gotta hook me up!" He spoke into the telephone: "Guess who wit me in the tank?"

Although he didn't smoke his own product, Kwan smoked nearly half an ounce of marijuana a day, usually in cigar-size joints, rolled in tobacco-leaf cigar papers, which were available under the counter in most Korean markets around the city. That he bought his pot from his crack source left him perpetually in debt—like the old mining ditty, he owed his soul to the company store. You could probably say that it was his pot habit that had got him arrested late last evening. He'd smoked a big blunt and nodded out—while parked at the curb outside 7-Eleven, waiting for his homey to return with a stash of munchies, window down, vehicle reeking. At which time a cop strolled past, on his way into the store. A fruit too ripe not too pluck, even on a coffee break.

Just then an alarm sounded, a metallic ring like a high school bell. The blue cell door slid open with an automated *shush*.

In filed Waylon, followed by Louie and Beta Max. Like the Pope and Kwan, they were all three wearing plastic wristbands—last name, first name, date of birth, charges. As it happened, all of them had been charged with the same crime: possession of a controlled substance with intent to distribute. There was only one difference. The Pope and his people were arrested for possessing powder cocaine; Kwan was arrested for crack. To buy powder coke, a customer usually telephoned a beeper number to arrange pickup or delivery; others bought powder in neighborhood bars or trendy clubs. Powder coke was sold by the gram, for about a hundred dollars; you could usually get an eight ball, three and one-half grams, for $150, enough to snort all night with several friends. In contrast, crack was sold on street corners. Most of the users lived within stumbling distance of the supply. The average unit was a five-dollar rock, a little less than one-tenth of a gram. The high part of the high lasts upward of two minutes; the manic, jittery part lasts four hours. At night you could sometimes buy a five dollar rock for two dollars, but getting that kind of bargain usually necessitated a lot of bowing and scraping and pleading; the dealer might well make you bend over so he could kick you in your ass in front of all the other crackheads and dealers. For an ounce of powder cocaine—whether planted by the cops or not—the Pope and his merry men faced mandatory minimum sentences of fifty years. For an ounce of rock cocaine that the police had found in his SUV, Kwan faced a mandatory minimum sentence of life without possibility of parole. Some people insisted that the difference in prison time had been legislated because powder coke was the drug of choice of the upper class and rock coke was the drug of the poor. Nobody disagreed.

Waylon sat down next to the Pope on the bench, shrugged off his Burberry raincoat, placed it over the wet spot on the Pope's trouser leg. He touched the Pope's forehead gently with the back of his hand. "You didn't remember to bring your meds, did you? I should have reminded you. There was so much happening. I wish I could have—"

The Pope rested his hand on Waylon's shoulder. "Don't fault yourself for things you cannot control, my son. You've always done your best. Come meet my new friend." He indicated Kwan. "He's familiar with our work. He wants to become a member of the church."

"He sells rock up on Fourteenth and Q," Beta Max said. Without his video camera to hide his face, which was sharp-featured and boyish, he looked very much like the person he was—a preacher's son from Enid, Oklahoma, who dressed like a member of a satanic cult. (In truth he was an existentialist and an atheist.)

Kwan maintained his pose on the bench, his face frozen in an expression of menace and hauteur. He had no idea what to make of the Pope and his crew. In his entire lifetime, he'd been inside only one white person's house—Seede's. He knew nothing of white people except what he'd seen on movies and TV. He sucked his teeth, brushed an imaginary piece of lint off his shoulder. *These mothafuckas crazy.*

"How long until we can get out of here, counselor?" the Pope asked Waylon.

The lawyer did a mental double take. The Pope asking a straightforward question: not a good sign. "From here, they'll take us to be processed—mug shots and fingerprints," he explained dispassionately, finding comfort in lawyer mode. "Then they'll move us upstairs. We'll be arraigned tomorrow morning. I can represent us, *pro se,* no problem."

"That's great, toots."

"Well, yes, it *is* great," Waylon said, measuring his enthusiasm. "But getting out, that's a little bit trickier, I'm afraid. It will depend upon what they set as bond and whether we can raise the cash. And it will also depend upon—and this is a big one—whether or not the DA is gonna flag you as a three-strikes case. If they do, I'm afraid we're going to be looking at an extended stay in custody."

"We're all gonna be stuck in here?"

Long pause, long face. "Probably just you, your holiness."

The Pope of Pot said nothing. The life went out of his eyes.

Waylon took the Pope's hands in his own. "Right now, what I think we need to do first is get you into the hospital wing. They have really good facilities up on the eighth floor. You'll have a soft bed, your own telephone and TV, round-the-clock nursing—"

As Waylon spoke, Louie the albino, sans rabbit fur hat, moved about the room in a crablike fashion, opening the wadded brown paper bags, looking for one that still contained a jail-issue baloney sandwich. In the vicinity of Kwan's bench, he picked up a bag, unwadded it, peered inside. "Whoa!" he exclaimed. "Check it out!"

Like a boy with a box of Cracker Jacks, he held aloft his prize.

Six inches in overall length, it appeared to be some sort of found-art assemblage of broken office supplies—the top and bottom halves of a ballpoint pen, two pencils broken into four pieces, several rubber bands.

"*Zip gun,*" pronounced Waylon.

Kwan swooped down from his perch and snatched the object from Louie's hand.

Waylon took a step forward. "I'll take that," he said with authority.

Kwan resumed his squatting position on the bench. He held the gun high and sideways, like a character in a movie. He played it across the cell.

With some effort, the Pope rose to his feet and moved unsteadily toward Kwan, listing a bit to one side as he went, owing to the slope of the floor. On his face was an expression of utter disappointment. "You planning on busting out of here with that, Mr. Capone?"

"Give it up," advised Waylon.

The Pope opened his arms beseechingly. "We're all fighting the same battle against injustice, my son. We can't be enemies. We must be allies. We're like homeys, *capisce*? We have to work together. The man is out to get us. He's railroaded me and my people. We don't belong in this jail. And neither, I'm sure, do you. You seem like a fine young person—and handsome too, with the most lovely eyes. Stick with us. Waylon here is a lawyer. He will lead us out of harm's way. God the all-powerful does what he wants, when and where he wants, in the style he would have it. And that's a good beginning, toots. Now hand me that thing, will you please?"

At that very instant, four floors above, in the state-of-the-art command center of the DCCJ, a guard with the improbable name of O. K. Jones glanced up at the bank of video screens that occupied the entire wall to his left. On one of the screens, marked "Tank 22," he observed a young black male who appeared to be wielding a handgun.

Jones hit the panic button on the top of the console.

An alarm sounded, a piercing double wail, evocative of the car chase scenes in old James Bond movies: *wee-ahh, wee-ahh!*

Within minutes the jail's elite tactical response team was surging down the first floor hallway, two by two in lockstep, a tidal wave of adrenalized manflesh, all of them wearing identical black jumpsuits and black motorcycle helmets with mirrored visors, their black Gore-Tex boots slapping urgently against the concrete floor. The lead element carried riot shields, built especially for use in prison settings. Fabricated from bulletproof Lexan, the front of the shield was crosshatched with silver tape. With the press of a button, a deputy could send fifty thousand volts coursing through the body of an unruly inmate. Bringing up the rear of the eight-man contingent were two officers carrying weapons that looked, on first inspection, like some kind of cartoon version of thirties-era tommy guns. The ammo, worn across their chests in crossed bandoliers, was called "rubber projectile batons." There were two varieties. The lower energy round could pierce a mattress.

Reaching *Tank 22,* the squad commander barked something into his headset. The school bell sounded again, blending with the deafening *wee-ahh*. The blue metal door slid open.

The Pope of Pot raised his hands weakly. "Howdy, honey, howdy."

The tactical response team rushed inside.

21

Bo Franklin parted his meaty lips to accept the stem of his water pipe. He raised his butane lighter—a metallic click, the whoosh of pressurized gas, an ice blue cone of fire . . .

Abruptly he doused the flame and looked up thoughtfully at Seede, who was sitting in the chair opposite. "It wasn't till about the third time I smoked that I really got off," he said, gesturing with the pipe. "I mean, all the way off."

"*All the Way Off,*" Seede repeated, a tone of recognition. "The title of your second album."

Franklin looked pleased. It had been more than a decade since he was last on stage in his trademark jumpsuit and shoulder-length African hair extensions—women used to throw their panties. He hadn't been seen in public since his parole from Folsom State Prison. Few were aware he'd had his hip replaced or that he'd returned to his home town to recuperate. During his recovery, he'd had a minor stroke.

"When are we talking about here?" Seede asked. "What was the time period?"

"It was right after *Frankenfunk* hit number one. So it had to be what—1983? No. Eighty-two. January of eighty-two, I think it was. After New Year's. Or maybe it was right after Valentine's Day."

"They say that if you can remember the eighties, you weren't really there."

"One thing I do remember clearly: a messenger came from the record company. He handed me an envelope. Inside was a check for $1.8 million."

"That's not the kind of thing you forget."

"It was funny, cause at the time, I had no money. I had this huge check, but I had to borrow two bucks from one of the guys to go buy cigarettes."

"So we're talking about freebase, right? This was *before* commercial crack hit the streets—that didn't get going until about 1986. Did you cook it up yourself?"

"I hired this dude to cook for me, an older brother. We called him Chef Boyardee. Back in the day, he worked for this big coke dealer. He'd go with him to all the buys to test the shit. He'd weigh out a couple grams of the product and cook it up—baking soda and water, applied to heat. Is that what you used? I don't suppose you used no ether. That shit hard to come by anymore."

"Baking soda and water," Seede confirmed. "I think you get a better yield with Evian instead of tap. I use a glass jar and a pot of boiling water."

Franklin raised an eyebrow, impressed. "Chef Boyardee would cook the shit for the dealer, then he'd weigh the come-back. That was your percentage purity. You cook three grams and get back two—that's 66 percent pure. Which, by the way, would be a rip-off. Back in the day it was probably 80 percent, close to 90—people wasn't so greedy then. After they weighed the shit, they'd throw it away. You couldn't snort it. It was too coarse. Sometimes I think about it—all the damn freebase people done throwed in the trash."

"I wonder who first figured out you could smoke it?"

"Some sprung motherfucker, fo sho. Someone who needed another hit."

"Human ingenuity."

"Know what I'm sayin?"

"Actually," Seede said, "it isn't only humans who like to get high. You know how coke was discovered? People in the Andes mountains noticed their llamas were eating it all the time—man just followed their lead. Elephants have been observed eating fermented fruit until they fall over. Same with birds and other species—flying into trees, stumbling off cliffs, you name it. There's this scientist at UCLA who wrote a book about it. He says that getting high is a natural animal urge."

"I can't argue with dat."

"So what about Chef Boyardee?"

"I hired him away from Sly Stone—doubled his salary. Put him on the payroll with full benefits. He was worth it too. He showed me the right way to smoke."

"What do you mean, the *right* way?"

"Anything worth doin . . . you know what I'm sayin?"

"What were you doing wrong?"

"I was hittin it too hard, sucking it all through the screen; a lot of my hit was ending up as residue. And then after I took the hit, I was doin what you call *fuckin off the high*. Meaning that I wasn't letting it settle into my brain right, wasn't taking full advantage."

"Not getting a good rush?"

"Not getting the full ride, let's say."

"Can you describe that first real time you were talking about? What did *All the Way Off* mean to you?"

Franklin replaced the lighter and the pipe on the arm of his chair. He let his hand fall into his lap, squeezed himself absently. "It was like . . . *Motherfuck!* Know what I'm sayin?"

"I think I do, yeah. Can you give me a little more detail?"

Franklin picked up the lighter, clicked it on and off a few times. "I don't know. It's like an orgasm. A whole body orgasm. You feel it all over, not just down low, in your privates."

"Go on."

He clicked the lighter on and off, on and off, looking for the right words. "It's like . . . a bolt of lightning. It hits you in the top of your head and then drills a tunnel clear down to your groin, like drilling for oil, you know what I'm sayin? And then it strikes, and all the oil comes gushing up through your body and out your ears." He made a whooshing noise, like the sound of a jet passing overhead. "Or, I don't know . . . maybe it's like everything is rushing *in*. Like if there's music playing, your ears open up and all the music is amplified and sucked inside. It's hard to describe. It's intense. Your whole body just lights up. It makes this, like, sign of the cross inside of you"—he crossed the air before him, like a priest at mass—"this big, hot, electric cross."

"Crucified on the electric cross," Seede recited, another piece of lyric.

Franklin nodded.

"Can you give me more specifics about the exact feeling of the high?"

"More specifics? I don't know. It's just a whole other dimension. It's hard to describe. You can talk shit to death, you know what I'm sayin? It's not like I was no drug virgin, neither. I grew up in this neighborhood around all kinda drugs; we dibbled and dabbled our whole lives. I first smoked weed when I was nine. I had a motherfuckin heroin habit when I was sixteen. Went to my aunt's house in North Carolina and kicked the shit cold turkey, came back home for summer football practice, motherfuckin two-a-days. I've done mescaline and peyote. I've taken soma pills. I've done amyl nitrate and acid and you name it, man. I've done every kind of drug that comes in a plant, and I've smoked or chewed every kind of herb from Africa you could think of. I've smoked every kind of hashish—Afghan, Moroccan, Nepalese. I've done all kinds of opiates: heroin, morphine, opium, Dilaudid. I've done it all. Methedrine and Benzedrine . . . I don't think there's anything—drug, booze, beer, Wild Irish Rose, Robitusson, Romilar, quaaludes, Valium, Halcion—that I haven't tried. But this shit . . . This shit was different. I was like, *Motherfuck! I got to share this shit with the entire planet*."

"*Planet Rock*." Seede said. "I always thought it was talking about rock and roll. That's what all the critics said."

"People can think what they want. There's nothing you can do about it no way."

Seede looked down and checked his tape recorder. The little sprockets turned. "So what was the wildest thing you ever did while smoking coke?"

A wet laugh, followed by a phlegmy cough. "You know what? That's just the kind of question you expect from a reporter." He said the word with obvious distaste. "*What's the wildest* . . . *What's the best* . . . *What's your favorite* . . . When someone asks me a question like that, you know the first thing that happens? My mind goes totally blank. Because that shit ain't the point, know what I'm sayin? Lemme tell you somethin, Appleseed, from the perspective of the interview*ee*. If you don't ask the right kind of questions, you just get the same old answers. You never gonna learn nothin. With rock cocaine—crack, freebase, what have you—you do a blast, you get the rush, and then the first thing that comes to your mind is doing something sexual, you know what I'm sayin? Something deviated from the norm. Something freaky. And it's gotta be right away. This second. Without delay. It's like that old commercial." He sang the melody, a black snake moan: "*It's gotta be sweet and it's gotta be a lot and you gotta have it now*. All the shit you ever fantasized about. Shit you didn't even know you was fantasizin about. It all comes into your mind. You don't wanna think about nothin else. You cain't think about nothin else. It deliver you straight to the devil's door."

Seede reached into his coat, which was lying across the ottoman, and extracted a notebook. "Funny you should say that. There's this quote I found in the Library of Congress." He turned the pages. "About what it feels like to smoke coke."

"And?"

"It's attributed to Lucifer."

"You mean, like, *the* Lucifer?"

"I couldn't find reference to any other Lucifer. It's from a translation of a scholarly article written by a Peruvian academic. Instead of freebase or crack, he calls it 'pasta.' After a hit of pasta, he quotes Lucifer as writing, 'a sweet taste of sex impregnates the immediate atmosphere—but not a normal sex . . . rather, a prohibited sex, sinful as the thousand promises of the exotic Babylonian prostitute.'"

"Lucifer on crack," Franklin said skeptically.

"Suckin the devil's dick: isn't that what some people call smoking crack? Maybe the derivation—you know, maybe there's a connection."

"I've always heard it called the *glass dick*. Suckin on the *glass* dick."

"Same difference, I suppose."

"I suppose . . ."

Seede searched his mind for his next question. He kept coming back to the same one. "Now I'm really curious," he said. "What *is* the wildest thing you've ever done on coke?"

Relenting: "I like smoking with a woman and having a tube and blowing the smoke up her pussy. Is that the kinda stuff you're looking for?"

Seede looked at him, dumbfounded.

"Okay, check it out," Franklin said, amused, adjusting himself in his chair. "You get a length of tube. You can get it anywhere. You can get the hose from the back of a toilet, or you can use the straws from McDonald's, or you can use the kind of clear plastic tubing they sell for aquariums—those are the best. You can get real long ones, or you can use shorter ones. I like a shorter one, so that you can be teasing the clit at the same time."

"Okay. What happens next?"

"You blow the smoke up inside."

"Mucus membranes," Seede said.

"That's right."

"And then what?"

The wet laugh: "Planet O, *baby*."

"Like the song."

Franklin picked up the pipe and the lighter and heated the bowl. "See, if you hit it right, you don't need no huge piece of rock." His tone was warm; obviously he was enjoying the attention. Something else Seede had learned along the way: the more you let people talk, the more attentively you listen, the more they will like you, the more they will tell. Franklin raised the stem to his lips and took a long, slow drag. The water in the pipe bubbled; the sound reminded Seede of a fish tank. The rock threw off tiny sparks, made a crackling sound as it burned—the origin of its street name.

Eyes closed, Franklin held the hit in his lungs for a longish period and then exhaled—a sustained, modulated, voluminous stream of clean white smoke. Followed by a deep inhalation of fresh air, another exhalation . . .

And then his eyes popped open.

He spoke with great gusto: "Sometimes I'd be with a bitch and she couldn't handle the shit. I'd give her the tube and she'd come so hard she'd fuckin stop breathing. I shit you not, her fuckin heart would stop. This happened like, four, five times. The girl would have this huge orgasm, and then she'd start convulsing. And then her eyes would roll back in her head, and she'd fuckin stop breathing. I had to use CPR. I had to get on her chest with the CPR and shit, I'd be doing motherfuckin mouth to mouth. I didn't even know how to do it but I was doing it, you know what I'm sayin? Pumping on they chests, putting ice on em, puttin ice up their pussy, bringing em back to life. Literally. Bringing these bitches back to motherfuckin life. And that shit happened to me like four, five, six times." He squeezed himself, as if he was testing the ripeness of a fruit. "*Six times I killed a bitch with an orgasm.*"

Franklin laughed his phlegmy laugh. He leaned forward, held out the lighter and the pipe. "Here you go, Appleseed. Have yourself a hit."

Seede eyeballed the pipe. He eyeballed Franklin.

And then Seede's pager went off—a shrill beeping that pierced the stillness of the darkened room.

22

By midday the heat had become ever more merciless. The sun leaned down oppressively upon the Rio Pulgas, steaming the brown river into a muddy broth. We were headed cautiously upstream in the little motor launch, myself at the helm, the antique one-lunger sputtering along at a measured pace. The banks of the river were hemmed in with bamboo and pandanus; behind that were seemingly endless hectares of giant spreading trees and tropical palms of all varieties. Parrots and other brilliant birds winged and chattered here and there; a colony of nests hung from the topmost branches of a great Santa Maria tree, set at a dizzying height to protect the eggs from the profusion of snakes and lizards and carnivorous rodents that dwelt below.

The lush beauty did little, however, to offset conditions that could only be described in terms of Dante's inferno: the sweat streaming from our faces; the soupy air increasingly hard to breathe; the enervation and general heaviness of limbs; the stinging swarms of mosquitoes, botlas flies, and Tabanidae that rendered our bodies and our faces covered with itching bumps. In addition, there was Stuke's malady, some sort of mysterious spider or insect bite that left his face bloated to twice its normal size. One thing was eminently clear: this awful tributary was aptly named —River of Small Biting Insects, indeed.

But we were closer now than ever to the promise of the Lost City; we forged ahead with little regard for our personal well-being. As I have long experienced, no great discovery comes without its personal price, its pound of flesh. A story without hardship is no story at all—if it is comfort and ease you seek, I bid you stay home by the fire. As we continued farther and farther upriver, we noticed that the waters were increasingly strewn with obstacles—rocks, sandbars, roots, gigantic mahogany trees carried downstream by the floods in the wet season. The current was strong. With the two dugouts in tow, navigation was ever more difficult. While my nerves were stretched to the breaking, I showed no signs of it. Mine was the face of the stoic; I was, after all, the leader of this expedition, motley though it was, its physical and spiritual center. Bobbie sat at my side, jaw set, fingers intertwined prayerfully on her lap. Stuke lay sprawled in the bow, useless after a double dose of laudanum. Ambrose had charge of the second dugout—being the larger, it held most of our stores.

Eventually we came to a bend in the river. Two fallen trees had left only a narrow passage in between. With much effort I managed to steer the launch through the channel without incident; the first dugout followed closely behind. We would not have the same luck with the second.

As it approached the channel between the two submerged trees, the second, larger dugout canoe impacted upon something beneath the water. An awful scraping sound was heard; the dugout lurched sideways, causing its stern to catch the current and swing about wildly. With a sickening crack, it struck a submerged tree and rolled over. Ambrose, the Carib boys, and most of our stores splashed into the turgid waters.

It was nearly sunset by the time we called to a halt our attempts at salvage. Owing to a fear of what they described as waterborne snakes and flesh-eating fish—and dragons and unicorns, as well, no doubt; from where I stood on the slippery clay banks, there was no evidence of any such—the effort by our crew was less than sterling. In the end the preponderance of our food and supplies was lost.

Frustrated and exhausted, feeling once again the curse of the heavens upon my head, the piteous laugher of Fate, I sat down on a log to collect my thoughts. If it is true what they say, that progress comes only through extreme hardship, then surely I was on the right road. Across the river, the sun was beginning to disappear below the canopy of trees. I took a deep breath and gathered myself, tried to remember my blessings. Over the years of my wanderings, far from the trappings of culture and civilization, the momentous spectacle of the setting sun has always provided succor to me. Just as the Parisians have their Louvre, the Madrileños their Prado, I have always looked to the western sky at sunset —a breathtaking canvas that changes from day to day, one perfect masterpiece following the next in endless succession. Whatever Time and Fate delivered to my feet, whatever hardships, whatever travails, I have always trusted, at the end of a long and difficult day, that Mother Nature would comfort me with her glories.

But now, looking to the horizon of treetops, I saw something different than expected—a daunting, blue-black mass of clouds.

Within minutes, the deluge was upon us.

The rain finally abated at about 2:30 a.m. We were soaked to the bone in the pitch dark; the insects treated themselves to a new round of feasting. We weathered the night as best we could, unable to get a fire started, huddled together for warmth, wrapped in the few sodden blankets that we had managed to salvage from the river. Ambrose and I shared one of the blankets; Bobbie took the other with Stuke, having volunteered to nurse the hapless watercolorist through his fevers—or so I believed at the time. Looking back, with the clear vision of hindsight, I can see now that this innocent and difficult evening—with all of us victim to the kind of hardship that bends the will—was the genesis of the supreme heartache to come.

The next day, when dawn broke, we stared hollow- eyed at one another: bitten from head to foot, covered in clay, we were a sight to behold, players in a tale of horror. In addition to the countless mosquito and other bug bites, all of us suffered from peculiar ulcerated sores, at the center of which could be seen emerging, like infant Galápagos turtles from their buried nests, some type of small flying insect. After considerable deliberation, Ambrose postulated that we had been set upon by a species which had laid its eggs beneath our skin. Of course, the effects were devastating. Imagine your own dermis as an incubator for a tiny, winged bug. One small stroke of luck to be noted: among the few items recovered from the river was a one-liter bottle of hydrogen peroxide. Under the doctor's direction, we spent the balance of the morning lancing egg sacs and cauterizing dermal eruptions.

With that unsavory task completed, we discussed the situation among ourselves and decided, due to the increasingly difficult prospects for navigation, to abandon the dugouts and the motor launch and continue by foot, carrying on our backs what little of our kit we had salvaged.

We pushed into the jungle, following a muddy track which appeared to parallel the river. So dense was the brush—a fiercely unwelcoming tangle of green scrub that encompassed the path like a tunnel—that the taller among us were forced to walk bent at the waist. There were thorns and stickers everywhere; we tried to keep as near as possible to the exact center of the wet and rutted path, lest our clothes and bodies be ripped and torn. One plant, a vine covered with hooked spicules, was capable of removing a square inch of skin at a rub. Worse were the spikes of the lancietta palm, two inches long. I will not here elaborate on the intricate spiderwebs that ensnarled, nor catalog the Brobdingnagian arachnids which inhabited them, thoughts of which still elicit, even as I write this many years later, an involuntary shudder. Nor will I mention the footprints on the trail—numerous and small, like children's.

As darkness fell, we hit a fork in the trail—which way to go? All of us were hungry and tired, pushed beyond the point of physical and mental exhaustion. Morale was low; the Caribs were near mutiny—it was no help that the rum had been lost in the river. Barely two days into our mission up the Rio Pulgas, we had already been visited by every sort of hardship one could imagine. Providentially, no one had died.

Steeling myself against the crushing weight of self-doubt, I ordered the company to make camp. I had no idea which fork in the trail we should take. I had no idea how far we had to go or what dangers we faced ahead of us. All I knew was that we had no other choice but to continue forward. To go back now would surely seal the death of my soul. I thought to myself—how much worse could it get?

And then, as if on cue, a party of savage Indians emerged ghostlike from the tangled underbrush, carrying blowguns and bows and arrows with colorful quills. Their teeth were sharp-ened into fangs; their noses were pierced with long bits of bone. None of them were greater than four feet in height.

We were at their mercy.

23

Seede strode with guilty urgency down the impossibly long central aisle of the newsroom of the *Washington Herald*, past row upon row of Formica-topped desks, each with its own identical two-line telephone and computer terminal. He carried his motorcycle helmet in one hand, a Styrofoam cup of coffee in the other. A copy of the morning's four-star final—the paper of record, containing all of the night's corrections and updates, as well as the latest sports scores—was folded under his arm. His navy surplus peacoat and hooded sweatshirt were unfastened, revealing a smart designer shirt and a skinny thrift-store tie—a nod, in spirit if not letter, to the *Herald*'s dress code, which mandated "attire appropriate for an unexpected interview with the president of the United States or other such dignitary."

To accommodate a full-time roster of nearly nine hundred reporters and editors, the *Herald*'s newsroom occupied an immense space, one full acre spread over the fifth floors of three adjoining buildings. Seede had begun working at the paper at the tender age of twenty-two—freshly sprung from an abortive three-week attempt at law school—as a copyboy on the graveyard shift. Eleven months later, after reporting and writing, during his off hours, a series of front-page articles that prompted a Senate investigation into misdealings at the Department of Agriculture, he was promoted to reporter. For a time thereafter, Seede was the talk of the newsroom, a featured lunch guest in the publisher's private dining room—the first male in twenty years to work his way up the ladder the old-fashioned way, sans internship or fancy j-school degree. That he had gotten the tip for the series while serving as a copyboy on the city desk—that he had taken down the details from a caller and kept it for himself, a gross violation of *Herald* policy—seemed only to enhance his standing.

Now, however, after seven years at the esteemed daily, with its glut of industry icons and regional all-stars plucked from lesser papers around the nation, Seede was still a junior staffer. A walk-on player who'd made the varsity against all odds, his career had stalled. Neither ethnic enough to warrant special consideration (there were already enough Jews in the news biz) nor patrician enough to curry the embrace of the blue bloods and Ivy Leaguers who held sway over the *Herald*'s institutional culture, Seede was still subject to weekend, holiday, and night duty, emergency calls at any hour.

Not that his work was subpar: over the last two months Seede had written thirteen front-page stories—more than one a week. All of them had been longish, quirky, well-written, self-generated features that inspired watercooler talk and radio call-in debates: a fourteen-year-old heroin addict; a high-priced callgirl who serviced clients on Capitol Hill, with a sidebar on a callboy; a suburban Fairfax woman who was forced by authorities to give up the menagerie she'd been raising in her backyard—a male lion, an Arabian stallion, a ram, and a male German shepherd; a weekend stay with a family of ten adopted children, all of them severely disabled. The one story with any real news value—about a promising high school basketball player who died of a crack overdose—had been optioned by a Hollywood producer. Seede had an agent, the handshake was done, the deal was in process. Even after splitting the money with the boy's family, there was a large paycheck in his future, the amount of which would equal seventeen years of salary at his present rate. Rather than endearing him to his coworkers at the *Herald,* the movie deal only served to further alienate Seede, as if his windfall had been a betrayal of all the underpaid Ivy League staffers who'd eschewed the prospects of big money in order to practice their noble profession. Of course, many of them had trust funds.

At eight in the morning the fifth floor was still deserted. Striding down the central aisle of the newsroom, Seede ventured a look to his right, toward editor country, at the heart of the vast room. Oddly, no one was yet on post.

Relieved, annoyed, he slowed his pace. *Who the hell paged me anyway?*

He hung a left down a secondary aisle, then a right, passing through the maze of desks, different colors for different sections—blue for National, green for Foreign, black for Metro, and so forth. Some of the staffers likened employment at the *Herald* to military service. There was much scurrying about and barking of orders, many layers of officer-editors, a cover-your-ass mentality, a long and distinct chain of command. Others compared it to a Big Eight accounting firm, a sweatshop, an Orwellian warehouse of clerks. Over the span of his tenure at the *Herald* —as his star dimmed, as his hairline receded, as his once-lauded craftiness and drive came to be seen as counterproductive to the greater good, as his ambitions turned toward something more literary than the yeoman hunt-and-peck of daily reportage—Seede had settled on his own mixed metaphor for employment at the *Herald:* a slave galleon where the prisoners manned keyboards instead of oars.

At length Seede reached his own desk in the Metro section, off in a secluded corner, shielded from the view of his editors by a large support beam onto which were tacked the usual assortment of notices, cartoons, and in-house ads. Conveniently near a printer, a copier, and the restrooms, the area was shared by Seede with three others, none of whom would likely be in until ten, the regular start time for most staffers.

He stowed his helmet beneath the desk, removed his coat and sweatshirt and draped them, still coupled, over the back of his chair. On top of the desk, he now noticed, was a box wrapped in plain brown paper, addressed by hand in block letters. It appeared to be a proper piece of mail, stamped and cancelled, yet it had no return address, a detail that gave him pause. Last year, in reaction to a feature he'd written about a poor black family's Thanksgiving dinner, Seede had received a shoebox containing hundreds of cockroaches, many of them still alive. After a story about a gay couple's battle with AIDS, he received a large rat in a Tupperware container. It had been dead for some time. There were maggots.

Seede picked up the box gingerly. It was heavy, probably five pounds. The contents inside shifted a bit with movement. He sniffed the top, pressed his ear to the side, listened. Hearing nothing, he set it down on the desktop.

He raised his ankle-high, Dr. Martens boot and placed it on the seat of his chair. Strapped to his calf was an eight-inch throwing knife, a skill he'd picked up a few years back while training with Navy Seals for a series. He used the knife to cut the shipping tape, returned it to the hi-tech scabbard with a securing *click*.

Inside the box was another box, this one gift wrapped with festive holiday paper, a snowy Christmas scene. Inside he found a round tin container. It had a card taped to the top: *Season's Greetings from the Fraternal Order of Police*.

Mixed nuts. Neatly separated into pie-wedge sections of cashews, Brazils, almonds, white pistachios. And three additional sections of spiced pecans in different flavors, Seede's favorite. He popped one into his mouth.

"There you are!"

A voice from behind, exasperated: the tidewater drawl of Seede's immediate supervisor, William "Buddy" McCarthy.

Seede spun around to face him. "Have a nut," he said, offering the tin. "Compliments of the FOP."

At forty-eight McCarthy bore more than a passing resemblance to Humpty Dumpty—ovoid torso, arms and legs like sticks. Once upon a time he'd been the celebrated young second in command of a midsize daily in Wilmington, Delaware. Having dreamed his whole life of working someday at the *Herald*—one of the top dailies in the world—McCarthy had agreed to come on board in the lowly position of assistant Virginia editor, having every confidence he'd work back up the ladder in no time. Eighteen years later, he had a wife and four boys, a house in the suburbs, an excellent package of salary and benefits. And he was assistant city editor, a lateral move, slightly upward owing to the primacy of city over suburbs. In seven more years he'd be eligible for an early buyout.

McCarthy pushed back the rumpled sleeve of his sport coat and checked his cheap digital watch, worn with the face inside his wrist. "I paged you fifty-one minutes ago," he informed Seede. "What took so long?"

"It's hard to find a working pay phone," Seede said, not untruthfully. While lying was a cardinal sin—and a firing offense—in the newsroom, creative use of language was a staple. One of his city-side colleagues had just done an exposé on the sorry state of the town's pay telephones. It was a fact that a working pay phone was hard to find. It was also a fact that Seede hadn't attempted to find one. "I figured it was quicker to come straight in."

"Where were you?"

Seede looked at him searchingly. "I'm pretty sure my shift doesn't begin until seven tonight."

"Unless otherwise directed," McCarthy quoted.

"Well, here I am. Direct."

Buddy McCarthy stared at him cockeyed. He had fourteen reporters in his platoon; with each of them he shared a unique, dysfunctional, codependent relationship. Seede was up to something, he was sure—he just couldn't put his finger on it. He held up a copy of the overnight memo. "What do you know about this bust on Fourteenth Street?"

"Bust on Fourteenth Street?"

"Isn't that your beat?"

"There were probably three dozen or more busts out there last night"—scatting, buying time, searching his gray matter for details—"the cops were out in force. Seasonal crackdown. They do it every year. As a matter of fact"—popping a spiced pecan into his mouth—"I heard from one of my sources about this new—"

"*What* are you *doing*?" interrupted McCarthy, aghast.

"What?"

"You can't eat those."

"I know it's early, but these cinnamon ones are great." He popped another. "You gotta try one."

"That's a gift from a source. You're not allowed to keep it!"

"A can of mixed nuts?"

"No gifts from sources," he recited. "No free meals, no free tickets, no drinks, no trips, no gratuities or special considerations of any kind. You know the rules."

"You think a can of mixed nuts is going to compromise my journalistic integrity?"

"It's not open to interpretation, Seede. There was a reminder last week from the ethics committee. The holiday memo? You didn't receive it?"

"I can't recall," Seede said, quoting Ronald Reagan's testimony before the Tower Commission regarding his involvement in the Iran-Contra scandal. Since the former president's addled performance two years earlier, it had become one of the newsroom's favorite retorts. Seede sat down in his swivel chair, hooked his boot around the *Herald*-issue wastebasket under the desk, and pulled it out. He took a last spiced pecan and popped it into his mouth. Then he upended the tin into the wastebasket.

"*What are you doing now?*"

"What do you mean?"

"You can't do *that.*"

"You said I couldn't keep it."

"You're supposed to give it to charity."

Seede peered mournfully into the wastebasket. He looked up at McCarthy. He shrugged.

"Jesus Christ, Seede. Why can't you just grow the fuck up? You have a good deal here, better than you know. Why do you always have to gimme all this . . . *attitude.*"

"What *attitude?*"

"The one that tells me you don't care about keeping your job."

Seede's brow beetled. "You're saying you're gonna fire me?"

McCarthy crossed his arms, reset his feet. "I'm saying something like that is not beyond the realm of possibility if you don't do what you're supposed to do."

Seede shook his head sorrowfully. "Maybe I should just quit."

McCarthy gave him a look like he'd just lost his mind. The *Herald* was at the pinnacle of the newspaper profession. Where was there to go from here? To the same kind of bullshit at the *New York Examiner*? Many became disillusioned with the *Herald*, but few ever left. "Don't you have a family to support, hotshot? A daughter? How far do you think that Hollywood money is going to take you? You'll probably pay 35 percent in taxes off the top. Do you have any idea how much auto insurance for a sixteen-year-old costs? You know what a semester of college goes for these days? I hope you're considering opening a tax-deferred college fund with some of that money. It's a struggle out there, Seede. In a few years you'll wake up and realize it. You'll be facing down an avalanche of responsibility. You have to plan for the future. It'll be here before you know it, pal."

Seede said nothing. What could he say? That he'd been thinking a lot lately about just this sort of thing? That he had seen the Ghost of Christmas Future and it looked a lot like William "Buddy" McCarthy?

The ovoid editor glared at Seede, a low wattage beam of long-simmering resentment. He knew what it was like to be young and full of promise. "So what's it gonna be? Are you quitting or are you working?"

Seede let the tin fall into the wastebasket; the sound echoed loudly across the huge empty room. "I'm all yours, boss."

"Okay," McCarthy said, trying to sound definitive, not quite sure if he was being had. Forty-eight years old and here he was, the first person in the newsroom every morning, dealing with these young assholes.

"Okay," repeated Seede, not so definitive, either. Twenty-nine years old and here *he* was, doing the bidding of others, taking orders from this has-been. How had it come to this? Who would have imagined that working here would be so claustrophobic, so constraining, so dull and demoralizing. He had talent. He had ambition. He had ideas. He wanted to do what *he* wanted to do. It was becoming increasingly clear that working for the *Herald* was not it.

"So . . . this bust on Fourteenth Street," McCarthy said, looking through his bifocals at a printout. "The overnight memo, if you would ever read it, mentions an arrest at a storefront operation run by that marijuana clown . . . What does he call himself?"

"The Pope of Pot?"

"Right. Apparently the good pontiff was busted last night with a major quantity of cocaine."

"Cocaine? Are you sure?"

"How did we miss this one, Seede? I thought, after last time, you were going to keep a close eye on this."

"Like I explained *last time:* the cops didn't notify *any* print people about that bust. That was strictly made for TV. The DA hates the Pope. He's been going after him full throttle."

"Well it sounds like they've got him now."

"Except for one thing: the Pope is totally against hard drugs. He's been arrested for picking up used syringes in the park and handing them over to the cops. The Pope dealing coke? That makes no sense at all."

Despite everything, Seede found himself rising to the occasion, performing as he'd been trained, briefing his editor concisely about the situation at hand. Since college, and before his marriage to Dulcy, the *Herald* had comprised the sum total of his adult life experience. For the first four years, he'd scarcely taken even a day off. He'd worked, shared meals, partied, played sports, had sex with, and generally spent most of his time with other reporters. When he introduced himself—Jonathan Seede from the *Washington Herald*—he liked to joke that *from the Washington Herald* was his family name.

"He was some kind of midlevel bureaucrat at the Department of Agriculture . . . Treasury . . . one of those, I forget which," Seede continued. "After twenty-some years of service, one day he just up and quit. Eventually he landed in Amsterdam—that's where he got into the marijuana business. But it's not just pot with him. He's got this whole utopian vision thing going. And nonprofit status as a church. He actually feeds a lot of people. Underneath it all he's a do-gooder. A little loony, but harmless. But I'll tell you this: his pot isn't harmless. Strictly the highest quality, people say, designer product with names like Purple Haze and Tripto-ganja. He sells to all the celebs who come through town. He claims to have cops and judges and senators as regular customers. You just call his toll-free number and a bicycle messenger comes out and—"

McCarthy's eyes saucered. "Cops and judges, you say? Senators? Buying marijuana?"

He sat his ample posterior on the edge of Seede's desk, leaned in conspiratorially. "When can I have *that* story?"

24

There was a knock on the door of Metcalfe's study. Thornton Desmond gripped the armrests of his chair as if they were parallel bars, planted his feet at shoulder width. With the advance of age, with his thickening catalog of chronic aches, pains, stiffnesses, and bodily failures, the simple act of rising from a chair had become a complex gymnastic feat—the approach, the execution, the landing. Grunting, he rocked forward and pushed himself up.

He opened the door to find one of Metcalfe's corps of messengers, a tall young woman wearing a one-piece lycra uniform and a pillbox hat. Behind her, with his black pompadour and trench coat, was Detective Massimo Bandini, the cop from Internal Affairs.

Metcalfe looked up from his place at the library table, where he'd been reading from one of his grandfather's journals. "Do you have it?" he asked excitedly.

The messenger frowned. "He says it got away."

"Got away?" Metcalfe looked crestfallen, like a seven-year-old who'd been expecting a pony for his birthday.

"I'd characterize it more as: *temporarily eluded us,*" Bandini corrected.

"What the fuck does that mean?"

"Prior to zero hour, sir, intelligence had the object in plain view—on top of a cabinet in the storefront on Fourteenth Street. But when we executed the raid, it was no longer *in situ*. Someone may have been tipped off. We're checking now for any breeches of security that may have occurred within our operation —though that is unlikely. The only people who were aware of the plan in advance were my partner and myself. Even as we speak, every effort is being made to recover the object. It's a small town. It shouldn't take long."

"This kind of incompetence really annoys me, detective. When I hired you, I thought I was getting the best."

Bandini took umbrage. He was already out on a limb for this guy—he did not ordinarily bend the rules. On the contrary, he worked for Internal Affairs; he was about *enforcing* the rules, keeping things on the up and up. But Metcalfe was a most unusual man, a very rich man. He played golf with Margaret Thatcher, squash with Steven Spielberg. He exchanged favorite video games with the crown prince of Japan and favorite racing camels with members of Saudi royalty. Often he'd show up unannounced in an inner-city neighborhood and give out hundred-dollar bills. Scores of African villages owed their water wells to his philanthropic whim. He had the power of money, the power of association, the power of good intentions. Despite his small stature, he was truly larger than life. He had a way of getting people to do the things he wanted.

But that didn't mean Bandini had been bought. Over the course of his involvement with this case, the detective had developed a few questions of his own. "What *I'm* wondering," Bandini said pointedly, "is why you waited so many years to look into your own background. Weren't you curious about your grandfather before now?"

"The best defense is a good offense, is that it, detective?"

"By the time you called me in—"

"I believe it is my privilege to conduct such matters as I please," Metcalfe interrupted. "This isn't a criminal case. This is you moonlighting for me in your off-time, conducting a private investigation."

"I understand that. And we've come a long way, considering how cold the trail was to begin with. Finding those papers and journals, I told my men, that took some damn fine investigative work."

"And you are to be complimented for your brilliance, detective. I know you've already been well paid. And you will be paid even more when you *complete* the job you started."

"The fact is, sir, at this point, certain lines have been crossed, and you need to know that."

"I understand. I appreciate your efforts. I know you will do the right thing as regards the law. But the question remains: how long until I have the Master Skull in my possession?"

"No more than forty-eight hours, sir."

"I have your word?"

"I guarantee it."

"In that case . . ." Metcalfe said dismissively, turning his attention back to the journal.

Bandini made to leave, then stopped himself. "One more thing, Mr. Metcalfe."

Without looking up: "Yes, detective?"

"Sometimes, in the course of an investigation, we get what we like to call 'by-product.'"

"By-product?"

"Investigational by-product. It's like turning over a rock. You're looking for one thing, but sometimes you find things you weren't trying to find, things you weren't expecting."

His full attention now: "Yes?"

"How to say this . . ."

"Just say it, detective."

"We believe you have a child, Mr. Metcalfe."

"That's impossible."

"No, sir. It is quite possible." He flipped a few pages in his notebook. "A daughter. Born October 7, 1967, in Cape Canaveral, Florida. I believe you were there for a space launch in late January of that year."

Metcalfe looked stunned. "Not a launch. I was checking out Apollo 1. They were still testing. There was a fire. All three astronauts died."

"You were there at the invitation of the mission commander, Virgil Grissom."

"One hell of a man," Metcalfe said, a look of sadness curtaining his face. And then: "Good *Lord*. How does this happen? I have a child and no one tells me? What kind of woman . . . How sure is this, detective?"

"If you'd care to submit to a blood test, I could have our lab work up the DNA. My partner will be contacting the young woman very soon"—Bandini paused to gauge the reaction—"unless you'd prefer he didn't. I could reach out to him and wave him off. There's still time."

"No, no," Metcalfe said. "Let's do it. I'll messenger a blood sample to you by this afternoon."

"Hopefully we'll have more conclusive results for you by tomorrow, sir."

"Find that skull. You gave me your word . . . forty-eight hours."

25

Salem crossed the lobby of the Capitol City Motor Lodge, doing her best to ignore the rheumy leers of the resident pensioners and old farts who passed their days playing Tonk around the card table in the corner. Pausing at the glass door of the diner, she signaled the creepy Indian guy behind the front desk. He smiled crookedly, issued a fey little wave. The lock buzzed. She pushed her way inside.

The diner was a lovely relic, red Naugahyde and tarnished chrome, with tableside jukeboxes, three songs for a quarter. The rumble of the morning traffic outside on New York Avenue was palpable underfoot; the smells of bacon grease and cumin commingled in the air with exhaust fumes. Brenda was sitting in a booth at the rear, nursing a mug of coffee.

"Sorry I'm late," Salem said, sliding in opposite.

"Not late. I ain't even ordered yet." Brenda had olive skin and sparkling black eyes that commanded attention. "So how'd you get past management?" she asked.

Salem smirked. "I gave him a little sumpn-sumpn to help him sleep, just like you suggested."

"A little warm milk?"

"*A man with a hard dick is a tool,*" Salem quoted.

"Who-eva tole you that?" Brenda giggled.

Salem gave her friend a high five. "I think it was you, sista."

When Salem had first shown up in town, the new girl on the Strip, Brenda and her two partners had been the first to befriend her. On the street, the trio of independents were known as Charlie's Angels. Nichelle was a blonde, a few degrees south of wholesome. Soledad was deep ebony with braided hair extensions. They'd hooked up with Brenda, who was Salvadorian and Vietnamese, in Las Vegas a few years ago. Sharing expenses, watching each other's backs, the trio had worked in Chicago and Atlantic City before coming to DC. Because they had no pimp, Jamal called them renegade hos. He thought they were a bad influence on Salem.

As green as she was, Salem knew differently. There were constant variables on the street—foul weather, guard dogs, angry residents, undercover cops, sicko tricks, crackheads, peeping toms, thieves. From his seat in the Lincoln, Jamal could do only so much to protect her. Witness the bust of Debbie. You needed a partner on the track, a buddy, an extra pair of eyes. Someone to lend you a condom or a pair of panty hose. Someone who'd last seen you getting into a car with a stranger, who could pick him out of a lineup. Someone to invite along on a three way or a bachelor party—those were the highest paying gigs besides all-nighters, but they could get unruly, being so outnumbered in a room. It was hard to explain, but to Salem, working the street, giving a blow job in a car, just you and a nervous john, well . . . It felt a lot safer to her than stripping. A room full of men, together, drunk, watching a naked girl dance. What was supposed to happen next? The whole equation made no sense to her.

Having undertaken her new career with little research or consideration, Salem had quickly discovered there was much she didn't know. There is, after all, an art to every pursuit, no matter how high or low. Lucky for her, Brenda was a nurturing type, willing to share trade secrets: which corners attracted what kinds of tricks; which cars the undercovers always drove; which parking lots and alleyways were safe for transactions; which downtown hotels would call the cops; which bouncers in which clubs would allow you to use their bathrooms—there was one guy, at the Silver Dollar, who would even let you take a trick into the storeroom for a small fee.

Over the last several weeks, as they'd click-clacked together along the sidewalks in their four-inch heels, Brenda had kept up a running Socratic commentary, a sort of crash course in the modern practice of the world's oldest profession: Use the opportunity of removing a trick's pants to check for cleanliness, sores, or off-odors. Use a red-wrapped Trojan, nonlubricated and extra durable. Conceal the condom in your palm, roll it on with lips and teeth; the less obvious you are with the condom the better—it cuts down on arguments. No condom, no sex, no exceptions. Steer tricks toward the half-and-half, a blow job followed by intercourse—it takes only a little longer, but you can charge four times as much. Also it gets them to your motel room—you can charge a usage fee. Riffling their pockets when they go to the bathroom is another option. What are they gonna do? Call the police?

Always take the top during intercourse. Put a hand on the trick's shoulder, your knees outside his hips, your feet inside his knees, allowing for maximum control and serving to keep the trick from kissing you. Always refuse to do it doggy style—the trick has too much control, too much access to your neck. Carry a single-edged razor inside a pack of matches in your purse. Never shower with a trick after sex: a man always lasts longer the second time around; after he's done, he won't want to pay for it. Always get the money up front. And no refunds—ever.

Now, at the table, Salem took notice of something new about her friend. "*Oh . . . my . . . God!*" she gushed. She took Brenda's left hand. "Look at that *rock*!"

Salem turned the ring this way and that, a three-quarter-carat solitaire with a thin fourteen-carat gold band. It sparkled in the harsh lighting of the diner, a literal diamond in the rough. "*I can't believe you have an engagement ring on your finger!*" Salem squealed. She half stood and reached across the table to hug her friend.

"Can you believe it?" Brenda asked.

"Here come the bride!"

"He's driving back down next week to take me home wit him."

"To Philly?"

"Not Philly. Some suburb outside Philly. I don't remember the name."

"Headed for that white picket fence, baby."

"That's right."

"I knew he was a keeper the first time I met him."

Brenda hugged herself. "You know it, girl."

"What about Soledad and Nichelle?" asked Salem.

"What about them? They big girls," Brenda said soberly. "They can take care each other." She took a sip of coffee. "I'm ready for the next chapter, know what I'm sayin? *More* than ready. This shit gettin *old*. Been old for a while now."

"Change is good," Salem assured her. "I'm glad I'm outta Miami—*fo real*."

"I still can't imagine you with long red hair. To me you're such a blonde!"

"Sometime I look in the mirror and I kinda scare myself . . . It like, who da fuck dat?"

"Hey girls, what'll it be?"

The waiter wore his dreadlocks tied up high on his head with a colorful scarf—Bob Marley meets Carmen Miranda. His name was Ivan. He was famous in some circles for his weekly appearances at J. Edgar's, a drag joint located kitty-corner from the massive downtown headquarters of the Federal Bureau of Investigation. Like the club, the FBI building was named for its former director, J. Edgar Hoover, who enjoyed a bit of drag himself, it is said. In his signature piece, Ivan dressed like a cafeteria lady and lip-synched the song "Hot Lunch" from the movie *Fame*. As he sang, he made ham sandwiches on his lunch cart and tossed them into the audience.

"I'll have the steak and eggs, over easy, with hash browns and whole wheat toast," Brenda said.

"Make it two," Salem said. "Scrambled. And black coffee, please."

After Ivan had retreated, Brenda leaned across the table. "So what up wit you? You doin okay?"

"I'm fine—you know," Salem said. "A hellacious bruise on my right ass cheek. But I got a great night's sleep." She stretched her arms and yawned contentedly.

"What about South Beach? Have you heard anything?"

"Knock on wood." Salem rapped her temple.

"You never told me: who was this guy anyway?"

"You mean Roberto?"

"Yeah—the guy who got killed."

Salem glanced around the restaurant. Since she'd arrived in town she'd constantly wondered: how do you know for sure if you're being followed? She hadn't seen anyone tailing her, but then again, if whoever was following her was good at his job, how could she tell he was there? She looked uncomfortably at Brenda. "I'd rather not talk about it," she said.

"Come *on*—what else we gonna talk about?"

"Your engagement?"

"We done talked about that."

Salem sighed. For as long as she could remember, people had been pressuring her into doing things she didn't want to do. For some reason she always did them anyway. "I met him in this club. I'd been seeing him for about three months. I figured he was high up in drugs *some* kinda way. Cuban and rich and living in Miami with no visible means of support, what else could he be? He was in his forties, I guess. Late forties. A little bit of love handles, but not too bad, he worked out, you know? And he drove this really cool Lamborghini. Bright yellow."

"Flashy," Brenda said.

"Flashy," Salem confirmed.

"And lemme guess—small dick."

Salem giggled. "Small but thick, like a sausage." She used her thumb and forefinger to illustrate. "And kinda loud. One of them grunters, you know what I mean? *Uhhhhh, uhhhhh, uhhhhh!*"

Brenda rolled her eyes. "At least he didn't have no pencil dick."

Salem laughed.

"Like a fuckin tampon up in there."

"Know what I'm sayin?"

"So what happened?" Brenda pressed.

"With what?"

"With Roberto."

"I don't know. I saw him once a week. Usually Thursdays, late. One night he was at my condo . . . this was what, two weeks ago? Almost three now . . . It seems like a year. We was drinking champs and doing some lines, like usual, that's what we always did. I was in the bathroom taking a pee—*trying* to take a pee. You know how it hard sometimes to pee when you been doing coke? Like you really hafta go but you can't, so you sit there and wait, like, forever? Well, I'm sittin there lookin at *Cosmo* and I hear this giant crashing sound, breaking glass. It was like a hurricane had hit, you know what I'm sayin? Like all hell broke loose—yellin and bangin, all kindsa shit. I didn't know what the fuck. I ran into the closet and hid."

"And then what?"

"I heard these bangs, like gunshots. I was too scared to move. I stayed there for like two hours. I didn't have no watch, I wasn't really sure what time it was when I went to the bathroom. You know how it do—time get away from you when you're partyin."

"One minute it midnight, the next it four A.M."

"*Um-hum,*" Salem confirmed. "And then I didn't hear nothin for a long time, so I tiptoed into the living room. It wasn't nothin but a two-bedroom place, but it had this giant window in the livin room—a view of the ocean, downtown, all the twinkling lights. It was completely shattered. The wind was blowin the curtains in, like in the movies, you know, after some disaster. And there were these ropes. You could see they were still tied to the roof. My place was on the twenty-first floor, one level down. There's a pool up there. Whoever it was musta swung down through the window."

"That some commando shit right there," Brenda said.

"Know what I'm sayin?"

"Sweet crib, though."

"Belonged to the dentist. This Jewish guy. He was totally in love with me. He used to come over in the middle of the night in his robe and pajamas. He'd tell his wife he couldn't sleep and was going out for a drive."

"So what about Roberto?"

"He was dead on the floor. I'm pretty sure he was dead. I didn't take his pulse or nothin, but his chest wasn't moving. There was a bullet hole in his forehead."

"They must not have knowed you were there. Or maybe they didn't care. You didn't see nothin no way."

"I wasn't takin no chances. I packed a bag and drove the Lamborghini to the Greyhound station."

"The Lamborghini?"

Salem smirked. "I always wanted to drive it but he never let me."

The women dissolved into giggles—giddy peals of sisterly laughter that echoed around the shiny and aromatic confines of the nearly empty diner, then slowly died, giving way to the quiet din of the restaurant, the clatter of silverware on plates, the song on the jukebox, "Billy Jean."

They sat a few moments nursing their private thoughts. Salem looked toward the kitchen, wondering what happened to her coffee.

And then a man entered the diner—a balding Irish guy in a suede jacket. He walked straight toward them, sidled up to the table. Smiling pleasantly, he reached into his pocket and pulled out a gold badge.

"Good morning, ladies." It was Detective O'Rourke, Bandini's partner from Internal Affairs. "Are you Salem Irene Clark?" he asked.

Salem looked at Brenda for advice. Brenda's eyes told her: *Shit! Don't ask me!*

"Am I under arres, officer?" Salem asked.

"Under *arres*?" he repeated, lampooning her fake ghetto accent. "*Shiiit,* girlfrien. This be your lucky day."

26

Sojii awoke in near darkness. The air on her face was cold, but she was warm beneath a heavy blanket. Beside the bed was a plastic milk crate. On top of the crate was a small Tensor lamp and an alarm clock. The numbers glowed red: 1:37 P.M.

She turned on the lamp and sat up, crossed her legs Indian style, considered her next move. The room was small and windowless with a low ceiling—not much larger than the queen-sized mattress upon which she'd been sleeping. The effect was womblike or claustrophobic, something in between. She was dressed once again in her pink angora sweater and antique bell-bottom jeans. She noticed a sweatshirt at the foot of the bed; she slid over and put it on, flipped up the hood. She looked around for her shoes. They were nowhere in evidence.

Three of the walls had doors. She reached for the nearest knob.

A walk-in closet, several wire hangers, two yellow tennis balls gathering dust in the corner.

The second door opened into a large room—rectangular, dampish, with a bay window at the front, what the *Herald* classifieds called an English basement. Track lighting illuminated the whitewashed brick; a small but serviceable Pullman kitchen ran along one wall. Through iron bars on the front windows, which were small and high and close to the ceiling, Sojii could see parked cars, a pair of legs walking past. The front door was contiguous to the bay, to the right.

The charcoal-colored industrial carpeting was awash with toys. There was a willy-nilly quality to their abandonment, a feeling of things hastily left: a partially demolished assemblage of oversize Legos, a crate of Matchbox cars, overturned, a three-foot basketball hoop, a scattering of Nerf balls, a toy electric guitar, an assortment of drums, several cook pots, three large wooden spoons. At the center of the room, parked nose to nose, were a blue Big Wheel trike and a green plastic vehicle that resembled a tractor, a red horn at the center of its steering wheel. Sojii reached down and jabbed the marshmallowy protuberance —it let out a wheezy *squeak*.

Atop a kindergarten-size table, attended by two chairs, was a collection of art supplies. Sojii picked up a can of Play-Doh, emptied the contents into her palm. Squiggles of hot pink and electric green squished out between her fingers, cool and pliable and familiar. She smiled with delight.

"Look who's finally awake."

It was Seede. He was standing in the doorway of the bedroom from whence she'd come. He checked his watch. "I take it you slept well."

She stared at him.

"You don't remember last night?"

She rolled the Play-Doh into a ball, mushed it back into the can. "I . . . I don't know. I was having these, like, really weird dreams."

Seede stroked his beard, an involuntary gesture, a sort of space retainer—your next statement here. *Maybe this wasn't such a great idea after all.* He'd done this favor for Waylon because, well, for several reasons. Back when he was a city attorney, Waylon had been an important source; with his help Seede had broken a number of stories, gotten jailhouse access to several high-profile criminals. Seede knew the Pope too, and not just from interviews. He had dialed the toll-free number many times. More often he simply walked the three blocks to the church to cop in person. He enjoyed hanging out with the Pope. His farrago of mixed messages resonated with Seede, who'd written his undergraduate thesis on utopian communities in nineteenth-century America. Like the Pope, Seede believed in the perfectibility of the human spirit; it was *people* he found hard to take—so petty and hateful, focused on the wrong stuff, their insecurities overruling their more noble instincts. The Pope always talked about buying his own island and living in peace with others of his own selection. It seemed like a great idea.

"My name is Jonathan Seede," he told the girl, as he had the night before, when he had practically carried her from the Pope's attic hideaway to his house. "This is my place. We're a couple of blocks north of the church. Waylon called me last night from the lockup and asked me to get you out of there. I never knew about the attic. The swinging fridge? Pretty high-tech for such a dump."

She fitted the top onto the Play-Doh can, returned it to the table. "Now what?" she asked dejectedly.

Seede looked her over. She didn't seem like a druggie or a hustler. She was poised and collected. And unbelievably beautiful, he could not help noticing. "Can I ask you a question?"

Sojii shrugged, noncommittal.

"Why were you hiding up there? Are you in trouble? Is there something I need to know?"

She sat down in one of the little chairs. "The last thing I remember, the cops were at the door of the church. Waylon made me go upstairs to hide. And then—" She bit her bottom lip, which was moist and pillowy, the color of a good fillet steak cooked medium rare, in contrast to her upper lip, which was darker, more like medium well.

"Go on . . ." Seede prompted.

"I don't know. It was really weird. There was this weird beach. And I was . . . I must have fallen asleep. Maybe I was dreaming." She looked up at him, suddenly alarmed. "What happened to Mickey and them?"

"According to the cops, they raided the church and found a quantity of cocaine—though Waylon didn't bother to mention that part when he called. For some reason, two detectives from Internal Affairs made the bust. Usually IAD only investigates other cops. Mickey and Waylon were arrested."

"Louie and Beta Max too?"

"I don't have all the names. I'm going down there this afternoon to check the police report—you have to do it in person. But I do know that a group of people were taken into custody at the church, and that the Pope and Waylon were among them. According to my sources, they're being held right now at the DCCJ."

"What's that?"

"After you're arrested and questioned by the police, you're taken from the precinct house to the DC Central Jail, where they process you into the system. After that, you go before a judge and have an arraignment. More than likely, that'll be tomorrow morning at superior court. We'll know then if they make bail."

Sojii stacked and arranged the cans of Play-Doh, six in all, a child's activity. Seede thought of Jake. He liked to do the same thing. Stack the cans, knock them over. Seede felt a dull pain radiating from the vicinity of his solar plexus, a palpable sorrow, an emptiness. He wondered where the boy was right now, what he was doing. He had never wanted a kid, he'd been pretty adamant about it. There was so much in life he was aiming to do, he felt like he was still a kid himself. But when you love a woman and she wants a child, you really have no choice, you are a passenger on a runaway train. The last twenty-seven months had been the most wrenching of his existence; he had suffered mightily at the expense of that child. But now that Jake was gone, Seede missed the little booger.

"How old are you?" he asked Sojii.

"Sixteen."

Something else Waylon hadn't mentioned. "You're a runaway?"

"Not exactly."

"What, then, *exactly*?"

"It's complicated."

"I have time."

"After my father died, the court ordered me to live with some relatives in Chicago—my mother's family. I don't know them. I have never even *met* them. I was on the way there when I got to DC. I was supposed to change buses but I didn't. That's when I met the Pope—at the Greyhound terminal. Waylon's gonna help me file some papers to become a . . . whatdoyoucallit?"

Searching the rough-textured stucco ceiling for a particular piece of legal vocabulary she was after, Sojii absently pushed back the hood of her sweatshirt and stretched herself, elbows akimbo. She gathered her long chestnut hair into a high ponytail, the way girls do.

Seede felt his breath catch, as if he'd just been plunged into the freezing ocean.

"Emancipated minor," she said at last, proud of herself. She let her hair fall, a shimmering cascade. Of course she noticed Seede's reaction. Ever since she was little, men had stared. Like someone born blind or deaf, she was used to it; it was the way things were.

"How many kids do you have?" she asked.

"Um . . . one," he stammered.

"A boy?"

Recovering: "Jake."

"Where is he now?"

"You ask a lot of questions."

"Me? What about you?"

A goofy smile—a grown man bewitched. "Occupational hazard, I suppose."

"What occupation?"

"I'm a newspaper reporter. For the *Herald*."

Impressed: "The *Washington Herald*?"

"It sounds a lot better than it is."

She looked at him with consternation. "Are reporters supposed to be doing favors for people in jail?"

"What do you mean?"

"You know what the Pope sells, right?"

"After that live bust on CNN, the entire world knows what he sells."

"Exactly."

"So?"

"So why are you helping?"

"I'm not helping. I'm researching a story."

"I'm research?"

"You're a source."

"And it's okay if you let a source stay in your house?"

"You do what you have to do. Shades of gray, you understand?"

Sojii's voice grew whimsical. "It's nice down here. Your son is lucky." From a coffee can on the table she picked out a paintbrush, tickled her palm with the tip. She replaced it in the can, picked up a rolling pin. "How old is he?"

"Eighteen months—a year and a half. In the world of babies, for some reason, the time is always counted in months. Maybe that's why it seems to pass so slowly. I feel like I've been a father for eighteen *years*."

She measured the weight of the rolling pin in her palm. "Isn't this thing a little big for him?"

"You do it with him. Like, you make stuff with the Play-Doh —little men and whatnot—and he smooshes them. You should see him. He laughs like it's the funniest thing that ever happened."

"So you're divorced?"

Seede crossed the room to the kitchen, took a seat on a barstool by the counter. "If you don't mind me asking, what's your background?"

"My background?"

"You know, your ethnicity, race—whatever you want to call it. What are you?"

"What do I look like?"

He studied her face, a free pass to stare. "Kind of Asian? But also kind of African-American, you know, black. With a hint of Semitic . . . Arab or Jewish? I can't tell. Eyes your color could be Afghani, like that girl on the cover of *National Geographic*. Did you ever see that? Your nose is kind of Asian, but your hair and skin tone—"

A sudden squall of anger: "Why do people have to be put in categories?" she demanded. "What difference does it make anyway?"

"I didn't mean . . . I just, well . . ." He started again: "No. People do not have to be put in categories if they don't want to be. It's just, you know, you're unique. Very beautiful, if you don't mind me saying so."

Sojii removed a pair of blunt-edged scissors from the coffee can, began cutting a sheet of green construction paper.

"What about your mother?" he asked.

"What about her?"

"Why can't you go live with her?"

"She left me with my dad when I was six months old."

"And you haven't seen her since?"

"I'm hungry," she said. "Can we get something to eat?"

He ran a few restaurant choices through his mind, then thought better of it. "It's probably best if you lay low, at least until I figure out what's going on with the Pope and all. This whole coke thing, the bust—something's off, you know? It doesn't sound right to me. You like eggs? I could make you an omelet."

"The Pope is *really* anticoke," Sojii said. "He hates crack. He says it all the time, how it ruined the neighborhood *and* the neighbors."

"I know," Seede said. "I can't understand how he—"

Just then, from the vicinity of the small bedroom where Sojii had slept, there came a very strange sound—something that might be heard in a zoo at feeding time.

Seede turned his head toward the noise. "That sounded like a—"

And there it was again, unmistakable: the agitated screech of a large jungle cat, a panther or a jaguar perhaps, something of that order, aroused and very close.

Seede's eyes widened. He hooked his heel onto the top rung of the barstool, extracted his knife from its ankle sheath. He moved carefully toward the bedroom.

Sojii brushed past him and entered the room. She sat down on the bed, reached for her backpack, which was sitting on the floor near the plastic milk crate. By the light of the lamp, she unzipped the top compartment, took out her CD player, a pair of headphones, and several CD jewel cases and placed them beside her on the bed.

Then she removed the Master Skull. "I think it was this," she said, holding it up for Seede's inspection.

PART THREE

27

A battered taxi, blue on white, pulled to the curb at the northeast corner of Wisconsin Avenue and M Street NW, the crossroads of Georgetown, Washington's upscale tourist district, some eighteen blocks from the Strip. It was ten o'clock on Thursday morning. The back passenger-side door opened with a metallic groan; a brown leather ankle boot emerged, pointy-toed with a fun little heel.

Stepping over a yellow tie left abandoned in the gutter—artifact of an expense-account nightcrawl by some lobbyist or conventioneer through the Irish pubs, discos, and fern bars hereabouts—Salem gained the high ground of the sidewalk. She was wearing a calf-length lambskin coat with oversize shoulder pads that rather dwarfed her pale, swanlike neck. The wind was gusty but the styling mousse held her white-blonde hair fast, short spikes upthrust jauntily, a fitting metaphor for Salem herself, who had come far and suffered much in the short course of her lifetime.

She twirled around slowly on tiptoe, gathering her bearings, visualizing the map she'd studied earlier in her room, a page from a Fodor's guidebook to Washington, DC. She'd found the brand-new paperback abandoned on a bench at the bus station in

Miami. Freshly on the run—not sure, exactly, *where* she was running—she'd taken the book as a sign. At the other end of the journey she'd found Jamal, who'd bought her this expensive coat, stylish but unlined, no match for the temperature, which hovered around forty degrees, not counting windchill.

Putting the Potomac River at her back, she headed up Wisconsin Avenue at the leisurely but determined pace of a seasoned window-shopper. A Christmas carol emanated from an outdoor speaker somewhere; the aromas of pine needles and Godiva chocolates, imported perfume and sugary ice cream waffle cones mixed in the air with stale dishwater, auto exhaust, urine, the sweat smell of boiled hot dogs wafting from the umbrella cart across the street, attended by a kohl-eyed Somali refugee. According to the Fodor's—Salem had read it twice on the two-day trip north—Georgetown was once a bustling seaport, the largest exporter of tobacco in a new nation whose largest export was tobacco. The city had also done a heavy trade in human chattel: a major slave auction house had been located just a few blocks north. Nearly 250 years after its founding, Georgetown was still a thriving commercial center, a sprawling outdoor shopping and entertainment mall, decorated merrily for the season in a colonial Christmas theme. The stores and bars and restaurants were housed in rows of joined but mismatched buildings, evidence of the march of time and taste: saltbox colonial beside domed Federal beside seventies glass and steel beside eighties nouveau Victorian, these last with their precious round crosshair windows peering down like eyes from the dormers.

She walked past Hats in the Belfry, past Britches for Men, her image reflected in the large storefront windows. Past a flower stand, sweet pollen tickling her nose, past White Castle Hamburgers, the facade rendered in the customary blue and white tile, the unmistakably delicious smell of grilled onions. Past an ice cream shop, a leather shop, a jewelry shop. At Cindy's Slipper, her cadence faltered.

More than anything, Salem loved shoes. Pumps and slingbacks, cowboy boots and knee-high lace-ups, stiletto heels and fuzzy slippers, sandals and loafers and sneakers—you could never have enough shoes. Shoes made the outfit. Shoes revealed the inner woman. Shoes calmed the restive female soul. Shoes were dependable; they never disappointed you. If they fit once, they always fit, no matter how bloated or fat or ugly or evil you might be feeling on a given day. Likewise, if they didn't fit you could be sure they never would, no matter how much you loved them or wished otherwise. It was a lesson about life that Salem was still trying to learn: wrong choices stay wrong. When she'd lived in South Beach, whenever she felt blue, she would drive her Corvette—titled in the name of the auto dealer who visited every Wednesday at lunchtime—to the mall in Bal Harbour and buy herself some new shoes. By the time she fled town she'd amassed a collection that numbered 134 pairs, each in its original box, carefully stacked by color and type in the walk-in closet of her condo. Of all her actions over the last several years, she had only one regret: leaving those shoes behind. She shuddered to imagine what had become of them. The condo, she figured, had been repossessed by the dentist. Poor man, she'd never had a chance to say good-bye. She felt bad about the body and all that blood on the white shag carpet. Lord knows what he told his wife. Maybe she ended up with the shoes.

As Salem eyeballed the offerings in the window—considering each shoe, trying it on mentally—a group of Japanese tourists shuffled down the sidewalk behind her. She watched their reflections as they went by, all of them in their late teens or early twenties, all of them wearing stiff new blue jeans and clean new Nikes, all of them sporting asymmetrical punk hairdos, infused with streaks of red and green and blue. They moved en masse, giggling and talking and smoking cigarettes, their heads tilted toward the epicenter of the group, as if networked together.

She checked her own hair in the window, fussed with several spikes, then cocked her hip, a model's pose—her whole life, people always said she should be a model. She smoothed the epic lapels of her coat, the leather cold and creamy to her touch. Leaning closer to check her makeup, she could see the beginnings of fine lines in the various localities around her face that registered emotion. She was twenty-four years old. Eight years ago, when she was in high school, she won a prize from NASA for an essay about her dream of becoming an astronaut, part of a team, perhaps, that would settle the moon.

She checked her watch, started up the street again—she didn't want to be late. She walked past an antique jewelry store, past Martha's Knitting Shoppe, a couple of restaurants, a delicious long-legged stride. Past more men's clothing stores, all owned by the same Iranian family—post-Ayatollah, they preferred to be called Persian. Past a Korean woman behind a folding table, selling scarves, gloves, and hats. A group of black teens break-dancing on a piece of cardboard. A movie theater where Bob Guccione's *Caligula* had been playing exclusively for nearly a decade. Every night during the second reel, the distinguished actor John Gielgud would slit his wrists and bleed out peacefully into a warm bath. No doubt he wished the movie would do the same. Past two men dismounting Harley-Davidsons. One wore chaps, the other sported a Nazi helmet. They walked off together in a southerly direction, holding hands.

At the intersection of Wisconsin and O, on the southwestern corner, was the site of the former slave auction. According to her guidebook, the slave dealers would march their chattel up the steep hill from the docks in lines of ten or more, men and women and children, chained neck to neck . Salem wondered what it felt like coming up the hill she'd just walked, chained to your mother or your brother, chained to your man. Then she thought about slavery in general, wondered about the difference between being sold and selling yourself. In place of the auction house was now a Gap clothing store. The company was pushing a layered look for winter—a clever ploy: to be in style you had to buy several pieces.

At R Street, she stopped and pulled a business card from her pocket. A gold shield was embossed on the front: Det. John O'Rourke, Internal Affairs. On the back was an address, handwritten. After some consideration, she turned east.

In short order the neighborhood became residential. Large houses, a canopy of stately bare trees—upper Georgetown, the ancestral home of Washington's political elite. The air smelled clean, birds twittered and doves cooed, the din of traffic could scarcely be heard. Salem slowed her pace, taking in the majesty of her surroundings, the clip-clop of her chunky heels on the cobblestones evoking a bygone era.

Presently she arrived at her destination: 3128 R Street NW. A two-story brick carriage house hunkered at the corner of the property; the roof of the main house was visible behind an ivy-covered wall.

As instructed, she rang the bell marked SERVICE.

28

Seede and Jamal were sitting at the window counter of a carryout joint on U Street, nursing cups of coffee. In the downtime between breakfast and lunch the place was deserted. The owner was busy in the storeroom.

Across the street, a scruffy white man turned the corner at Ninth and headed west on U, muttering to himself as he went. His hands were stuffed deep into the pockets of his olive drab overcoat, his head was bent into the blustery wind. He moved gingerly, as if his knees hurt, as if he was walking on eggs.

"There he go," announced Jamal, tapping his fingernail on the glass. There was a mixture of pride and wonder in his friendly basso profundo, like a tour guide at a ghetto franchise of Lion Country Safari. He tapped the crystal of his counterfeit Rolex Oyster. "Exactly 10:20. Same as every morning."

Seede checked his own watch, playfully awed. "You da man, Mr. Alfred." He chucked Jamal on the shoulder of his three-piece suit, this one a burnt sienna pinstripe.

Jamal placed his right hand over his heart and bowed his head, a display of graciousness common among Arab men, something he'd picked up at Club Gemini. "From each according to his abilities, my brother."

The carryout in which they were sitting was called Ma's Place. It was owned by a mutual friend. To Seede and Jamal, he was known as Wayne Tony. To others he was known variously as Anthony Wayne, Wayne Anthony, Tony Morgan, Tony Wayne, Morgan Anthony. The first time Seede asked for his phone number, Wayne Tony thought for a second, then rattled off ten digits. "Write it down in pencil," he'd advised.

From what Seede had gathered over the years, Wayne Tony was the ancestor of freed slaves from North Carolina who had migrated north after the Civil War. He'd attended American University on scholarship but never graduated. He'd sold real estate and fine vintage sports cars—restored Nash-Healeys and MGs. He'd worked as a news cameraman and as a paralegal. He'd owned a store in Georgetown offering pricey antiquities from Morocco. He'd exported used copy machines to South Africa, factory-second T-shirts to Nigeria, previously owned Toyotas to Central America. He'd imported Mexican diazepam and black tar heroin, Colombian cocaine (through Dominican middlemen), Jamaican marijuana, Afghani hashish. Given a little advance notice, he could procure for you a driver's license or a passport, a handgun, a crew of illegal immigrants to remodel your kitchen, one thousand pounds of frozen chicken wings, a homeless couple with a newborn baby to caretake your construction site.

Wayne Tony's current pet project was this soul food carryout called Ma's Place, set in a three-story townhouse on the nine hundred block of U Street NW, a few steps down from sidewalk level. Named for his mother, a retired public school teacher, Ma's Place catered to the lunch crowd associated with nearby Howard University, the historic seat of black learning, and Howard University Hospital, six blocks northeast. During the Jazz Age, this portion of U Street had bustled with hotels, clubs, and other establishments, most of them black owned, all of them grown up around the centerpiece of the storied Lincoln Theatre and

Colonnade, which itself was now boarded, the plywood covered with gang graffiti and concert posters, many of them featuring bands that played go-go, the homegrown musical genre that employed plastic paint buckets and metal trash can tops in the rhythm section. A group of investors was said to be planning to purchase the theater for restoration, part of a comprehensive redevelopment scheme for this segment of U Street, which jazz singer Pearl Bailey once called "the Black Broadway."

At least that's what Wayne Tony had heard. With Ma's Place, he was hoping to get in on the ground floor of a future that still seemed far distant. By dusk the block was given over to the heroin trade; Wayne Tony lowered the riot shutters. No one around at night had money to spend on food.

From their vantage point in the front window, Seede and Jamal watched as the scraggly white guy—known in the neighborhood as Larry the Pharmacist—made his way slowly westward across the bleak urban tundra, slew-foot in canvas high-top sneakers, his ratty ponytail whipping behind him like a ship's pennant in a stiff blow. He passed Lou-Ella Tailor . . . Aida's House of Beauty . . . a Rastafarian-owned bakery with a poster of Haile Selassie in the front window. Pieces of newspaper and trash blew down the sidewalk like tumbleweeds.

"So what do you think?" Seede asked Jamal.

"Go ask him."

"What should I say?"

Jamal took a sip of his coffee. "Just tell him I wanna see him and that I'm waiting in here."

"He won't mind?"

"As long as he got a place to do his business he cool."

"Here's okay?"

"Just *go,*" Jamal said. This time his basso profundo was not so friendly.

29

Sojii passed through the curtain of colorful glass beads that hung inside the doorway of Mystic Eye Books, followed closely by Jim Freeman.

The air inside the store was thick with the morning's ritual offering of burnt sage; candles twinkled throughout. New Age music—synthesizer and tabla drum—noodled along the cramped and dusty aisles. There were display tables of personal altar supplies, incense and aromatherapy oils, amulets and charms, lifelike synthetic skulls (with and without trepanation holes), and tourist-quality novelties (parking meter Buddhas, alien key chains, mood rings). A pantheon of deities, fierce and beatific, of every size and material, presided over all—Vishnus and Satans, Quan Yins, Marys, and Hatshepsuts. According to a sign above the cash register, if they didn't have your particular god or goddess in stock, they'd special order.

Sojii's long hair was tied up in a bun beneath one of Seede's old watch caps. She was wearing one of Freeman's winter coats, a down parka he'd purchased some years ago for a romantic getaway to the Catskills—he'd never forget the look on the night clerk's face when he and Tom arrived to claim their heart-shaped tub. Sojii's backpack was slung over her left shoulder. It sagged with the weight of its cargo.

Freeman was dressed in what he liked to call his Realtor drag—navy blue blazer, gray worsted slacks, silk rep tie, tasseled cordovan loafers. The belt of his leather-trimmed Cortefiel trench coat was fastened into a loop behind his back, as prescribed in the latest issue of *GQ* magazine, known among his friends as "the gay Bible." He pointed toward a glass display case, indicating a foot-high statuette—a voluptuous female with a mane of wild red hair, wielding a trident, wearing only a black face mask and a black body harness. "What is *she,* the goddess of S and M?"

"Celt," Sojii said authoritatively. "Dragons, wizards, goddesses—they use a lot of that kind of imagery."

"Weren't the Celts the ones who wore the hoods like the Ku Klux Klan?"

"Those were druids. They were priests."

"The ones who built Stonehenge?"

"Actually, they found Stonehenge already built. Nobody knows who built it."

Freeman shuddered voluntarily. "That kind of stuff always gives me the creeps."

"What kind of stuff?"

"Unsolved mysteries, strange coincidences, the unknown." He sang the theme of *The Twilight Zone*. "Do do do do . . ."

"Sometimes, the *known* can be even creepier."

"What do you mean?"

"Like the fact that a lot of the Celtic beliefs were absorbed into Christianity."

"Weren't the Celts, like, pagans?"

"Yes."

"So how is it that Christianity could absorb their beliefs—didn't they end up burning a lot of pagans at the stake?"

"They wanted converts so they borrowed stuff that was familiar. Most of the key dates from the Celtic year were assimilated into the Christian calendar, the one we use now. Their celebration of winter solstice—they called it Yule—became Christmas. Their celebration of the spring equinox became Easter. They called it Eostre." She spelled it out for him.

"I thought Christmas and Easter commemorated the exact dates of the birth and resurrection of Christ."

Sojii shot him a look, a distinctly teenage expression: *Duh.*

Freeman shot one back, a distinctly gay male expression: *Don't even try it, girlfriend.* "You don't really believe in all this crapola, do you?"

Sojii's eyes dropped. She appeared to cave in upon herself.

Freeman felt horrible. The girl seemed so poised and strident that it was easy to forget she was only sixteen. Hoping to set things right, he pointed to another display case. "Who's she?" he asked, his tone overly interested.

"Ishtar," she answered halfheartedly. *Like I didn't hear what he just said?* "She's Babylonian. The goddess of love."

"The original cruel mistress . . ."

An earthy voice, full of mirth and condescension, carrying with it the scent of patchouli.

Freeman and Sojii turned.

She was forty-ish and zaftig, with long blue hair and Cleopatra bangs. A Wiccan pentagram hung from a chain around her neck.

Sojii allowed herself to be hugged, albeit briefly.

"We're thinking of adopting her," the woman said effusively to Freeman. She winked at Sojii. "She practically lives here."

The woman reached over and pulled the watch cap from Sojii's head, made a fuss of smoothing the fine, flyaway hairs. "Who's your handsome friend?" she asked.

Sojii had met Freeman only about an hour earlier, when Seede had dropped her off at his house for safekeeping. Though Seede had been vague with his instructions—not to mention jittery and out of focus, in Freeman's opinion—he'd made one thing pretty clear: Sojii should stay put on Corcoran Street until he returned.

Freeman stuck out his hand and introduced himself.

"Ava Diner," the woman replied, taking his hand.

"A pleasure, Ava Diner." As he'd learned some time ago at a sales retreat, Freeman repeated the full name of his new acquaintance. While experts insisted that the early years of a person's life were the most formative, Freeman liked to believe that a person could continue to form himself over the course of his entire lifetime. He'd spent the first eighteen years at home, true. But now, at thirty-five, he'd lived away from home almost as long. Why shouldn't those years be just as influential? Since college, he'd studied Transcendental Meditation, Tai Kwan Do, and EST. He'd taken assertiveness training, visited the Chopra Center and Canyon Ranch, tried every diet and health regimen that came down the pike. He'd taken an entire catalog of courses, from a three-month cooking fellowship at Cordon Bleu to a DC Free College class on cloisonné. As he liked to say: "Life is an ongoing process." Nowadays, when he looked in the full-length mirror in his third floor loft bedroom, furnished entirely from Roche-Bobois, he saw nothing of his upbringing, and he was pleased.

Ava's smile was a tad too large. Her teeth were a tad too small. Despite her Halloween airs, she put Freeman in mind of an evangelical Christian. She clasped her hands upon her breast prayerfully, turned her attention to Sojii. "So what brings you in so early today?"

The girl hesitated, unsure exactly where to begin. It had taken a lot of convincing to get Freeman to come here against

Seede's wishes: *It's really important; it's only five blocks; it's totally safe; no one's ever in the store; the people who work there are friends.* Now she was having second thoughts.

Ava turned to Freeman. "She comes in every afternoon, sits on the floor and reads till closing time. Quiet as a mouse. And never the same section two days in a row."

"Not every afternoon," Sojii objected.

Ava bowed to the teenager. "Okay, a lot of afternoons. Many afternoons. Refresh my memory: what was it last time?"

"I can't remember."

"What do you mean you can't remember? You never forget anything," Ava chided. Addressing Freeman: "A mind like a sponge, this one." Back to Sojii: "Go ahead, impress us: it's good for your self-esteem."

"Carl Jung," Sojii said dispassionately, a child called upon to perform. "This thing about the Holy Grail."

"What thing?"

Rolling her eyes: "Jung thought that the quest for the Holy Grail symbolized a person's need to move beyond the collective beliefs of the group," she recited. "A person's higher calling, he said, is to create an individual life."

"A path of one's own," Ava said sagely.

"Free from dogma and expectations," Sojii added.

"Sounds like the hippies," Freeman said. "*Do your own thing.*" He turned to Sojii. "I used to be a long-haired hippie freak myself. Hair down to here in a braid." He put a hand behind his back, just above the waist. "People would always come up behind me and tug on it. I remember this one time—"

"Actually, the hippie movement did have a lot to do with the New Age movement," Ava said. "It all started with the Beatles. They got into the Maharishi, and pretty soon everybody was tuning to Eastern thought—the meditation, the yoga, the—"

"Tune in and turn on," Freeman said brightly. "Or was it turn on and tune out?"

Ava frowned. "It wasn't about drugs, although drugs have always played a part, especially in the shamanistic cultures. Drugs served to open people's minds to the possibilities, yes. But even Castaneda gave up on drugs and moved to higher plains of awareness. He started looking inside. And backward. That's the whole thing: New Age thought is not really new. It's about rediscovery of the past. It's about going backward to get forward. Some scientists believe that our ancestors possessed certain abilities that we don't have anymore. Physical abilities. Psychic and spiritual abilities. Use it or lose it, you know? Things atrophy. Evolution can mean de-evolution too. Isn't it true that—"

"Excuse me, Ava?"

In the manner of someone accustomed to being interrupted, the older woman didn't miss a beat: "Yes, Sojii?"

"Didn't you say that Geoff is into crystals and stuff?"

"He works with crystals, yes, if that's what you mean. Crystal is your best source for energy and clear vision. Nowadays, they use crystals in computers for memory."

"To store information," Freeman concurred.

"That's right."

"But don't they grow the crystals for computers nowadays?" Freeman asked.

"In giant autoclaves," Ava said. "But the essential ingredient is still a tiny piece of natural high-quality quartz. You need quartz to grow quartz. It can't be synthesized."

"Do you mean, like, crystal balls?" Sojii pointed to a display case full of them. "I always thought those were just kitsch."

"Those are glass, not crystal. Crystals are way more powerful. What you can do with them depends upon how you're wired."

"And Geoff is wired for crystals?"

"He doesn't like to advertise it, but yes, he's particularly gifted with crystal."

Sojii cut her eyes toward Freeman, a look of vindication: a strong part of her argument for coming here had been her dire need to consult an expert . . . though she hadn't explained exactly why or about what. Addressing Ava: "You think I could talk to Geoff?"

"Well, he usually sees clients on Mondays and Wednesdays. Lemme go get his appointment book. When do you think you would want to come see him?"

"How about now?" She took the older woman's hands in her own. "Please? It's *really* important."

30

Larry the Pharmacist entered Ma's Place ahead of Seede. His face was sallow and deeply lined; his eyes were hidden behind thick, photo-gray lenses. He turned immediately to Jamal: "Is there someplace I can do this?"

Jamal directed the threesome away from the front window, to a counter in the back of the restaurant. Larry the Pharmacist chose a stool and sat down, unzipped his army surplus jacket, retrieved from the front pocket a white plastic box—three by five by two inches deep—and placed it upon the orange Formica counter. Inside was a travel alarm clock and six identical wax paper bindles, each about the size of a postage stamp.

The bindles were folded in half and then half again, secured with a slice of Scotch tape; inside each was one tenth of a gram of China White heroin. Grown and refined in the Golden Triangle region of Southeast Asia, most likely Burma, it had been smuggled to the eastern seaboard of the United States by Nigerian traffickers. In the last ten years, the purity of street heroin in Washington had risen from roughly 3 percent to nearly 40, a fact attributed to increased competition from growers in South America and Afghanistan. On the front of each bag was a red stamp—a cartoon rendering of a lil' devil, complete with horns, tail, and pitchfork—the symbol of the Hellraiser brand, distributed by the T Street Crew, a crack gang that had recently diversified into heroin. Cheap and plentiful, heroin was a perfect compliment to crack, providing a tranquilizing effect that killed the jittery edge. Unlike crack, however, heroin was physically addictive. Junkies and scientists agree that the only drug harder to kick than heroin is nicotine, available on practically every corner in America.

Larry the Pharmacist propped open the digital clock, removed two bags of dope, placed them carefully to the right of the clock. He reached into the breast pocket of his coat, withdrew a pair of stainless steel surgical scissors and a grade school–variety Bic pen, this one missing its ink cartridge—a transparent plastic tube with a tiny air hole machined into the side. He placed them both on the counter next to the dope.

He chose the bag closest to the clock, tapped it lightly on the counter three times—*tap, tap, tap*—to settle the powder. Picked up the scissors, snipped the Scotch tape, put the scissors back down. Unfolded the bag, flicked it twice with the long nail of his middle finger—*flick, flick*—eyeballed the count. There was a practiced grace to his movements, a sense of ritual, of choreography, of clinical precision. And also a sense that he was handling something cherished and fragile, something very dear.

He picked up the scissors again, cut off the top of the bag. Traded the scissors for the Bic pen and raised it to his nose, taking care to cover the small hole in the side of the tube with his fingertip. Checked the clock—10:36. "This will hit me in exactly twelve minutes," he announced. Inserted the Bic into the bag and sniffed—a single strong inhalation. He switched nostrils, sniffed again.

Now he looked up and spoke to Seede directly, making eye contact for the first time. "You feel your nose burn. And then you get this smell, an aroma like . . . I always say it smells like those gel-cap vitamins you buy in a natural food store. Is this the sort of thing you want to know?"

Seede stroked his beard. The truth was, he didn't know exactly *what* he wanted to know. It took time to develop a piece. You had to let things simmer. You had to trust your instincts. So far in his research, Seede had gathered a lot of material on the federal government's war on drugs—hard data and firsthand reporting. He had some strong opinions and anecdotal information about the dangers of prohibition (how denial leads to fixation and abuse), and also about the impact of the Just Say No mentality on American life. With a little reflection, he would also admit that this book project was being driven, in no small part, by the way he perceived he was being treated at home—the way he was being ignored and taken for granted at home—as if to say, *Okay, if you don't love me, I'll write a book and achieve literary success and the larger world will love me*; as if to say, *Okay, let's see how deep into hell I must descend before you put aside your selfish preoccupations long enough to see what's going on right beneath your nose, ha ha, fuck you, you don't give a shit about me anyway!*

What sort of thing did he want to know? He wasn't totally sure yet. But he did know this: he was on the trail of certain broad notions and vague truths that he was positive would lead him somewhere vital, and he was pledged to proceed, putting one foot in front of the other, following his instincts until he got there. Sometimes, he figured, you don't know what you're onto, you just know you're onto something. You have to trust yourself. You have to dare to be bad. You have to take the chance that you might fail.

He pulled his tape recorder from his coat pocket. He held it up for Larry the Pharmacist to see. "You're doing great. Mind if I record?"

Larry dipped his Bic pen inside the bag again and sniffed, lighter this time, more prolonged, rooting for errant grains. "Heroin restores my normal physiological function," he said, placing the

Bic down on the counter. "Without heroin, I have no sex drive, I have no desire for food, I have no energy. But when I snort heroin, if you wired me up and monitored my vital signs, you would find that exactly twelve minutes after administration of the drug all my functions return to normal. When I turned the corner from Ninth on to U this morning, I felt about seventy years old." He checked his clock—10:38. "Ten minutes from now, I will feel about thirty. Another bag, I'll feel twenty-five." He popped the empty bindle into his mouth and commenced chewing.

"How old are you, actually?" Seede asked.

"Sixty-two on October second."

"Have you always snorted? I thought people with hard-core habits usually—"

"I stopped injecting on December fifteenth of last year. That was the day my brother died." He removed the soggy bindle from his mouth and placed it on the counter. "See, I came into the kitchen at 3:15 in the morning and his head was on the table. It was late. I thought he was asleep. I tried to wake him. He looked so . . ." He faltered, struggling to find the words. His photo-gray lenses had lightened; Seede could see a tear forming in the corner of his muddy brown eye, the pupil of which was stopped down to the approximate diameter of a finishing nail.

"When my brother died my life essentially came to an end," Larry continued. "Technically, my heart is beating. But really I died on December 15, 1991, a Sunday, at 3:15 A.M. I loved my brother—actually, he was my stepbrother, and also my best friend. His name was Michael—did I say that? He was a phenomenal man, worthy of a biography. He had an IQ of 165—well into genius level. He was a master of astronomy, a brilliant pharmaceutical chemist. I myself have a doctorate in biochemistry; people have said I am rather brilliant. But I'm nothing compared to Michael. He could read, write, and speak six languages. He graduated Caltech with honors. He studied photochemistry under Dr. George S. Hammond, the world's foremost authority on the subject. That's like studying radio with Marconi—it gives you an idea of the kind of intellect I'm talking about. Would you believe that Michael once conceived a synthesis of methamphetamine from beta styrene? If you know anything about chemistry, that's almost unbelievable. The structure of beta styrene is about as far from methamphetamine as you can imagine. If I had a quartz crystal in my hand and told you I could make methamphetamine out of it, you'd laugh me out of the room. But he actually conceived it—he never had a chance to test it, but it made sense, he'd mapped it out, he'd made diagrams: it obeyed the laws of chemistry. No one had ever even *thought* to look in that direction. He was quite a guy. A brilliant man. And he looked great in a Santa suit."

Up to that point, Seede had been following. "A Santa suit?"

Larry the Pharmacist smiled, a memory only he could see. Then his smile faded. He shook his head mournfully. He reached over and picked up the second wax paper bindle, tapped it lightly on the counter three times—*tap, tap, tap*. Snipped the Scotch tape, unfolded the bag, flicked it twice—*flick, flick*—with the long nail of his middle finger. Eyeballed the count, cut the top with the scissors. Checked the clock—10:52. Pointed the Bic at Seede.

"I came into the kitchen at 3:15 in the morning, and his head was on the table. I thought he was asleep, I tried to wake him. I managed to get his eyes open and they flickered a little bit, but then he died. Quite remarkable, actually. It was immediately apparent. I didn't even have to check the pulse. He took one last deep breath and he exhaled and that was it. Very final. A very final sound: there was no mistaking it. The absolute sound of the end.

"I held him in my arms for I don't know how long, just staring into his eyes, thinking about . . . I don't know what I was thinking about. Wondering what it was going to be like without this person who was so close to me, the only person, the only one left who cared. Thinking to myself that my life was over, I guess. And that's when it came to me. It was like: *Wait a minute! Holy shit! Remember John Belushi?* When he died of an overdose, the girl who'd furnished him with the drugs was charged with his murder. In this case, it was also clear: I had furnished the drugs. *I* was the one! Had I not given him the forty dollars, he would never have bought those four bags of dope. He would never have died. The chain of responsibility for his death led directly to me. I was a murderer.

"He'd been clean for a while, see. He'd been in detox, he'd been on methadone. And then I gave him that little taste in the bathroom stall at the Air and Space Museum—that's where he was working as a Santa, outside the museum, collecting money in one of those kettles for the Salvation Army. He was on his break. I just gave him a little taste. The tiniest little snort. I was so happy that day. Feeling festive, I guess—the both of us were. It's supposed to be a season of joy, is it not? I always loved going to the museum and seeing Lindbergh's plane hanging in the lobby, and John Glenn's Mercury capsule. And I guess that little taste got him going again, even though he assured me it wouldn't. Because I asked, you know, it's not like I didn't think of it. I said, 'Is this gonna knock you off the wagon or anything?' And he was like, 'No way—it's under control.' He should have known his tolerance was down. He couldn't have *not* known. He was a brilliant chemist. I can't for the life of me think of any reason he would have had to take his own life on purpose."

"So what did you do?"

"What did I do? I'll tell you what I did. And this is shocking. I didn't read about this in any book; this is my life I'm telling you about. This is God's honest truth. I took my brother's dead body out of my apartment, Michael's body. He was still warm. Humid, you might call it, like the way someone feels sleeping next to you under the sheets. I loved him, yes, but the thing is, he was deceased—there was nothing further I could do. And I knew if they found him in my apartment, I could face a murder beef. The evidence of my guilt was right there on the table—one and a half bindles of dope. The syringe was mine too. It was still in his arm. I could not go back to prison. I cannot. I had no other choice. I put him in the elevator in his pajama bottoms. I pressed the B, for basement."

A single tear, fat and solitary, dripped from the corner of Larry's eye and flowed along a deep furrow in his cheek, like rainwater through a desert wash, then plunged off his jawline, free-falling through the cold, greasy atmosphere of Ma's Place, splashing onto the dirty linoleum floor. Seede reached over and placed a hand on Larry's shoulder, gave him a couple of pats. Some time ago Seede had been at the Library of Congress, waiting for some periodicals he'd ordered to come down from the stacks. Idly he'd picked up a random book on a table and begun paging through. It turned out to be a volume of Scottish legends. In days of yore, apparently, in Scottish villages, there was always a man who served as the village sin eater. When someone died, the relatives would lay a feast atop the body. They would invite the sin eater to come to the house and consume the feast, symbolically absorbing into himself any sins the deceased had committed over the course of his or her lifetime, clearing his way into heaven. Reading this, Seede was struck by the parallels to his own job—although in his case, he serviced the living. He listened. He validated. He gave voice. He absorbed pain—so many murders and assaults, so many lies and scandals, so much misfortune and injustice. Over the years, it had begun to accumulate, like toxins in his liver.

"What happened after that?" Seede asked.

"I did what all dope fiends do in a crisis: I shot up. And then I left the building. I didn't want to be around when the cops arrived."

"I'm guessing you took the stairs," Jamal said, chuckling at his own bon mot.

Oblivious, Larry dipped his Bic into his bindle and sniffed. Seede looked to Jamal with a pregnant expression. Jamal took a swig of his coffee, addressed their guest. "You still doing any commerce?" he asked.

Larry switched nostrils and sniffed again. "Not a whole lot. How much are you looking to get?"

Jamal eyeballed Seede. "What do you think, two dimes?"

"What do *you* think?" Seede asked Larry the Pharmacist.

Larry the Pharmacist popped the empty bindle into his mouth, commenced chewing. "You ever use heroin before?"

Seede shook his head no.

"What else do you have on board?"

"On board?"

"What other chemicals are in your system right now?"

"Since when?"

"Say, the last twenty-four hours."

"Dimetapp—that's an allergy medication, an antihistamine. And let's see: four, eight, um . . . about fourteen milligrams of Xanax, and about an eightball of street crack." He thought a moment. "And a couple of joints, some wine. Does nicotine and caffeine count?"

"*Yoooooo!*" Jamal sang appreciatively. "Unsafe at any speed!"

"Actually, I'm functioning at a pretty high level." Seede's tone was that of a researcher, assessing the state of a lab animal. "I had another front-page story on Sunday."

"You been going to work every day?"

"Pretty much. None of my eagle-eyed investigative colleagues suspect a thing—everybody in the newsroom looks like shit. I'm beginning to believe what they say: the most obvious is the least obvious. It certainly bears out in this case. I don't think anyone suspects—except my wife, although she has no idea how long it's been going on and to what extent."

"And since she gone at the moment—"

"I'd try a dime to start," Larry the Pharmacist said. "That's about a tenth of a gram, a hundred milligrams. Hellraiser is running about 37.5 percent pure. You'd be ingesting only about thirty-eight milligrams of pure heroin. It's not that much. Enough to get you off, give you a little taste. It certainly won't kill you. Unless . . ." His voice trailed off.

Alarmed: "Unless what?"

"Unless you have a systemic intolerance to opiates. You don't, do you? It's pretty rare."

Seede's eyes widened. "Not that I know of."

Jamal chuckled again and took a swig of his coffee. "Don't worry. We can have you at Howard Hospital in two minutes." He looked at Larry. "They say the brain can go without oxygen for what, five minutes?"

"I believe that's correct," Larry confirmed.

"How long do you think it would take to acquire a habit?" Seede asked.

Larry the Pharmacist looked at him gravely. "I wouldn't recommend it," he said.

31

Salem followed the butler into the crystal chamber. The motorized ceiling was partially retracted, revealing a glass-and-steel roof, the wan winter sky above.

They were greeted by Bert Metcalfe. He was wearing a royal blue workout suit and white Reebok trainers. A terry-cloth towel was draped over his neck; drops of perspiration roosted amidst the swirling curls at his temples.

"Hello, Salem," he said warmly.

The hand he offered was small and stubby, with tufts of fine black hair growing like sea grass along the fleshy dunes of his knuckles. She chose to leave it where it was.

Metcalfe's hand dropped lifelessly to his side, like a duck caught midflight by a load of no. 3 buckshot. "You *are* Salem Irene Clark, are you not?"

She drew back one side of her long coat like a stage curtain, pinned it to her hip with a fist, revealing a chic little black dress that clung to her thin but shapely form. "I'm whoever you want me to be, baby."

Metcalfe cut his eyes to Desmond and then back to Salem. In his mind, this scene had unfolded a bit differently. Maybe he should have let the detective fill her in. He dabbed his forehead with the towel. "I know who you are," he said earnestly.

"I'm sure you do, baby," Salem said. "And I'm gonna get to know *you* real good too." She drew back the other flap of her coat, pinned it with her other fist.

"No, no, no," he said, struggling to make himself understood. "I don't want to have *sex* with you. I just want to talk."

"It's yo money."

Exasperated, he put his own two fists on his hips. "How much?"

Salem considered what the market would bear. She wondered what "just talk" was really going to entail. He was obviously loaded. But something about the whole scene felt really weird. Not dangerous exactly. Just off. That he knew her name—that was explainable: the cop had told him. Rich folk always have cops around to help with their dirty work. The skull thingies everywhere didn't help. Neither did this guy. What was he, a midget or something? The usual stuff she could handle—the blow jobs and straight sex, the groping in the front seats of cars—when it came right down to it, it wasn't much different from high school dating. It wasn't until the freak show started—the tandem dates, the dirty talk—that she began to really feel like a ho (instead of like someone just pretending to be one).

"Perhaps I need to speak to your *pimp* about the financial arrangements?" Metcalfe said, mistaking her reticence for ploy. The stress on the word carried an accusatory tone, modulated with a hint of worry that seemed inappropriate to Salem, especially under the circumstances.

"You can talk to *me,*" she said, raising her index finger in admonition. The nail was long and sharp, painted red. "And he ain't my pimp," she said, waggling the finger in the air, meanwhile swiveling her head contrapuntally. "He my *security.*"

A feeling of sadness overcame Metcalfe. He remembered her now, the mother. Her name was Suzy, a leggy bottle blonde with baby doll eyes and a raspy, cigarette voice. She'd worked as a bartender in a tavern patronized by NASA employees. Metcalfe had gone there with some ground-control types. The next day his friend Grissom was incinerated on the launchpad; in his shock and grief he'd never given the woman another thought. But why hadn't she contacted him? It made no sense. She must have had other lovers. She must not have believed the child was his. Certainly she'd known who he was and could have found him—his visit to Canaveral had been noted in the local press. Why not let him know? Why not ask for money? How strange it was to think that all these years he'd had a child in the world and hadn't known. And this is what had become of her. And this is how easy it was to communicate. It seemed so sad and ironic. He wished now that he'd prepared more for this meeting, maybe done a little reading on the subjects of fatherhood and reunions—all sorts of relevant topics came to mind.

"You're safe now," he said, striking a parental tone, his voice full of emotion. He reached up and placed his stubby but well-meaning paw atop her admonishing, red-painted fingernail, steered the hand back down to her side. "I know what happened in Miami. I know about the shooting in the condo. I can help you."

Salem stepped backward, out of range of his touch. *How the fuck does he know all this?* She gave her voice a hard edge; her eyes took cover behind a ghetto squint, lids crinkled, the effect somewhat offset by her lush Max Factor lashes. "You wanna date or not? Cause I gotta be goin. I got an appointment downtown, know what I'm sayin?"

Metcalfe sighed. "Give her the money, Desmond."

A standard payroll envelope, nearly two inches thick. Salem opened the flap, thumbed the stack of bills inside. She'd left

South Beach almost three weeks ago. There'd been no sign of the men who killed Roberto, no sign of anyone following her. Maybe this little guy was right. Maybe she was safe. Maybe her trail was cold by now. Maybe the whole thing had been a huge mistake. Maybe they'd never even realized she'd been hiding in the closet. Maybe they didn't care. Or maybe they did. Who knew? One thing was sure: there was a lot of money in this envelope. More than she'd ever seen at one time. More than enough for a ticket to California, a start on a new life.

"These are all *fifties*," she said, incredulous, pronouncing the second *f* in fifties—her ghetto inflection momentarily forgotten.

"Tea for two, please, Thornton," Metcalfe ordered.

32

Geoff Greene, the proprietor of Mystic Eye Books, leaned back in his desk chair, appraising the young girl before him with a connoisseur's eye. He was a handsome older man, chiseled and craggy, a type you might find acting in a daytime soap. His thinning hair was expensively cut; his cashmere turtleneck was threadbare at the elbows. A two-day stubble of salt-and-pepper beard camouflaged the gentle erosion of his jawline. "Your name is Sojii?" he asked.

"Ava introduced us once. I was in the shop, and you were—"

"And you are . . . ?" Greene waved his antique half-glasses imperiously in the direction of her companion.

"James Freeman, Mr. Greene." He'd insisted on following her up the stairs, along the dark corridor to this back office. He proffered his hand and a winning smile. "Don't mind me: I'm just along for the ride."

The room was small and dusty, with books everywhere—crammed into shelves, stacked waist-high around the floor, balanced on the arms of chairs, piled atop the large desk behind which Greene was sitting. Scattered here and there were fallen deities, breakage from the bookstore—a Buddha with no head, a Jesus with one arm, two halves of a Ganesha serving as paperweights. From this unlikely headquarters, Greene did a brisk and lucrative trade in rare texts and high-end religious relics. Self-educated in his field, he'd gotten his start peddling illustrated Bibles door to door in a beat-up VW bug. While he did boast a sizable personal collection of important artifacts, the rarest and most valuable of which were kept in a vault in the basement, he served more often as a middleman, working the dark margins between the mercenary adventurers who acquired the stuff and the wealthy zealots who conspired to possess it. He gestured to a pair of chairs. Freeman removed a stack of books to the floor and sat down in one. Sojii perched on the edge of the other.

"Ava tells me you're interested in crystals," Greene said.

"Crystal *skulls,*" Sojii clarified.

"Crystal skulls?" The smile overlarge.

"You know—like a skull made out of a large piece of crystal rock?"

He smiled again, a toothy display of expensive bridgework that resembled a primate fear grimace. "What a coincidence," he said, indicating the array of books spread before him on his desk. "I was just doing some research on that very topic."

"Small world," said Freeman. He liked the looks of this guy, but that was about it.

"What do you want to know?" Greene asked Sojii.

A long beat, eyes downcast. Then her emerald irises rose and sought his grays. "Everything?"

Greene smiled again, closer to genuine this time, disarmed by her youth and beauty. He fitted his glasses to the tip of his nose, pulled out a book from the pile on his desk. "According to various legends, there are as many as fourteen ancient skulls," he said, locating a page. He commenced reading: "Crafted of precious or semiprecious minerals, in lifelike human proportions, they are said to be able to speak or sing or otherwise communicate, sometimes in birdsong or other animal sounds. A fifteenth skull is known as the Master Skull. All of the skulls are said to contain important information about the origins, purpose, and destiny of mankind—answers to some of the greatest mysteries of life and the universe."

"How do you know which is which?" Sojii asked.

"For one thing, they're made of different materials," he said. "Some are crystal—three of them, I believe, including the Master Skull, which is said to be the most valuable. Then there's a jade skull, a rose quartz skull, one of lapis, so on. According to the legends, they're meant to be used in groups of five with a crystal skull central to each grouping."

"Whose legends?" Freeman asked.

"That's what's interesting," Greene said, looking over the top of his glasses. "Versions of the same stories are found in different cultures." He ticked them off on his fingers. "The Mayans and the Aztecs in Central America. The Pueblo Indians in the southwest United States. The Cherokees of the northeast, the Canadian tribes. All of them have legends about skulls. All of them have legends about visitors from the sky or from the sea. The British Museum has a crystal skull. As does the Smithsonian—that one is said to be cursed. But most of the fifteen skulls are privately owned. They're very valuable. As you could imagine, there are a lot of counterfeits on the market."

"How do you know which are the counterfeits and which are real?" Sojii asked.

Greene leaned forward. "Why are you so interested in all this anyway?"

Uncertain: "I just am?"

"You haven't seen one, have you?"

Her backpack was on the floor between her feet. "What if I have?"

"For one thing, you might be on the verge of becoming a very wealthy young woman."

Unblinking: "What if it's not mine?"

"These skulls have enormous scientific value," he said gravely. "Religious, historic, scientific—you name it, Sojii. If you know where one is, it is your civic duty to come forward and tell."

She glanced at Freeman and then back at Greene, considering. Then she reached down and unzipped her backpack. She placed the skull upon the desk.

It was a marvelous object, absolutely flawless, anatomically correct. The cranium was transparent, cool to the touch. The eye sockets glowed softly, reflecting the available light. The details of the teeth were precise, the cheekbones were exquisite, the surface was as smooth as glass. Deep within the skull could be seen a series of tiny bubbles, laid out in a gently curving plain, glittering within the mass of the crystal like stars.

Visibly moved, Greene picked it up with both hands, turned it reverently this way and that. A rainbow of refracted light played across the rugged screen of his face. Until yesterday, when Detective Bandini had called, Greene had never given much thought to crystal skulls. He had collaborated intermittently with Bandini since the early eighties, when the cop, working robbery at the time, had sought Greene's advice on a series of break-ins at churches. Of course, Greene had heard of crystal skulls; he had replicas for sale in his store. But typically that sort of product wasn't on his radar. He usually concentrated on more mainstream items—ancient texts, rare icons, paintings, and the like. As he told Bandini: he'd heard nothing specific, black market *or* otherwise. Bandini thanked him and hung up, but not before mentioning—rather pointedly, Greene thought—that a large reward for information was being offered by a private party. With the holiday lull at hand, Greene had decided to nose around a bit. Like he always said: nothing comes to those who wait.

"This is the Master Skull, isn't it?" Sojii asked.

"It's supposedly a woman," Greene said. "In the mid-1920s, a forensics guy from the New York City Police Department drew an artist's conception from a photograph. He used the bone structure to extrapolate her features."

Greene pulled another book from the pile on his desk, flipped through the pages, found the drawing. He held it up for his visitors to see.

"*Whoa*," Freeman exclaimed. "She looks *exactly* like you, Sojii."

"The eyes and the cheekbones especially," Greene agreed.

It was Sojii's turn to be skeptical. "And this was supposedly made on another planet?"

Greene threw up his hands, partly in acknowledgment of the volumes crowded into his dusty office, symbolic of mankind's collective wisdom, partly in acknowledgment of the great mysteries that mankind's collective wisdom hadn't yet managed to explain. "Some say beings from outer space brought the Master Skull and its brothers and sisters to Earth millenniums ago." His voice sounded neutral, just relating the facts, unbelievable as they might sound. "Others say the skulls were fashioned by the inhabitants of Atlantis in the hours or days before their civilization was wiped out. Some believe the Atlanteans were the descendants of colonists from another planet. The earliest known reference comes from Plato, circa 350 B.C."

"Plato wrote about Atlantis?" Freeman snorted.

"It's in a book called *Timaeus*," Greene said, digging for another volume. "He writes of an Athenian named Solon, a wise man who traveled through Egypt. At a place called Sais, Solon meets an old priest. The priest tells him that compared to the Egyptians, the Greeks have little knowledge of the great events of ancient history. He goes on to tell Solon a story about a long lost island in the middle of the ocean.

"Plato quotes the priest," Greene said, finding the place, reading aloud: "'On this island of Atlantis had arisen a powerful and remarkable dynasty of kings. . . .'" He skipped ahead, "'. . . which arrogantly advanced from its base in the Atlantic Ocean to attack the cities of Europe and Asia.'"

He flipped a little further in the text. "'There were earthquakes and floods of extraordinary violence, and in a single dreadful day and night . . . Atlantis was swallowed by the sea and vanished.'" He raised his head from the text to gauge the impact on his visitors, who were visibly rapt. "The priest goes on to tell Solon," he continued, "'You and your fellow citizens are descended from the few survivors that remained, but you know nothing about it because so many succeeding generations left no record in writing.'"

"Why weren't the skulls lost with everything else?" Freeman asked.

"Supposedly, the Atlanteans knew they were doomed. They wanted to preserve their culture. They put all of their collected knowledge into the skulls and sent them off to different parts of the world. That's the story anyway. One of the stories. Some people believe that the Atlanteans may have been responsible for the unlikely leaps of technology made by many of the Earth's great civilizations. Like the Mayans. The way their culture seemed to sprout up out of nothing."

Sojii riveted him with an intense stare. "So is this the Master Skull or not?"

Greene pulled out another book, found a section of high-quality color plates. He held it up. "What do *you* think?"

She read aloud the caption beneath: "Discovered in the jungles of Belize."

"In 1915," Greene added. "It was called British Honduras at the time."

"Just below Mexico," Sojii said.

"On the Caribbean coast. Where Atlantis was supposed to have been."

Sojii turned the page. A photograph of a tall, thin, serious man. He is standing in the jungle, squinting against the bright sun, wearing a floppy hat, jodhpurs, knee-high boots. A fancy, long-stemmed tobacco pipe is angled out and down from his mouth. She read: "Bertram Metcalfe."

"He's the one who found it," said Greene. "Or actually, it was his daughter. His adopted daughter—there is some evidence that he fathered a child with her, though he never claimed parenthood or even saw the child, apparently. They found the skull in a place called Tumbaatum, which is Mayan for 'City of Fallen Stones.' It's quite a story," he said, selecting another text, a brittle old book. "A disastrous expedition through the jungle. Crocodiles and predatory insects. Injury, delirium, a love triangle . . . you name it."

Greene opened the book, obviously a valuable limited edition, hand-sewn, leather-bound. "This is a diary. It was self-published by a man named H. R. Stuke. He was a Cornish watercolor artist. There are some of his prints and sketches included as well. Apparently he signed on with the expedition at the last minute. This Metcalfe guy was short on funds; Stuke was an Eton kid with a sizable trust fund."

He paged through the book with care, mindful of the brittle binding. "According to Stuke, after hiking for weeks through the treacherous rain forest, Metcalfe literally stumbled upon the city: he tripped over one of the fallen stones buried within the thick underbrush and hit his head. He was gravely injured—from the sound of it, he suffered a minor stroke and was debilitated for some time. Stuke says that he had no choice but to assume command of the expedition. He hired scores of natives from the surrounding tribe and began clearing the underbrush. They hacked away with machetes and native stone implements for several months trying to reclaim the city from the jungle. Finally, he decided to set a fire."

He read from Stuke's diary: "'The inferno raged for several days and nights like a mighty blast furnace, spewing out white hot ash and spitting red embers all around, nearly choking the very life breath from our party of explorers and native tribesmen. As the holocaust swept onward, the mythical city was slowly revealed, like a vision from a fairy tale . . .

"'In its totality, we would eventually calculate, Tumbaatum occupied some six square miles. There were pyramids, palaces, houses, subterranean chambers. A huge amphitheater appeared as if it were designed to hold more than ten thousand people. The magnitude of the labor that must have been required is almost beyond computation: the only tools available during that era were flint axes and chisels, of which we found many at the site. One morning, in imitation of the workers or slaves who built the place, I set out to square a block of stone with one of these implements. The task took me an entire day.'"

"You said the daughter found the skull?" Sojii asked.

"Adopted daughter. Her name was Roberta. They called her Bobbie. She was probably just about your age at the time—how old are you?"

"Sixteen."

"She was maybe a year older. Old enough, apparently, to fall in love with Stuke—or at least, he was in love with her. He never says it in his journal, but it seems pretty clear—some of his prose gets pretty purple," Greene sniggered. "About a year after the skull was found, Stuke and Metcalfe fought a pistol duel on a street in downtown Belize. Bobbie ended up sailing back to England—pregnant, some say. Stuke's shoulder was shattered; Metcalfe was an expert marksman. Stuke never painted again."

"How did she find the skull?"

"One morning, according to Stuke's diary, Bobbie woke up early and climbed to the top of the central pyramid. Metcalfe had forbidden her to go up there—it was more than fifteen stories high. But she got it in her mind to go, and go she did. She is portrayed as a tough little nut, not shy about voicing her opinion.

"Anyway, one morning, as the rest of camp still slept, Bobbie climbed to the top of the pyramid." He picked up the story on the page: "'The climb was difficult but she was in excellent shape. Once at the summit, she sat for a long time, entranced with the beauty and the wildlife, the birds and monkeys, the vast canopy of the rain forest stretching around her for miles, the closest part of it charred from the fire we'd set, which luckily had been doused after several days by the first driving rains of monsoon season. (Frankly, the idea that we would have to put it out never occurred to me.) As the sun rose higher overhead, she became aware of something glittering—something way down inside the pyramid. She could see it shining through a deep fissure . . .'"

"It took the party several weeks to enlarge the hole," Greene narrated, turning the pages. "When everything was ready, Bobbie volunteered to retrieve the skull."

He read again: "'Slowly, hand over hand, the natives let her down, feetfirst, into the opening, which was certainly more than fifty meters in depth. She was a leggy thing, long of limb and finger; a sprite, barely eight stone. Her eyes shined fearlessly, ferociously, utterly dedicated to the task. Taking no chances, I insisted on utilizing some twenty of our diminutive brown employees for the task, ten on either of the two ropes. Their skin glistened with the weight of their responsibility, for everyone in the party, Christian and heathen alike, had the utmost regard for this wonderful young woman, whose ready smile and intelligent blue eyes had seen us all through the darkest of times.'"

Greene skipped ahead. "'With due haste, Bobbie was pulled back to the surface. Flush with her accomplishment, she removed the object from beneath her blouse, where she had held it for safekeeping, and raised it aloft. In hushed silence we gazed at this strange object, mesmerized by the way it refracted the rays of the sun, sending forth great rainbows of light. Then, spontaneously, the native workers erupted with joy. They laughed and cried, kissed the ground, hugged one another, as if an ancient memory had been triggered, as if each of them knew intuitively of this crystal icon, that it was a significant part of their past, a long lost deity finally returned home.

"'When evening fell and the first stars appeared in the sky, Metcalfe—finally up and around after months of debilitation, he was acting his part as Cock of the Walk—placed the skull upon a makeshift altar the natives had built. Fires were lit all around. There was drumming and chanting and singing. Dancers appeared from the shadows, decorated with the plumes of jungle birds and the skins of jaguars. The celebration went on for days, drawing natives from other villages, bringing all work at the dig to a complete halt."

"How do we know this really happened?" Sojii asked.

"The only other account we know of is Metcalfe's. His personal papers are said to be privately held. I'll tell you one thing I *do* know for sure: up until you took that skull out of your bag" —he indicated the Master Skull, still sitting on his desk—"it had been missing for seventy years."

"But it's been on the Pope's desk ever since I've known him."

"The Pope?"

"The Pope of Pot. He has a church on Fourteenth and P."

"I don't know anything about him," Greene said dismissively. "All I know is that people have been searching for this thing for years. Someone is offering a lot of money for information about it."

"What is it supposed to be used for, exactly?" Freeman asked.

Greene pulled out another book, this one more modern. "Back in the early twenties, before it went missing, Metcalfe took the skull to be examined by ocular scientists in Germany. They ran a complete battery of tests."

"And?"

"For one thing, they found that the skull was made of pure, natural quartz, which doesn't age, so you can't tell how old it is, not even with carbon dating. But the weirdest thing was this: even under extreme magnification, the scientists could find no evidence at all of what they call 'tool chatter'—a telltale pattern of repetitive scratch marks left by the makers."

"Meaning . . . ?"

"Meaning that the scientists couldn't figure out *how* the skull was actually made. There was no evidence of any type of hand craftsmanship or machine work or anything. It's like, *poof,* you know? Like it just materialized in its present form."

"That's what the scientists concluded?" Freeman asked. "That it just materialized?"

"Actually, no," Greene said. "There was a big dustup over the report. The official version ended up concluding that the Master Skull had been made by hand—by slowly and patiently rubbing and polishing a large quartz rock with a mixture of sand and water."

Sojii shook her head emphatically: *no way*. "That would have taken *years*!"

"Three hundred years," Greene said. "That was their estimation."

33

Sidestepping an unattended gurney—the patient/inmate in full restraints; on his face the terrified befuddlement of a wounded animal ensnared in a trap—Seede approached the reception desk on the fifth floor hospital ward of the DC Central Jail.

He carried his pad, pen, and tape recorder. The rest of his stuff was stowed in a locker downstairs in visitor intake. Around his neck dangled his Certified Media Credential, known as a CMC, a three-by-five-inch laminated card issued by the Metropolitan Police Department after a rigorous background check. The CMC provided official access to crime scenes, precinct houses, and government buildings. It also exempted its holder from the usual routine searches of person and personal effects.

The cinder block walls up here were painted a darling shade of little boy blue; the air smelled of ammonia and industrial deodorizer, the familiar bouquet of a modern health care facility, with a slight after-nose of dirty mop. Seede shifted his paraphernalia awkwardly to one hand, separated the paperwork he'd been given downstairs, proffered it to the khaki-uniformed guard.

The guard glanced down at the sheets of paper, then down a bit further, toward the miniature television that was peeking out from the bottom drawer of his desk. A popular game show played at low volume. Transfixed, he tipped back his baseball-style cap—the most expensive in the catalog, the bill embroidered with fancy gold scrollwork known as scrambled eggs—and scratched absently at the top of his balding head.

Seede's own balding head was glistening with sweat; his complexion was alarmingly green. His mouth was dry and foul-tasting; a leaf of something earlier ingested was lodged between his cheek and gum. Beneath his V-neck sweater and button-fly jeans, his T-shirt and briefs were soaked. Standing as he was beneath a large air vent, part of the network of exposed ductwork and hanging sprinklers and suspended lighting that gave the vaulted reception area the feel of a chic converted warehouse space, he was beginning to feel a chill.

While Larry the Pharmacist had warned him of the possible side effects for first time users, Seede had been surprised by the intensity of his reaction. He'd come here directly by cab from Ma's Place—a thirty-minute ride across the Anacostia River into far southeast Washington—with no particular ill effects. In fact, he'd found the cocktail of heroin and crack, known on the streets as a speedball, to be exceedingly pleasant. To his great relief, the jittery edge of the cocaine high, the prolonged and jangled trough that followed each fleeting orgasmic spike—the intensity and duration of which diminished incrementally as the binge continued—was now completely gone. Gone too was the insistent need for constant maintenance, the all-consuming urge for more, a hunger that manifested itself as a yawning pit in the middle of his gut, as a constant carping voice in the back of his head, growing ever louder and more demanding. After a couple days without sleep, he'd noticed, he'd start getting traces of phantasm, trails and flashes of movement around the room, convoluted aural hallucinations, shadowy people who weren't really there. The voice in the back of his head would begin to sound like Elvis. It would sing the same song over and over, a bastardized bit from *Bye Bye Birdie: One more hit, oh baby, one more hit / Oh oh oh / Gimme one more hit*.

But as he was juddering across the pocked and pitted surface of the John Philip Sousa Bridge, lounging in the backseat of the cab on the way to the DCCJ, a ten-dollar bindle of Hellraiser heroin surging through his bloodstream, a perfect synergy had been momentarily achieved. Seede had the sensation that he was floating on a small raft in a large pool on a perfect day. The chronic stiffness in his neck and shoulders was gone; his jaw had ceased to clench. He closed his eyes and savored the golden upside of the crack high: a grandiose state of grace he'd been chasing, to the tune of four hundred dollars a day (the maximum allowable ATM withdrawal; there had to be some rules), for the past two months—a feeling of promise and possibility, of visionary entitlement, of personal and artistic luminosity, of unwavering belief in himself and all that he was out to achieve. (Accompanied, meanwhile, by a constant nagging tingle in his crotch: nine weeks and five days since he'd last had sex with a person who was not himself.)

By the time he'd arrived at the DCCJ and paid the cabbie, Seede was feeling unusually copacetic, albeit no less aroused: the amorphous cocaine tingle having been augmented, he couldn't help but notice, by a very specific heroin itch, localized on the underside of his penis, in a patch of sensitive skin just below the clefted rim of the glans. Fighting the urge to grab himself like Michael Jackson—a level of self-control that some of the other visitors to the jail appeared unable to muster—Seede had entered the DCCJ and followed his usual routine: he'd checked in with the duty sergeant at visitor intake, exchanged the requisite jocular banter, signed the log, received his locker assignment, hung up his coat, the inside pocket of which contained the remaining bindle of heroin, about a gram of his home-cooked freebase, and a crack pipe fashioned from aluminum foil and other household products.

And then, without warning, an intense wave of prickly heat washed over his head. He broke out in a vicious sweat; a rush of nausea nearly buckled his knees. He stumbled to the visitors' restroom—a popular site for unofficial conjugal trysts, providentially unoccupied—and spewed forth a bilious projectile of vomit, a slight bit of which could be seen on the tip of his black Dr. Martens boot.

Now, after standing nearly two full minutes before the reception desk on the fifth floor hospital ward, waiting for the guard to acknowledge his presence, Seede could hear the game show theme song filtering up from the bottom drawer, signaling a commercial break. The guard picked up the telephone, spoke a few words, hung up. He looked at Seede, nodded indifferently toward a pair of double doors to his right, the entry into the ward proper. Seede ventured a supplicating smile.

Returning his attention to the television, the guard crossed his arms over his chest and leaned back slowly in his chair—gunmetal gray with black Naugahyde upholstery—shifting his ample weight gradually aft, until the two front legs lifted off the floor. He teetered at the fulcrum for an instant, frozen in weightless repose, like a living monument, like a statue at the center of one of Washington's celebrated traffic circles, this one a memorial to the government's army of entitled employees, a unionized everyman with a lifetime job, astride his trusty throne. And then the chair found its tipping point and resumed its quiet ride through space, a neat arc of about fifteen inches, the crown of the metal frame coming at last to rest with a muffled *thunk* against the little boy blue cinder block, where a dark scuff on the wall told of many a similar feat. His eyes still glued to his television, he reached over with his right hand and pressed a button on the wall. The doors swung inward.

34

Metcalfe led Salem toward an alcove on the far side of the crystal chamber. En route they passed the westernmost pedestal, on which was sitting the skull crafted of rose quartz, known as the Templar. As she went by, Salem felt the way you feel when you're stopped at a traffic light and you look up and someone in another car is staring at you—a cold tingle crept along her spine.

The alcove harbored a facing pair of chrome and leather loveseats, the space between occupied by a fifties-era boomerang coffee table, smoked-glass with an ebony base. Salem chose one of the loveseats. Metcalfe sat opposite.

"So," he said, "here we are."

Noncommittal: "Mmm-hum."

"You like the sofas?" He patted a cushion with his palm. "They're French. Le Corbusier."

"I like leather."

"I can see. That's a nice coat."

She gathered the soft lapels beneath her neck. "Lambskin."

He dabbed his forehead with the towel. She smiled thinly.

"I guess I'll just start," he said.

"It's yo money."

He cleared his throat. "What do you know about your father?"

Salem recrossed her legs. "My real name is Jennifer. I was molested by my uncle when I was seven. When I was ten, I was sent to a Catholic orphanage. The mother superior—"

He gave her a look.

"Wha?"

"The truth, perhaps? And you can drop the white-girl-talkin-black routine. I know you grew up in south Florida."

She studied her nails.

"I think I've more than paid for the privilege, don't you?"

The envelope was resting in her lap. It had an appealing heft. She supposed he had a point. "What do you want to know?"

"Let's start with your biological father. What information do you have about him?"

"Not much."

"What did your mother tell you?"

"What's to tell? He knocked up my mother with me. She claims he died in a car accident before I was born."

"She claims?"

"That's what she told me."

"But you don't believe it."

"I think my mother was trying to do me a favor. Or maybe she was trying to rewrite history. Or maybe she was delusional. I don't know exactly. I was trying to be a kid at the time."

"What do you think?"

"I think she made a lot of bad choices in her life."

"About your father, I mean. What do you think about him?"

"I think that men leave. They're irresponsible. They're cowards who act like bullies to cover up."

"My, my . . ."

"You asked."

"So I did. What else?"

"I think that men are only interested in women for one thing. I think our whole society is based on it."

"On what?"

"On men being in control. On men lording over women. Making sure they always have women available to service their needs."

"That seems an unusual point of view for a prostitute."

"If you ask me, I have a good vantage point."

"Flat on your back?"

If looks could kill . . .

He raised a hand in peace. "Sorry. That was out of line."

She shrugged, cut her eyes to the floor.

"Have you ever given any thought," he asked, "to the reasons why relations between the sexes may have developed the way they have?"

"Because men will put their dicks in any hole they can find?"

"Yeah, yeah, I know: all men are jerks. We're critical and controlling. We're intimidating, unyielding, exploitative, and unreasonable. We're the source of all the world's problems."

"And?" She looked up at the glass roof. The sky over this town was always gray. It made her feel heavy. She missed the blue.

Metcalfe leaned forward in his seat, allowing his feet to touch the floor. "What do you know about the origins of our species?"

She looked at him as if a tree was growing out of his head. "You mean, like, Adam and Eve?"

"More like preagriculture, when our ancestors were living in caves and trees."

"What about it?"

"At that point of our development, according to anthropologists, people lived in matriarchal societies. That means the *women* were in charge. Society revolved around them."

"Sounds like paradise."

"Let me ask you this: have you ever found it difficult to get along with other women?"

"That doesn't change the fact that men are jerks."

"Maybe men are the way they are because women are the way they are."

Crossing her arms: "What is that supposed to mean?"

"Put it like this," he said. "In the early years of human evolution, females were the dominant sex. Women's evolutionary function was to make babies. Naturally, society revolved around them. Women took multiple male partners in order to insure the continuation of the species. They had sex with anyone who appealed to them; fertilization was their uppermost goal, their biological imperative. Men brought them food, fought one another for mating privileges. Women called the shots. They had the power."

"So what happened?"

"Women invented agriculture."

"Agriculture?"

"One of a series of laborsaving innovations developed through the ages which had the unintended consequence of tying women down rather than freeing them up. With the rise of agriculture, the nomadic, hunter-gatherer lifestyle came to an end; people started living in villages. Men's crucial role as the provider was no longer central to survival. In fact, men had no crucial role at all."

"Besides sperm donor."

"Exactly. Women did the farming, the cooking, the child rearing—the survival of the species rested solely with them. The home and hearth became the center of the universe, a territory presided over by women. Men came home for meals and sleep and sex during the estrus—you know how that goes: women really are receptive to men for only what? About four days a month? When they're ovulating? The rest of the time they could care less."

The corners of her mouth turned up into a smirk. "More like: could do without."

"But those four days are powerful. I read somewhere that something like nine out of every ten young women who lose their virginity with unprotected sex end up becoming pregnant. Most of them say, when surveyed, that they didn't have any intention of having sex, they were just carried away by the moment. What that means, generally, is that their good sense was overcome by their hormones—they couldn't help themselves. It's chemical, don't you see? Women are driven by an engine they can't control."

Not at all pleased by the insinuation: "So?"

"So here you had all these men with nothing to do, no real role to play in society. Not only that, but the women kind of lorded over them, treated them like children—you know how women do. Men felt unnecessary. They felt underfoot and unappreciated."

"What's the point?"

"That's when men took to spending their days away from hearth and home, away from the women and the children. They'd collect down by the river, in a clearing in the forest—the ancient equivalent of the corner liquor store, the Moose Lodge, the office. With no pressing duties to perform, men had lots of free time to brood and commiserate about the way the women treated them, about their basic lack of purpose in the grander scheme. While brooding, they needed something to fill the hours. They busied themselves inventing things. They came up with religion, politics, philosophy, and education. They created sports, war, music, literature, and crafts: complex systems and pursuits that existed in a world totally outside of the household. A world designed to supersede the natural authority that women held at home. A world, simply, where men were in charge."

She chewed it over for a few beats. "So you're saying that our whole way of life is based on men being bored and horny."

"More like insecure and pissed off."

"Because their women wouldn't give 'em any pussy?"

"Because they knew deep down that they were good for only one thing."

Salem couldn't help but laugh.

35

The call came crackling through his new custom-fitted polymer earbud, a female voice over the hailing frequency, the staticky techno singsong of central dispatch: "Unit Three-Sixteen Alpha."

Officer Perdue Hatfield, Unit 316A, recoiled from the unaccustomed aural assault, the pain evident on his broad face, the Rockwellesque freckles across his cheeks flushing in protest. The earphones had just been issued to all beat cops, amid much fanfare and press ("MPD Cuts Noise Pollution in Neighborhoods," trumpeted the *Herald* that morning), the latest innovation in hearing technology, another vital new law enforcement asset, $147 per unit, wholesale.

He reached for the microphone clipped to the left epaulet of his waterproof, winter-weight uniform coat, beneath which he wore his armored, bulletproof vest. He had the physique of a man who spent the bulk of his free time lifting heavy weights in the basement gym at the precinct house, shopping for vitamins and protein supplements, and reading bodybuilder magazines. His thick fingers poked out luridly from fingerless gloves. He pressed the button on the microphone. "This is Three-Sixteen Alpha. Go ahead."

"Check the welfare: 1304 T Street Northwest."

"Copy that," Hatfield said. "Thirteen zero four, T-Tango."

"Roger, Three-Sixteen Alpha. RP reports baby crying."

Puzzled, he adjusted his hat. "Repeat?"

"Baby . . . crying," the dispatcher said. "See the resident manager. There are no further details at this time."

Hatfield pursed his lips and spat a brown stream of tobacco juice into the gutter. *Check the welfare:* he hated those calls. They always sounded innocuous, but you never knew what you'd get. Old man on garage floor all night, too proud to call for help. Teenager giving birth in restroom at Popeye's. Woman holding iron skillet; boyfriend's brain splattered across kitchen. Originally, when he went into police work, Hatfield's motivations had been pretty straightforward. Like it said on his badge: TO PROTECT AND SERVE. Most cops will tell you the same thing—they always wanted to be a cop. As a boy Perdie Hatfield refused to go anywhere without his twin Hasbro six-shooters, the faux leather holsters secured around his chubby thighs with strips of rawhide, an innovation he jerry-rigged himself. (Back home, they'd have said nigger-rigged.) In neighborhood games he always cast himself as the hero, saving his girl cousins from pretend villains: to this day he could recall the sweet and powdery scent of his favorite cousin, Bonita—blonde and beautiful, one year older, mature for her age—as he untied the ropes from her hands and feet and carried her pretend-limp body to safety. Later, when he joined the marines, literally to see the world, he learned something more about himself: he enjoyed living by the rules, specific rules you could memorize and observe. Rules created precision. Rules gave you a standard to live by. Rules made your purpose clear. He hated when things were out of sync, when standards were violated. It was a visceral reaction, a physical discomfort that he felt when, say, one hanger was facing inward when all the others were facing outward, or when he saw someone throwing litter out a car window on a highway, or when someone acted like a bully. To Perdue Hatfield, there were right ways and wrong ways in this world, absolute values, lines in the sand. Shades of gray made him uncomfortable.

Unfortunately, in real life everything was a shade of gray. No crime was ever clear-cut, no two witnesses ever told the same story. More often than not, at a crime scene, Hatfield didn't know who to believe—five years into his career, it sounded to him like everyone was lying.

"Three-Sixteen Alpha responding," Hatfield said into his microphone. The tone of his voice was grim.

Flicking on his mental array of sirens and lights, Hatfield turned north onto Fourteenth Street, his powerful body canted slightly forward, his pace steady and rhythmic, his pumping arms cocked akimbo to accommodate his gear: a black leather utility belt with its many ingenious pouches and loops; a 9mm Glock sidearm; extra clips of hollow point ammo; a can of Mace brand pepper spray; a steel and leather blackjack, known in the training manual as a "personal self-defense fighting tool"; an ebonized hardwood, military-style nightstick—a model made popular by the Los Angeles police, as featured in the videotaped beating of black motorist Rodney Glenn King.

Dangling from a braided leather cord was another important tool of modern law enforcement: his summons book. Hatfield's unofficial quota for parking tickets was ten per shift. A day's paid leave was quietly awarded each month to the high ticket-writer in the precinct. With every other step, the summons book swung on its cord and knocked against Hatfield's muscular left thigh, adding a faint, percussive *thunk* to the symphony of his gear: the purposeful *thwap* of his black Danner combat boots against the sidewalk, hard rubber on cold cement; the *jangle* of his key chain; the *clink* of his handcuffs, stowed inside their own special pouch; the *clunk* of his nightstick, banging against the blue-black handle of his gun; the *swish* of the nylon fabric of his overcoat; the *rasp* of his trouser inseams, a poly-wool blend, custom made to accommodate his size.

In short order he was standing before the front door of 1304 T Street NW, a dilapidated house with a sagging roofline, white paint peeling from the brick.

A woman answered. She wore a colorful, African-print scarf around her head. Though she was no taller than five feet, her bosom was monumental. She crossed her arms beneath, lending structural support.

Hatfield tipped his cap, two fingers to the bill, another antiquated police custom he admired. "Afternoon, ma'am."

His years overseas notwithstanding, Hatfield's accent still carried the woodsy redneck singsong of his upbringing. He knew what it made people think. A few years back, he'd actually taken elocution lessons, hoping to lose his twang, figuring it would help his chances of advancing through the ranks. Then one day, he was walking down Fourteenth Street and this black dude called him a cracker. He didn't know the guy; they'd never had any dealings. Just a random act of hatred; the level of vitriol knocked him sideways. A lot worse things had been said to Hatfield over time, to be sure. But this one unprovoked act had really got him thinking. People made such a big deal about skin color these days. Why should *he* be judged for the color of his? Or by his accent—his double modals and lax vowels, his use of *y'all* as a second person plural? If it was fine for all the so-called minority races to embrace their "roots," why shouldn't he be able to embrace his?

The woman pulled open the door the rest of the way and admitted him into the foyer.

"Somebody called the police?" he asked.

"Upstairs, 3B." She was missing a lower front tooth.

"What's the problem?"

She regarded him blankly, not quite sure how much to say. Cops: they show up to help you, and the next thing you know they're ransacking your place and taking your man to the lockup. "It dat baby upstairs," she said finally. "Won't stop cryin."

Speaking the native dialect: "Where da momma at?"

Her eyes were large and black in her puffy face, heavily outlined with mascara, giving her the look of an overfed Cleopatra. "She onea dem hos. Ain't nobody seen her fo a while."

He looked around the foyer, rundown but not unclean. "You the resident manager?"

"That chile *always* makin a racket." She shifted a hand to her hip. Deprived of its undercarriage, her bosom shifted, setting in motion a series of epidermal waves, a sloshing effect, like water being carried in a bucket.

Hatfield tried not to stare. "How old is the baby?"

"Two and a half, three. Still in diapers."

He cocked his head toward the stairwell and listened. He heard water running, the theme from a soap opera, the clink and clank of pots and pans, the subsonic rumble of a rap song, the din of midafternoon traffic rushing by outside . . . but no crying baby. He bid her to show him the way.

Together the two climbed the stairs to apartment 3B. Hatfield removed his hat, pressed his ear to the door.

An odor was evident, putrid and sulfurous, not uncommon in these ghetto rooming houses—a plumbing failure, perhaps, left too long to fester. The way these people lived floored him sometimes. It's not like he was raised rich. It's not like he was no snob; he'd gone to bed hungry many a night when his father was laid off. Some of the people back in the hollow didn't even have indoor plumbing. But at least they had the self-respect to keep their outhouses clean. He could hear the television, but no crying baby. He knocked, a polite rap with the knuckle of his middle finger—*rap rap rap*. "Police. Open up."

Hearing no response, he replaced his hat, held out his hand to the resident manager. She pulled a key chain from the pocket of her housecoat, setting in motion another series of fleshy aftershocks.

With his right hand, Hatfield unholstered his Glock. With the left, he inserted the key into the brass depths of the cylinder. Slowly he opened the door.

The smell nearly knocked him down. "Like the barracks latrine after a bad night in Tijuana," the medical examiner would later say.

Though it was thirty-five degrees outside, the room was unbearably hot and stuffy, and very dry, a condition attributable to the old-fashioned radiant heating system in the building; the hissing and knocking gave the scene an otherworldly quality. It appeared that the place had been searched. Drawers open, clothes spilling out. Bed stripped, pillows scattered, chair overturned. Cheerios and half-eaten crackers strewn everywhere. A soiled diaper abandoned on the plank floor. A purple plastic video cassette poking half out of the VCR, wrong side in. And everything sticky with reddish handprints and footprints, child-size, like a nursery school finger painting project run amok.

On the far side of the bed, in the rounded alcove formed by the bay window, Hatfield discovered the source of the smell.

Black female. Late twenties, early thirties. Dressed in a ratty, polyester-satin bathrobe. From the looks of things, she'd given herself a hot shot of heroin while seated on the bed. The spoon, lighter, and empty bindle of Hellraiser were still on the bedside table. Claimed by gravity, the body itself had tumbled forward, onto the floor. It was arranged now in what medical examiners call a "praying position"—a prostrate pose similar to the one assumed five times a day by adherents to Islam—her weight distributed evenly between her knees and her forehead, her arms acting as outriggers. The syringe remained where she'd left it, plunger down. She'd tied off with a Mickey Mouse jump rope.

From the looks of her fingertips—dry and leathery, wrinkled like raisins, the skin receding from the nails—she had been dead for several days. Her body had begun to mummify, the process accelerated by the dry environment. Leaking from her nose and mouth, forming a puddle on the floor, was a mixture of blood and gases, the by-product of putrefaction—a reddish, viscous discharge, known to MEs as "frothy purge."

On the floor near the body was another series of reddish prints—tiny frenetic paw prints, with roundish central pads radiating four sharp digits. A trail led from the body to the radiator and back. Looking closer, he could see bite marks on the victim's ears and lips—tiny nibbles, bloodless half-moons.

Hatfield stood like a statue, mouth agape, overcome.

And then it occurred to him.

The baby!

Something inside of Hatfield gave way, popped like a hamstring at a Sunday afternoon softball game.

Frantic, adrenalized, half blinded by tears of fear and rage, Hatfield searched the premises for the child, tossing aside sheets and mattress, re-riffling the drawers, throwing clothes and boxes out of the closet . . .

At last he found the boy in the kitchenette, in the cupboard beneath the sink. Naked and dirty, partially wrapped in a blanket, he was sucking his thumb, which was red and sticky with frothy purge.

Hatfield eased down onto the floor, like a nanny trying to win over a new charge. He took off his hat, put on his happiest face. "How you doin, bud?"

The boy looked back at him blankly, a toddler version of a thousand-yard stare.

36

An orderly in pink scrubs gestured in Seede's direction with a tapered ebony hand. Seede figured him for a man but it was hard to be certain. The hair was gathered into a nappy top-knot; the slinky, swivel-hipped walk recalled Diana Ross in her prime. Seede followed him down a long corridor. They passed a series of medical observation cells. Each had a metal door and a large one-way viewing window on which the name and booking number of the patient/inmate were handwritten in nonpermanent marker, a neatly applied schoolteacher cursive that seemed out of place in its surroundings.

The orderly stopped at cell 17: *Rubin, Michael David #90194.* He keyed the lock, opened the door for Seede. "You got fifteen minutes, baby," he said in a smoky voice.

A TV hung from the ceiling; on the bedside table was a phone with no dialing mechanism—incoming calls only. In the far corner was the standard aluminum sink and toilet combo, this one retrofitted with a seat. The Pope of Pot looked small in the big hospital bed. His head was elevated; he was wired to an array of machines. Seede hadn't seen him since the Fourth of July Smoke Out in Lafayette Park. He had always seemed so large: a big man with big appetites and big ideas, many of them absolutely crazy. The difference was disconcerting. It looked as if he'd been shrunk.

"Pope? Are you awake?"

The Pope of Pot opened his eyes. "Howdy, honey, howdy," he rasped. An oxygen tube was strapped beneath his bulbous nose; he had a three-day growth of stubble. He worked his mouth, searching for moisture.

"I'm Jonathan Seede from the *Washington Herald*. Do you remember me?"

The Pope squinted in Seede's direction. Without his thick glasses, his eyes looked small and far away. "Could you pour me a drink, toots?"

Seede set down his reporting stuff on the bedside table. He found a pitcher of water, filled a paper cup. With effort, the Pope turned his head and drank from a straw. The way his lips pooched, greedy and helpless, reminded Seede of his son at the breast. "I take it the service in here isn't exactly papal," he said.

The Pope attempted a smile. "Bless you, my child."

Seede dragged over a chair and sat down by the bed, opened his notebook. It was warm in the room. He still felt clammy but the nausea had pretty much abated. He kind of needed a hit of crack—he could feel the emptiness gathering in his gut—but the H was doing a decent job of keeping it at bay. "I still can't believe the judge remanded you," Seede said. "I wouldn't say you're a big threat to the community."

"All hate is just fear," the Pope said. "All fear is insecurity."

Seede wrote it down.

The Pope's bedsheet was pulled only to his waist. A thatch of curly hair covered his chest and abdomen. Here and there, like clearings in a jungle seen from the air, were an assortment of scars—knife slashes, punctures, medical entries, scallop-shaped bullet wounds—monuments to his eventful days in the drug trade in Amsterdam, New York, and DC. In his hand he discovered a coarse brown paper towel; he attempted to wipe the cottony residue from the corners of his mouth. "The people I was arrested with—do you know what happened to them? Are they still in jail?"

"Waylon was released this morning."

"What about the others?"

"All their bonds were posted by"—he thumbed through his notebook—"the Realized Fantasy Trust."

The Pope closed his eyes, a measure of relief. "At least some things are as they should be."

"Can I ask you a question?"

"I am an open book."

"The police report says they found an ounce of cocaine at your church. You're charged with possession of coke with intent to distribute. I know in the past you've demonstrated publicly against hard drugs, especially cocaine. Can you explain what you were doing with so much coke at the storefront?"

"Preposterous," the Pope said dismissively. "The police planted that coke. No doubt it was stolen too."

"Stolen?"

"The police think they're entitled to free drugs. They go around stealing whatever they want."

"You have firsthand knowledge of police stealing drugs?"

"Of course: when they raided the church, they took seven pounds of my sacrament, but they only charged me with possession of *four* pounds."

Seede studied him for a few seconds, trying to figure out what the Pope was trying to say. "Isn't that better for you? You're charged with less weight. That should be better for your case, right?"

"Do the math," the Pope said, with all the derision he could muster. "Three pounds are missing. If the cops want pot, they should have to pay for it like everyone else. I made a formal complaint to Internal Affairs."

"Internal Affairs?" Seede's eyebrows went up. He wrote IAD on his pad, underscored it three times. "I was wondering why you were busted by detectives from IAD. Those guys never make street arrests."

"I had invited the gentlemen to the church to discuss the return of my sacrament."

"So you had actually lodged an official complaint? Is there paperwork?"

"What's right is right. It's what the good Lord expects from us."

"And you're saying that because you lodged a complaint, they came to the church and planted coke and arrested you."

"Obviously you're a man of great intellect."

"What would you say," Seede asked, choosing his words with care, "if I told you it's a little hard to believe that the police would go to all that trouble just to take you down?"

A mournful expression descended over the Pope's face, like a curtain dropping on the last act. The light in his eyes dimmed.

And then a coughing fit ensued, a series of deep black hacks that rattled his entire body.

Seede stood by helplessly. "Do you want me to call someone?"

The Pope of Pot motioned for another drink of water. Seede directed the straw into his mouth, held the cup. He'd known the Pope now for a couple of years. His pot was always primo, his count was always honest, he always had something on hand. On nights he visited, Seede would hang out with Waylon and the rest, drinking hot chocolate, listening to the Pope hold forth as he delivered one of his seemingly daffy diatribes. Invariably, on the way home Seede would suddenly be struck by something the Pope had said. For the rest of the night, the next day, it would be lodged in his brain like a song heard on the clock radio first thing in the morning. In a town full of conventional wisdom, where the politicians talked in endless meaningless circles (punctuated with the usual fist bangs and semi-up-thrust thumbs), and where the journos and pundits gave credence to all the doublespeak by endlessly discussing and interpreting it, the Pope of Pot could sometimes be absolutely inspirational. He reminded Seede of Don Quixote, a personal hero since eleventh grade, when he read the book for Spanish 4.

Seede replaced the cup of water on the bedside table, rested his hand lightly, affectionately, on the Pope's forearm. The skin was soft and papery, freckled with brown age spots, the purple-red blossoms of broken blood vessels. "Why are you doing this to yourself?" he asked.

"I've done nothing, my son. I am the victim of foul play."

"Everyone says it: the Pope of Pot is his own worst enemy. The choices you make—it's mind-blowing. Handing out joints to people in line for the White House tour? What's the purpose of that? What statement does it make? What do you have to gain? You give the government no choice. It's like you're *asking* to be arrested. They hate you. They want to lock you up and throw away the key."

"Let them do what they must."

"Didn't your family used to have a factory in New Jersey? The Realized Fantasy Trust—that's family money, isn't it?"

"A modest sum, if you must know. Foundation garments. The bullet-boob look of the fifties? That was my father's design."

Seede chewed the top of his felt-tip pen, a perplexed look on his face. "I gotta tell you, Pope: your message isn't coming across. People don't understand what you're trying to accomplish. I don't even understand, and I'm *trying* to understand. You just seem childish and perverse. You flaunt everyone and everything. The city attorney told the judge, in open court, that you are"—he flipped through the pages of his notebook—"'dangerous to himself and others, most likely certifiably insane.'"

"Do you think I *like* being in here?" the Pope asked. "Do you think I like being everyone's pain in the ass?" As he spoke, the cottony strings at the corners of his mouth expanded and contracted. Seede had the urge to reach out and take the paper towel from the old man's hand and wipe his lips for him. "Believe me," the Pope continued, "it's not fun absorbing everyone's anger and defensiveness and animosity all the time. The name calling. The outright derision. What have I done to provoke such ire? People call and write letters. They go out of their way to hate. Do you think it's fun to read editorials in the newspapers that say nasty things about you? Do you think I don't notice the ridicule?"

"Things could be different," Seede said. "You're obviously a very intelligent man. A brilliant man. The things you say, some of your concepts and life lessons—you have original and interesting ideas. Some of that shit is amazing. Winning by example. The silent I-told-you-so. The Theory of Originals: be number one in a class of one—never compete with anyone but yourself. It really works. Like, since I've stopped competing with others and focused on myself, I have to tell you, my career has taken off. You told me that stuff last July; it sticks with you. It works. And that thing you just said—" forward a few pages in the notebook. "'All hate is just fear. All fear is insecurity.' Wow. I mean—that is so fucking true. It's fuckin elemental. Wisdom like that doesn't come around every day. Wisdom like that needs a bigger audience. Maybe you could focus your message a little better. Maybe you could quit the pot dealing. Maybe you could go about things in a different way. A way that people can understand. You could start a legitimate nonprofit organization. You could lobby Congress or hold seminars. You could be the Tony

Robbins Antichrist! There are lots of things you could do, most of which pay handsomely, none of which would require going to jail. Take a look at yourself, Pope. This isn't working for you. Something needs to change."

The Pope of Pot squinted in Seede's direction, trying to get a clearer view of misguided youth. "It's like this, toots," he sighed. "You're in a canoe without any paddles and the boat is just going. You're headed down the rapids and the current is strong. The water is breaking over the side. Your pants are soaked; your ass is wet. But you're going wherever you're supposed to be going. All you're doing is kind of hanging on for dear life, bailing as needed. Because there's a force at work that stands behind you and on top of everything, a force that is in fact more powerful than anything you can come up against—more powerful than the police, the laws, the federal government—more powerful than anything. You have to speak the truth when untruth is surrounding you. When there is insanity surrounding you, you have to communicate that. Somebody has to. There's a part in the Old Testament that says those who see danger approaching the village must blow the trumpet and warn the people. And if they don't blow the trumpet, the responsibility for the people's welfare—and the outcome—rests with them. I am trying to sound the alarm. The responsibility rests with me. I accept it."

Seede looked at his watch. His fifteen minutes were almost up; he hadn't even begun to open the door on the Pope's list of clients—his alleged role in selling marijuana to cops, judges, and congressmen—the reason his editor had sent him here in the first place. But the truth was, there was a bigger story here, maybe an important story, and it had nothing to do with who bought pot from the Pope. If you looked at Seede's recent string of front-page articles—at all of his articles, for that matter, all of the stories he'd done over the course of his career at the *Herald* —what you'd notice would be the fact that none of them had really *meant* much in the wider scheme of things. Yes, they were in turns bright, pithy, evocative, entertaining, investigative, gut wrenching, well written, newsworthy, and outrageous. But taken in sum, what was the meaning of all that piecemeal effort? What had it amounted to? A decent paycheck, yes. Lunches in the publisher's private office with community leaders. Some degree of social status. A house on Corcoran Street, one wife, one child, one car, one motorcycle. One Hollywood deal in the works. But now he was nearly thirty years old. The meter was running. He wanted to write something meaningful, something that would illuminate and entertain. Something that people would remember long after he was gone. Hopefully, this book of his was going to be the answer. Deep down he had the sense that the Pope needed to be an important part.

"Do you really want to die in jail, Pope?"

"What better place?"

"I don't know. The beach, maybe? Your own bed?"

"If I die in here, everyone will know that the government killed me for my beliefs."

"They'll know you died in jail—if it even makes the news."

"It'll make the news, I guarantee you that, toots. *Pot Pontiff Perishes in Prison*. No news editor in the world will be able to resist."

"They'll make total shit of you and all the things you stand for."

"But everyone will know. Everyone will know. Don't you see? The truth is the truth, no matter what. You have to be willing to die for what you believe in. You have to make your body a living sign."

At this last bit Seede's ears pricked up. He turned to a clean page in his notebook and wrote it down: *Make your body a living sign*.

37

Sojii alighted from the back passenger-side of a Japanese-made SUV driven by Geoff Greene, the proprietor of Mystic Eye Books. Jim Freeman shut the door, leaned into the front passenger window. "I think we could have managed the five blocks on foot," he said brightly.

"Don't be silly," Greene said. "I was going out anyway to do a few errands."

"We should get together sometime for dinner," Freeman enthused. Then he knocked himself lampoonishly in the forehead. "*Hellooooo!* What do you think about sushi? I just finished this great Japanese cooking class where we learned how to—"

"Is this your place?" Greene indicated the townhouse behind Sojii, who was standing on the sidewalk, her backpack slung over her shoulder, looking like she wanted to go inside. It was a narrow building, painted brick red with blue-gray trim. An antique iron staircase led up eight steps to the front gate.

"Oh, no, no, no!" Freeman laughed, his booming baritone giggle—perish the thought. "We're on the other side." He pointed over the top the vehicle to the opposite side of the street. "It's 1329."

Greene twisted around. "The white and gray one?"

"That's right. With the gingerbread eaves. It was built in 1880 by this—"

"Impressive," Greene pronounced. He twisted frontward again, indicated the house behind Sojii. "Who's is this?"

"Adorable, isn't it? He just had it pointed and painted this fall. He got it five years ago for . . . guess how much?"

The primate fear grimace: "Surprise me."

"One fifty," Freeman stage-whispered. "I could sell it tomorrow for more than twice that!"

"Amazing," Greene said. A lock of his expensively cut hair fell rakishly over one eye. "I take it the owner's a client?"

"Client slash friend. He worked with my ex at the *Herald*. I like to say I got custody of him in the divorce. You've probably read his byline: Jonathan Seede? He just optioned a story to Hollywood about—"

"Excuse me . . . Jim?" Sojii's head was recessed into the fluffy, borrowed coat like a turtle's into its shell.

Freeman half turned, attempting to triangulate the two conversations.

"It's cold out here," she said. "I'm gonna go in now."

"You don't want to come back to my place? I'll make you a nice snack."

"I'll probably just read or something."

"Okay, then," Freeman said. "I'll come get you for dinner. You have my number, right?"

"Nice meeting you, Sojii," Greene called out affably.

As Jim turned back to his grown-up conversation, the girl skipped down the several steps to the entrance of Seede's basement apartment. With some effort—one gate, one door, three keys, four locks—she let herself inside.

The place was as she'd left it, still life with Matchbox and

Lego. She walked toward the miniature table, shedding her coat and hat and muffler as she went. She sat down in one of the little chairs, cleared a space, took out the skull.

Sojii placed her hand on top. The crystal was smooth and cool. A tingle of energy ran through her fingertips and up her arm. The fine hair on the back of her neck stood at attention.

She stared deeply into the cranium, trying to focus all of her thought, trying to achieve a "watchful, vigilant silence," as Greene had suggested. In a few moments, the skull began to darken, the holographic clouds appeared. The dark spot became visible at the center. The spot grew slowly, gathering size and intensity, leaving a black void.

Impulsively she dipped her index finger into the void. The sensation was welcoming—and creepy. Like jumping into a muddy lake on a hot summer day, and then your feet touch the gooey bottom. With haste she withdrew.

Presently an image appeared.

A mountain ridge, a sheer cliff. Eagles soared, riding the updrafts. Clouds floated past. Hundreds of feet below, a sparkling lake was nestled like a giant sapphire into a basin of undulating green hills.

And then she was on the cliff.

Not just viewing it anymore but actually standing on the edge, hair blowing, raindrops on her cheeks.

And then she was standing beside the lake, the shoreline rendered in animated Disney hues. A path led into a dense alpine forest. It reminded her of Hansel and Gretel. She wondered if that was the idea.

In time, she came to a clearing, presided over by a modern building. Small but chic, it was built of glass and stone and dark wood.

Inside was a reception desk, a lobby bar, a pricey little boutique.

She entered the store, moved among the racks of clothing the way females do, not so much browsing the offerings as sojourning among them.

At the rear of the store, she came upon another shopper, an Asian woman in her midforties, perusing a circular rack of cute little tops. She had a prominent Semitic nose which lent to her face an odd, beautiful, asymmetrical quality. She slid the shiny metal hangers one by one along the rack, a distinctive scrape and tinkle, her head tilted appraisingly to one side.

Sojii recognized her instantly.

38

Head down, boots pounding the sidewalk, Perdue Hatfield marched full tilt in a southerly direction down Thirteenth Street.

At R Street he turned west. He'd seen a lot of gruesome stuff over time, plenty of blood and heartache, plenty of bodies, he'd even killed a man. The guy was high on PCP. It took four shots in the chest to knock him down. But this was different. No kid deserved to grow up with that kind of film inside his head. Hatfield wanted to scream, to jump up and down, to punch a wall, to hurt someone. He wanted to hold the boy and tell him everything would be alright. He wanted to bitch-stomp the corpse of the mother until it turned to bloody pulp. He wanted to be a million miles away, anywhere but here, with no one counting on him for anything.

"Whoa, big man, what's the hurry?"

John Steinschmidt was standing by the curb smoking a cigarette, wearing a cleric's collar and a cook's apron. His graying hair was low-parted into a sweeping comb-over. He had a tough, North Philly accent, flat *O*s and glottal stops, that put you in mind of a football coach.

Hatfield pulled to an abrupt stop. "Sorry, pastor," he drawled, a bit breathless. "I guess I was a little preoccupied."

"I guess *so*."

"What's with the getup?" Hatfield asked.

Steinschmidt wedged his index finger between his neck and his collar and pulled—slightly at first, feigning discomfort, and then harder, strangulation. "I was up on the Hill today—had to look suitably pious. We're trying to get a grant to build some low-income housing."

Hatfield knitted his brow. "Around here? That's the first I've heard of it."

Steinschmidt winked.

"What about the neighbors?"

A young woman walked past, headed east on the cobbled sidewalk, hurrying to beat the darkness home. She was wearing a camel-hair overcoat and Nike running shoes, white with neon yellow accents and a purple swoosh. Slung from various parts of her anatomy were her purse, her briefcase, her gym bag, a plastic sack of groceries—out of which jutted a baguette and two hothouse sunflowers—and a leather dog leash, attached at the other end to a brown rottweiler, a muscle-bound creature marching possessively at her side.

Steinschmidt waited until she was safely out of range. "There'll be some screeching and hollering, but we'll see it through. People like to do good, despite their selfish instincts. You just have to show them the way."

"We all know you're the master of that," Hatfield said.

Steinschmidt cracked a wry half smile.

The two men stood together in silence, each facing a different direction. A few steps away, lined along the brick wall in an orderly fashion, were two dozen women—despairing, demoralized, some of them clearly deranged—clutching suitcases, plastic bags, the sticky hands of small children with dark circles beneath their eyes. The sun was going down; another subfreezing night was at hand. Each shuffling step brought them closer to a tepid spaghetti dinner and a cleanish cot at Karen's Place, a shelter for homeless women housed in Steinschmidt's former church rectory. The hard-bitten but compassionate Lutheran sucked a last drag from his cigarette and flicked the butt into the street—a high, arching trajectory, like a shot from a flare gun. "The Green Party will be after me next," he said. "Don't you just love how recycling these days passes for social commitment?"

Hatfield smiled halfheartedly. He stopped by Karen's Place on a regular basis to chat with Steinschmidt; he was usually a much better audience. Though the gulf between their personal philosophies was wide—the pastor was a man who believed that the laws of man could be superseded—Hatfield felt a kinship with the plainspoken son of a German immigrant baker. In some ways, judging from the stories they'd exchanged, growing up in a tenement neighborhood in North Philadelphia had not been so much different than growing up in Hatfield's West Virginia hollow—just as insular and clannish.

Steinschmidt searched the cop's face, trying to take stock. "Are you okay?"

Avoiding his eyes: "Fine."

"Hmmm," grunted the pastor, unconvinced.

"What?"

"I guess it was pretty rough over there today."

Hatfield met his eyes. "You heard from Child Protective Services?"

"There's always room for one more."

"I told them to call you. When are they gonna transport him over?"

"Sometime tonight."

"Do they have a name yet?"

"He's still not talking. At this point he's a Johnnie Doe."

Just then the wind picked up, a rogue gust from the northeast that skittered the leaves and the trash. Steinschmidt's carefully lacquered comb-over was lifted from his head. It fluttered there for a few beats, one end rooted, luffing like a flag, exposing the shiny pate beneath.

"He'll be safe here with us," Steinschmidt assured the officer, meanwhile fingering his hair back into place. "Maybe they'll be able to locate some family."

Hatfield looked off down the block. The sky was darkening. The pink neon cross atop the Central Union Mission had been switched on; the words pulsed beneath: COME UNTO ME. Though he'd searched the apartment several times, he'd been unable to find any ID, official papers, or anything else that would help identify the boy—no mail, no bills, no papers or certificates. It was as if the occupants didn't really exist, not officially anyway. Neither were the other tenants or the manager much help. The room was let on a week-to-week cash basis, no paperwork was kept, no relationships were forged. There was no way of telling who the dead woman was or where she came from. And no one from either the police department or CPS was going to bust their butt to find out.

The pastor reached up and placed his hand upon the cop's ample shoulder. "Come on, big guy, lemme buy you and your black cloud a cup of coffee."

They walked through the alley, past the line of women, toward the back of the building, a wide, three-story townhouse, as were most of the others on this stretch of R Street, distinguished in real estate circles by its two homeless shelters: Karen's Place, for women and children, was on the east end; the Central Union Mission, for men, was on the west. Rounding out the assortment of properties on the block were a trio of abandoned buildings, the windows boarded, and several illegal rooming houses that catered to hookers, alkie pensioners, and welfare moms, some of whom supplemented their checks with part-time streetwalking. On the northeast corner of Fourteenth and R, opposite the mission, was the jewel of the neighborhood: the newly opened Elizabeth Taylor Medical Center, a gay-run free clinic and AIDS hospice. Freeman had been part of a committee responsible for persuading La Liz to attend the gala opening in person. As her companion for the event, she'd brought along her good friend Michael Jackson, who himself had brought his own companion, a chimpanzee named Bubbles. Jackson and the chimp looked resplendent in matching sequined military-style uniforms. Liz was timeless in Halston.

A staircase led to the basement door, then down two steps into the kitchen. The cooking staff—none of them, it appeared, far removed from the streets themselves—circulated purposefully around the room, wearing hairnets, tending huge cook pots with paddlelike utensils.

Steinschmidt drew two cups of coffee from a shiny urn. "It's funny," he said, with a hint of regret, "one of the main reasons I took this job in the first place was because Karen loved this house."

Hatfield leaned against a counter, conscious of being in the way. Even as he increased his mass, rep by rep, in the precinct weight room, he could never quite shake the feeling—developed during his childhood when the neighbor kids called him "Fatty" or "Oven Stuffer" (as in Perdue brand Oven Stuffer roasting hen) or just "Stuffy" (for short)—that people resented him for taking up too much space. No matter how much muscle he managed to build, no matter how cut his abs or expansive his pecs, deep down he would always be the little fatso who'd once shit his pants at school. That he'd had a stomach flu, that the teacher wouldn't excuse him to go to the bathroom, none of that seemed to countervail. Whenever he went back home, he had the sense that everyone he knew was remembering the burden he had carried through the balance of that day in sixth grade, a Wednesday, his sweater tied around his waist for camouflage. He certainly remembered. Maybe that's what they meant when they said you can't go home again. Especially not when you come from a town of ninety-four.

Hatfield removed his hat and squared it away, military-style, between his elbow and his side. "When did you first come to Washington?"

"Nineteen and seventy," Steinschmidt said fondly. Hatfield always found his football coach voice oddly soothing, like Spencer Tracy in *Boys Town*. "What a time that was. Historic. Exciting. Kind of the grand finale of the sixties, you know? Like the ending of a good fireworks display—all hell was breaking loose. And here we were, one mile from the Nixon White House, one mile from the devil himself! We held this little coffeehouse every week in the basement of the church. We called it the Café Iguana. We'd meet there and talk big talk. Roberta Flack got her start there. Marion Barry would show up with his radical homeboys. The government had our phones tapped, the whole nine. Once a night we'd turn on the house lights and ask all the FBI undercovers to stand up so we could give them a round of applause."

"Did you ever actually live here?"

"For fifteen years—until eighty-five. Probably right around the time you were getting to town, the early days of the Sanctuary Movement. The city was lousy with Central Americans fleeing the U.S.-sponsored bloodbaths in their countries. Remember Ollie North? Drugs for arms? They called it Iran-Contra—Contragate. These people's stories were un-frickin-believable. They had nowhere to go. And we had this huge, five-bedroom rectory and no little chicks in our nest, so to speak. Woodies donated a couple dozen sleeping bags. The Foam Store, over on Sixth and G, gave us a tower of foam pads. Next thing we knew, we had wall-to-wall people. We had a family of five that set up housekeeping in Karen's walk-in closet."

"So you never lived here again?"

It dawned on Steinschmidt that he'd been standing there running his mouth, still holding the two cups of coffee. "I kept promising Karen we would move back in," he said, handing Hatfield his cup. "But just about the time we were placing the last of the Central Americans—a lot of them ended up in the poultry industry on the Eastern Shore—Reagan flung open the doors of all the so-called mental wards. Virtually overnight the sidewalks and steam grates were filled with human beings who were basically unequipped to cope with everyday life. We had people sleeping on the steps, on the lawn, even in our car one time when Karen forgot to lock it. The first night we re-opened the shelter, we were filled to capacity. And we've never had an empty bed since. I used to joke with this friend of mine—Jerry Weiss? He's the general manager of the Madison Hotel. Great guy. He's donated a ton of stuff over the years—I used to tell him, 'Karen's Place has the highest occupancy rate in town.'"

Hatfield stared into the dark pool of his coffee. One by one, the little air bubbles popped. "How do you do it, pastor?"

"Do what in particular?"

Hatfield ran his palm across his bristly, sand-colored flattop.

"After what you saw today, Perdue, it's pretty normal to question your faith—even tough guys like you. All those muscles don't make you immune to pain."

"We were always brought up to believe that God would take care of things," Hatfield said bitterly. "*Let go and let God,* they told us. *Leave it in God's hands. Have faith in the Lord Jesus Christ.* How can you have faith in someone who allows such travesties to occur on his watch?"

A pained expression stretched Steinschmidt's doughy features. "God doesn't *allow* anything, Perdue, no matter what they tried to teach you back home—good Lord, all that fire and brimstone shit is like child abuse! It ruins people for life. God allows free will. He allows choice. Your choices have consequences. When you choose to inject heroin into your body, you're adding to the equation the possibility that your child might end up spending some quality time with your corpse. It's all in the Torah, the Old Testament. It says that you have a choice between the light side and the dark, between good and evil. Deuteronomy 30:19: 'I have set before you life and death, the blessing and the curse. *U'vacharta b'chaim, l'ma'an tichiyeh,*'" he said, quoting the Hebrew. "'Therefore choose life in order that you may live, you and your descendants.'"

"I was brought up to believe that God expects so much," Hatfield said. "I'm supposed to treat others as I would myself. I'm supposed to act in a just fashion. I risk my life every day to serve and protect my fellow man, to uphold the law. And I do it to the very best of my ability. Every single day I make the extra effort. I go the extra mile. Couldn't *He* work just a little bit harder? What the hell else has He got to do anyway?"

"You know damn well that's not what He does, Perdue. God doesn't wave his hand and fix stuff, despite what it says in all those pretty Bible stories. And neither can we. At Karen's, we feed and house a maximum of thirty-seven women and children. Every single night, 365 nights a year, thirty-seven women and children get something to eat, a place to shower, somewhere safe and warm to sleep. It doesn't change the world. It doesn't cure homelessness. But it does help a few real individuals in a concrete way, however briefly. And that's all you can do. That's *all* you can do. You have to let the big stuff take care of itself."

Hatfield looked at him. He didn't know what to say.

"Can I ask you something?"

Hatfield shrugged.

"Strictly as one service professional to another: when's the last time you went somewhere with a woman who wasn't wearing handcuffs?"

"Hmmm," Hatfield grunted, recalling the pastor's earlier sentiment.

"Seriously, Perdue. If I didn't have Karen, if I didn't have other people to talk to, other people in my life—not to mention vacations or getting-away time, processing time, healing time, time to be a human instead of a tin soldier in God's army—I think I would be a total waste-case. Because the script doesn't change. It always remains the same. We're humans: flawed creatures with good intentions, stuck together on the same planet, fighting our baser instincts, trying our best to get along."

"*Flawed* being the operative word."

"I'd bet, if you went back to biblical times—or to any time: the Middle Ages, the Wild West, pick your favorite epoch—if you could get into a time machine and travel back through the years, I bet you'd discover that people have always lived with this same acute sense of dread. The feeling that any minute the other shoe is going to drop. That something really bad is about to happen. *The sky is falling,* you know what I mean? It wasn't that long ago that vast populations were being wiped out by flu. Twenty-five years ago, kids in schools were being taught to duck and cover. Now the Evil Empire has been dismantled, and we're on to the next thing, AIDS. They say that by 2010, 89 percent of all people living on the continent of Africa will be infected. The very act that is supposed to sustain us—reproduction—is now *threatening* our existence."

Steinschmidt opened a cupboard, retrieved a pack of Oreo cookies, offered it to Hatfield, who declined. He hadn't eaten refined sugar in over two years. "Remember high school biology?" the pastor continued. "A healthy, well-adapted organism tends to increase in population. If that's true, then you have to say that the human race is flourishing. What are we up to now, about six billion?"

"Give or take a junkie mom or two," Hatfield said morosely. And then he added, "As I recall from high school, once the population of an organism gets over a certain level, doesn't society descend into chaos?"

The pastor helped himself to another Oreo, dunked it into his coffee. "Maybe this is just the way it's supposed to be," he said. "Maybe this is just our way, the human way. It ain't pretty, but we survive." He popped the soggy cookie into his mouth. "Despite ourselves, we muddle through."

Hatfield drained his cup, crunched it in his meaty fist. "It's a muddle, alright." He replaced his hat on his head. "Where do you keep your recycling bin around here?"

Steinschmidt reached out and relieved the cop of his trash. "We wouldn't want to choke any dolphins downstream, now, would we?"

39

"And then she, like, looks up at me," Sojii said breathlessly. "*Ohmigod!* I knew it was her."

"It was only a dream," said Jonathan Seede, comforting his beautiful young houseguest, trying to sound fatherly. "You're here now. You're safe. Everything will be okay—I'm sure of it."

The living room of Seede's house was dark and narrow. Amber rays from the streetlamp filtered through the slatted shutters, casting shadows against the wall. The television glowed snow, a video interrupted. Flames crackled in the fireplace, over which hung a blue glass art deco mirror. Despite the fire, the room remained chilly. With its plaster walls, high ceilings, and original, lead-counterweighted window frames—warped and leaky, they'd rattle theatrically in a storm—it was a difficult house to heat.

"But it wasn't a dream," Sojii insisted. "It was more like . . . this." She raised her hands, palms up, indicating the here and now. "It seemed normal, you know? Like I was definitely there, in this boutique. And so was she."

He settled back into the lumpy cleavage of the convertible futon sofa. It was Thursday night. His wife and son had been gone since Monday—what time, exactly, he wasn't sure. He'd awoken in the afternoon to an empty house, a note in the bathroom: "We'll call." The *We,* of course, meant Dulcy and Jake. Seeing it there, written on the page like that, *We* with a capital *W,* had made him feel very . . . something. Kind of liberated. Kind of alone. He wasn't sure exactly which. Over the course of his marriage, he'd never really embraced the notion that being someone's husband or father, being part of a family unit, could be nearly as important or fulfilling as the monumental task of becoming one's self—in his case, Jonathan Seede, celebrated writer. But seeing the note there on the counter, her toothbrush gone from the glass, the wicker basket on her side of the sink emptied of its usual payload of brushes and sponges and other pricey feminine grooming paraphernalia . . . Well, it definitely gave him pause. Their whereabouts was still unknown.

"You're sure it was your mother?" Seede asked.

"She looked just like her picture."

"When was the last time you saw her in person?"

"I was six months old. She left me with my dad and went backpacking around Europe. That's the story, anyway, the one my dad tells—" She corrected herself: "*Told.*" At this last bit, Seede became aware for the first time of the sadness she was carrying. Up until now, he'd taken this girl at face value: mature for her age and seemingly self-sufficient, she acted as if being orphaned and on the run was no big deal to her, something she was handling just fine. The fact was, Seede knew very little about teenagers, about kids of any sort, eighteen months of reluctant fatherhood notwithstanding. Such was not the case, of course, with Dulcy. That old saw about kids not coming with manuals? Not true anymore. Scattered about the Seede household were dozens of child-rearing books, each one proffering a slightly or radically different view, a dissonant chorus of contradictory opinions that served only to make each new parenting decision a monumental task: When to switch from nipple to formula.

When to add solid foods. Comfort him or let him cry? Pacifier or thumb? Family bed or marital bed? Nanny or daycare? Volumes dedicated to training your child to sleep through the night occupied an entire shelf of their own: the popular authors were Sears, Ferber, and someone who called herself the Baby Whisperer; Dulcy's guru of choice was the clownishly named T. Berry Brazelton, a one-man pediatric whirlwind whose distinguished credits included his appointment as the very first spokesman for Pampers.

Seede reached to the end table next to him for a Flintstones jelly glass, filled halfway with twenty-year-old Sandeman port. "When you saw your mom, were you actually looking into the skull?"

"That's how it starts. It's called *scrying*. First you're looking at this, like, 3-D movie. And then all of a sudden, you're, like, *in* it."

Seede buried his face in his hands, took a deep and audible breath. He needed a hit. His stash was almost gone. On some level, it never failed to shock him: what started out looking like an incredibly large pile of drugs always dwindled to nothing. It was time again to ask the crucial question: go to sleep or buy more drugs?

The trick was stopping. If he could take a couple of Xanax or Valium, and then manage to fight off the insistent, yammering voice (*One more hit, Oh baby one more hit*) long enough for the downers to take effect—twenty to thirty minutes at most—the current binge could be ended. Among all the drugs he'd done or studied, crack addiction was unique: you were addicted to crack (or powder coke) for only as long as you were actually doing it. Once you managed to stop and go to sleep, your pleasure center was able to reset itself—the slate could be wiped clean. You could skip a day or a week if you were so inclined. You could never again do it in your life. There were no physical withdrawal symptoms, no sickness or pain or tremors, though the first couple of days after a binge tended to be characterized by much eating and sleeping, accompanied by an overarching feeling of sadness and regret. The mental challenge of quitting was more difficult. While asleep, you would dream the next hit. While awake, you would fantasize it elaborately. The voice in the back of your head would plead. (This time quoting Spike Lee from *She's Gotta Have It:* Please, baby, please, baby, baby baby, please.) One hit and you were back on the ride.

Sojii took Seede's distraction for disbelief. "You heard it yourself last night," she said, exasperated. "Or maybe you still think that screech was some huge mutant alley cat behind the house."

"Look," he said, "I'm trying to believe you. I'm trying to wrap my mind around all this stuff. One thing you can be sure of: I am on your side. I'm out on a limb just having you here. You understand that, right? Harboring beautiful teenage runaways is not one of the privileges granted to journalists by the first amendment."

Embarrassed by the overt compliment from this older man—eyes were one thing, words another—Sojii angled her head down and away, letting her long chestnut hair come between them like a curtain of silken strands. From the near arm of the futon frame, Sojii availed herself of a small quilt, one of Dulcy's family heirlooms.

"So you're in the boutique with your mother," Seede said, picking up the thread. "What happened next."

Sojii unfolded the quilt, draped it over her legs. She wasn't sure what she thought about this guy. He seemed on the level. He worked at the *Herald;* she'd read some of his stories—pretty good. He knew Waylon and the Pope; he'd gone to great effort to get her out of the church; he seemed genuine about making her feel at home, about keeping her safe until they figured out what was going on with the skull and the Pope's arrest. But he was also kind of twitchy—speedy and clumsy and grandiose.

She'd been around the Strip long enough to know when somebody was on drugs.

At the same time, a lot of what Seede said made good sense. Some really weird stuff had been happening to her, especially since she'd come into contact with the Pope's skull. She needed someone to talk to. As depressing as it sounded, the truth was this: she had no one else but this stranger.

"So I'm in the boutique and I see her," she began again. "And I'm like, *Ohmigod!* My mouth dropped open." She buried her face in her hands. "I probably looked like a total *ugg*."

"I doubt that's possible," he said. "What did she do?"

"She gave me this, I don't know—this kind of dorky smile."

"Dorky how?"

"You know. The way grown-ups do. When they think they know something you don't."

"How did the conversation go?"

"She was like—" and here Sojii played the character of her mother, using a breathy voice, evoking a hippie chick from the sixties: "'The last time you saw me, you also knew me right away.'"

"And I said—" playing herself: "'The last time I saw you, I was six months old. You left me with my dad and took off.'

"And she's like, '*No,* the last time I saw you, you were four *years* old. You met me at the National Zoo. You ran right up to me in a crowd.'" Sojii switched back to her own voice: "It was weird. She had this, like, attitude."

"What do you mean?"

She tucked the quilt beneath her thighs, and then she set about smoothing the wrinkles with her palm, a painstaking process, like a worker skimming the surface of freshly poured concrete with a wooden float. "I don't know," she said at last, her voice filled with uncertainty. "Just an attitude and stuff. Like I'd done something to her."

"What did you say?"

"I told her to fuck off and go to hell."

"Really?"

She shook her head sheepishly, no.

"That's what you wanted to say?"

Nodding affirmative.

"What did you really say?"

"I don't know." She studied her nails, the remnants of black polish, commenced picking at one thumbnail with the other. "I think I said, like, 'This isn't even *real*.'"

"But you said it felt like it was real."

"It did."

He paused a moment, a bit lost. "So what did she say?"

"She was like"—the voice of the hippie chick again—"'It's real enough, isn't it? Here we are. We're together.'

"And I'm like: 'In a boutique?'

"And she's like: 'Maybe this is somewhere a mother and daughter are supposed to be together.'"

Seede reached to the end table again and opened a carved wooden box, retrieved a cigarette-size tube fashioned from a variety of household products: a ten-inch slice of Safeway brand aluminum foil, a wad of a Chore Boy copper scrubber, and a short length of half-inch plasticized electrical tape from Ace Hardware—this last bit functioning as a mouthpiece, a recent invention, the mother of which had been the painful blistering of his lips and gums. Still unsolved was the problem of his index finger, the flank of which had developed an ugly callus from exposure to flame: crusty and blackened and fissured, it looked more like the finger of a homeless man or an auto mechanic than that of a guy who typed for a living. A reciprocal callus, likewise blackened and fissured, had developed on the pad of the opposing digit. Kwan and his homeboys knew the condition as "Bic thumb."

"Did she say anything else?" Seede asked.

"We talked a while longer and stuff, I guess."

Weary of pulling teeth: "Anything specific?"

Relenting: "She said, like, how she left me with my dad because she thought it was best for me. And how it was a different era, you know, and how she was in a bad space and had low self-esteem. She was like"—doing her mother again—"'My therapist told me I had to commit to loving *myself* before I could properly love anyone *else*.'"

He opened his mouth and inserted his index finger partway, pretended to gag. "Sounds to me like a victim of psychobabble."

"That was her main thing." Sojii said, sitting forward, becoming animated. "How *she* was the victim. How *she* didn't know how to be a good mother because *her* mother had given *her* up."

"So she gives you up?"

Sojii raised her arms and gathered her hair into a ponytail, twisted it around itself in a deliberate fashion, like a magician doing a trick with scarves. The recalcitrant strands floated to rest around her face, which itself was configured into a diffident expression, as if to say, *Who the fuck cares?*

Seede stared. Not to belabor the point, but besides being underage and unsupervised, she was unbelievably lovely, truly a wonder of creation, her genes gathered serendipitously from the four corners of the globe. His heart fluttered, an involuntary ventricular contraction.

"I guess parents, you know, they don't, well . . ." He struggled to put together a string of words that would comfort her. "They don't always realize the kind of effect their selfishness has on their children. Sometimes, maybe, they're not even aware of it themselves. It's almost like . . ."

He felt another flutter—recognition.

And promptly changed the subject.

"In a way," he postulated, "it seems that this experience with the skull was good for you."

Defensively: "Good for me? What do you mean?"

"In a therapeutic sense. Perhaps this dream you had under the influence of the skull—"

"It wasn't a dream."

"This experience," he corrected himself. "This encounter, what have you—maybe the skull is intended to be some kind of . . . I don't know, I'm taking a guess here, but maybe it's designed to help people work out their"—he used his fingers like quotation marks—"personal issues."

A blank stare.

"Think about it like this," he said. "Look how fucked-up the world is. Maybe one big reason is people have too many personal demons that affect their dealings with everyone else. Taken on a massive scale, think of the damage. Have you ever heard the Pope talk about this? It's one of his little pearls. I think it goes: *All hate is just fear. All fear is insecurity.* When he said that, I don't know, it rang so true, made perfect sense. People's personal problems bleed over into every human interaction. It taints everything, the entire course of human events."

"You mean, like, the fact that Hitler only had one ball or whatever?"

"Something like that."

"What does that have to do with me?"

"Each of us has our own little sob story. Our own defining issue. I have one. You have one. We all do. Depending upon the person, it can be really bad—child abuse, death of a parent, abandonment. Or it can be pretty benign—Mommy always loved you best. But no matter where your trauma rates on the scale of real-life relativity, to *you,* it's always going to register a ten, because it's *yours*. What happened to you is the most important thing in your universe. It's what forms you, your own personal big bang. Take me for instance. I had parents who acted like I was more special than I really was; now I need the whole world to think so too—that's my sad story. Sounds like nothing, right? Believe me, something like that can take you pretty deep.

"You were abandoned by your mother. Not so benign. You have deep feelings of rejection. You can't trust anyone, including yourself. You've probably spent your entire life wondering what it would be like to finally lay eyes on her. Let me ask you this: How many times have you daydreamed that scene, a chance meeting somewhere with your long lost mom? How many times have you wondered what it would be like to finally talk to her, to be able to tell her a few things, get a few things off your chest, ask a few questions? With the skull, by whatever means, you kind of got the chance to do that. You got the chance to play out the scene. It's the unsaid stuff that haunts us, the stuff undone. That's what prevents us from moving on. Do you understand what I'm trying to say?"

She nodded yes, though noncommittally.

"Think of it like this," he said, becoming more sure as he went along, the logic of it seeming to crystallize as he talked it through. "Because of the skull, you've had a chance at"—using his fingers again as quotation marks—"closure. I know, it's a stupid, overused word, but it *is* an important concept. Because nothing is over until it's over. You haven't seen your mother since you were six months old. Don't you think you would have met her by now if you were going to? Thanks to the skull, at least you've had a simulated chance. You said yourself how real it felt."

Her eyes welled with tears.

He felt bad for upsetting her—he was only trying to help. He held his pipe before his mouth like a cigar and waggled his eyebrows up and down, a corny attempt at Groucho Marx. "Think of it this way, *schweet*heart" he said with Groucho's aplomb, "you've probably saved yourself a fortune on therapy."

She wiped her eyes the way women do, using a knuckle to squeegee the light spillage, carefully avoiding the mascara, even though she wasn't wearing any. From her own end table she picked up a mug of sweet milky tea, the front emblazoned with a likeness of former President Reagan.

Seede reached over to his box, which was made of redwood and lined with green felt, and picked up his last rock, round and white and crystalline, about the size of a baby's tooth. By now, the heroin had pretty much worn off. The empty feeling inside him was deepening into a chasm. It needed to be filled with smoke. It needed to be done now. He placed the rock in the pipe, picked up his butane lighter. A metallic click, the familiar hiss, a sound like a tiny jet engine. He trained the flame on the charred end of the pipe, moved it nimbly back and forth along the surface of the rock, like a dessert chef caramelizing a crème brûlée.

Sojii watched him intently. "That's crack, right?"

Seede doused the flame and looked up. "Technically, it's freebase."

"Why are you doing the lighter like that?"

"It primes the hit, melts it into the screen so it won't fall out." He clicked the lighter, put the pipe to his mouth . . .

"Can I try it?"

Seede doused the flame again. It had been nine weeks and six days since he had last touched a woman. Sojii's innocent emerald eyes sparkled.

"I think maybe it's time you went back downstairs," he said firmly.

40

Lightning struck the top of his head.

Coursed through his body, lit up his sex: *Ding!*

Seede's pelvis strained upward. He became aware of pleasure. Specific and localized. Tight, warm, wet. The electric tingle of nerve endings, each one singular and phosphorescent. His eyelids sprung open like window shades.

He noticed his right hand, abandoned, hovering midair, still holding the lighter. He returned it to the pocket of his sweatshirt, alongside a three-pack of Trojans, yet unopened, and then he placed the hand tentatively on her crown, the long blonde strands clingy with static, gripping as one might grip a basketball, fingertips spread, wishing he could slow the pace, not sure of the protocol, wishing she knew better the kind of thing he liked, more of a slow pushing down motion, as opposed to the frenetic pulling up. Her head felt lumpy in spots where the hair extensions had been attached with hot glue, cheaper than handsewn, though less permanent.

They were parked in a residential alley off Seventh Street, deep in heroin country, behind what appeared to be an abandoned house. The alley was strewn with trash and tires and old appliances. Around a charred steel drum was a circle of broken chairs and upended milk crates. Two abandoned vehicles seemed to be serving as residences. The place had the feel of a homeless encampment; in his haste to find a spot to park, Seede hadn't paid it much mind. A weed tree grew tall overhead. Its branches hung down like those of a weeping willow, dappling the amber light from the remaining streetlamp. The other, to the east, appeared to have been shot out.

He squeezed his eyes shut, trying to concentrate, to give himself over, to experience fully what he'd heretofore denied himself, a monumental feat of will given the proximity of the Strip and all its offerings. Sometimes, when he was at a bar, or at the movies, or out to dinner, or playing coed touch football, or standing in line at the post office, or walking around the newsroom (well, maybe not walking around the newsroom), he felt like he must be the only man on the planet who wasn't getting laid. What was wrong with him anyway? Why didn't his wife love him? Why couldn't she just break down once in a while and throw him a bone? He'd been a good husband—until recently, that is. Didn't he deserve better? In six years of marriage he had never strayed—not even during this long drought of physical affection that had slowly eaten away at his happiness and self-confidence, eaten away at the fabric of his being like a wasting disease, killing the very cells of himself, leaving instead this malignant need.

His pulse thumped behind his temples. His jaw was clenched; he forced it open. He took a deep breath through his nose: wood smoke and leaf rot, must and mold, auto exhaust, the cigarette smoldering in the ashtray, the medicinal smell of crack, her powdery sweet perfume, his body odor—sixty-some hours at this point without a shower or sleep. He leaned his head back against the cold surface of the window, his left shoulder wedged against the door, an awkward position that afforded this woman—street name Savannah, a friend of Jamal's he had interviewed once for a story—a better angle on her business, given the obstacles of stick shift and emergency brake between the bucket seats of his four-door Dodge Colt.

After seeing Sojii safely down the steps to his basement apartment—desperate though he might be, Seede was not about to feed crack to a minor, no matter how beautiful and willing—he'd found the car parked in its usual place in the garage, a brick suffix to the house, complete with remote-controlled door, an architecturally grandfathered setup much coveted in the neighborhood. The car was an '85 model, a zippy little econobox made for Dodge by Mitsubishi, painted an effervescent pinky yellow color called champagne, emblematic of the era of its manufacture, a time of junk bonds, expense-account caviar, and powder cocaine. That Dulcy did not take the car led Seede to conclude that she and Jake left by taxi. Surely they hadn't walked to the subway at Dupont Circle, six blocks across the frozen landscape. Maybe they'd been given a ride—he couldn't imagine where or by whom. Dulcy had no relatives in town, no friends. She always said, somewhat lamentably, that her closest girlfriend in DC was Jim Freeman. *She was always a man's woman,* Seede told himself. At which point another thought occurred: *Could she be having an affair?*

Reaching with his left hand into his other sweatshirt pocket, he pinched out a menthol cigarette, placed it between his lips, searched the confines of the driver's door pocket for his lighter, remembered the right sweatshirt pocket, located the lighter beside the condoms, lit the cigarette, careful to avoid Savannah's hair, no doubt flammable. The smoke loitered along the cheaply upholstered ceiling of the car, danced around the dome light. Seede tried to recall the last time he'd felt a woman's mouth on his penis. He thought of his wedding night and felt a twinge of guilt, followed by a flash of anger. *She's the one who fuckin left,* he told himself. He thought about all the times over the last year that he'd considered leaving. *Did I fuckin leave?* He thought about all the blow jobs he'd had over the course of his lifetime.

The brunette with braces at the rifle range at Camp Green Mountain. The redhead on the Spanish Club trip to Barcelona. The blonde in the front seat of the car at seventy miles per hour on the George Washington Parkway. Dulcy on their wedding night, looking up at him so lovingly, her lips full and slick, a gleam of contentment in her honey brown eyes, a goddamn sparkle. *This is what happens when you give them what they want.* Sadness rained down upon him, a cloudburst, a sudden squall. He felt lonely and misunderstood. He took another hit off his cigarette.

The head bobbed more slowly now; Seede's hips rose contrapuntally, a moist smacking sound, like someone chewing food with their mouth open. His breathing was shallow and effortful, like someone lifting weights. Seconds passed . . . one minute . . . two. His mind began to settle. The running internal commentary, the slide show of images, the dancing fountain of grandiose ideas—all of it began to subside, as if a hand somewhere was turning a series of dials, lowering the volume, dimming the lights . . . until stillness began to descend upon him, warm and syrupy, like the first faint tuggings of oncoming sleep, only instead of sleep it was pleasure. He gave himself over to her strong lips and muscular, swirling tongue, the excruciatingly luxuriant stretch of dermis, the electric tingle of nerve endings, her left hand squeezing, her right now cupping his balls.

Just then, outside the car, a fat orange alley cat—spotting a rat or a rival or a female in heat—jumped from a nearby garage roof . . . to a rickety fence rail . . . to a rusty metal trash can, landing a tad off balance, causing the lid to slip and fall, taking with it the fat orange cat, which shrieked, *Yeooooooooow!*—the lid clattering on the cobblestones like thunder.

Seede sat bolt upright. He swiveled his head around, bird-like, herky-jerky, checking his perimeter. With the sleeve of his sweatshirt, he wiped away the condensation from the window.

And there she was. Standing in the dappled shadows beneath the weed tree.

Her face was arranged into a hideous mask of hurt and anger and betrayal. Her toe was tapping, like Flo in *Andy Capp*. She held the boy on her hip, bundled in his snowsuit. The hood came to an elfin point at the top of his head. They had argued bitterly about purchasing the thing, which was stuffed with goose down and rated to negative ten degrees, another entry on a seemingly endless list of critical aftermarket add-ons: the safety locks on all the kitchen drawers and toilet seats; the plastic plugs in the electric sockets; the security gates on every landing of the carefully restored stairwell, the hinges of which needed to be secured to the antique hardwood with maiming metal screws. How much time had been devoted, over the last twenty-seven months, to researching and discussing and arguing and procuring and installing these and other must-have accessories? To schlepping them from place to place around the neighborhood, around the globe: strollers and car seats (different models for different age ranges); a portable high chair (the gay-owned restaurants in their neighborhood declined to keep them on hand); a portable playpen; the bulging backpack full of ointments and salves and diapers and bottles and emergency supplies; and, on one memorable trip into Heathrow Airport, a gallon-size ziplock freezer bag full of a crystalline white powder which happened to be infant formula. Lucky for Seede, the customs detectives assigned to strip-search and interrogate him were themselves beleaguered fathers of young children—were there any other kind?

Savannah looked up quizzically at Seede. She consulted the watch on her left wrist, in which hand she held his soft penis. "You think you can finish, baby?" There was a dubious tone in her voice.

Seede's chest vibrated as it heaved and fell. His eyes were twitchy. His pulse was racing, a timpani inside his skull. He ventured another glance out the window. Dulcy and the boy had dematerialized.

"You want another hit?" he croaked.

"Ten mo minutes," Savannah said, workmanlike, a bit annoyed. She took a drag off her cigarette, returned to her ministrations.

Seede took a long last drag from his own cigarette, pushed it through the slivered-open driver's window, leaned his head against the cold and soothing glass. He fished inside the door pocket for a film canister and his aluminum foil pipe, placed the pipe between his lips, let it dangle to one side like Bogart.

Working in the airspace above Savannah's head, he opened the film can and teased out a dove, a twenty dollar rock about the size of a molar—three days into this binge, large dosages were required to achieve a significant rush. He refit the lid, returned the canister to the door pocket, switched the pipe to his left hand, trembling, screen end up, recessed inside his fist for stability. Placed the rock on the Chore Boy screen, itself recessed inside the foil tube. Retrieved the lighter once more from his sweatshirt pocket. Melted the rock into the screen . . .

A long hit, impossibly long: chin uptilted, flame bright, a whooshing like a tiny jet engine, the rock crackling and popping, soot and sparks raining down upon his hands and cheeks. The molecules of cocaine alkaloid, rendered gaseous by the flame, traveled down his trachea and into his lungs, passing through vast fields of capillary-rich air sacs called alveoli, into the hot tributaries of his type O-positive blood—an invading force riding a commandeered fleet of protein particles, sailing full tilt into the gathering headwaters of his pulmonary vein and into his heart, to his brain, to his limbic system, buried deep within the two gray outer hemispheres of the cerebral cortex: the dark, moist realm of pain, pleasure, learning, and emotion.

(All in less than three seconds, according to a researcher Seede had consulted, who likened the process to "pounding a ten-penny nail made of pure cocaine directly into the pleasure center of your brain.")

Whereupon . . .

Lightning struck the top of his head.

His ears opened. His thoughts shattered into a million shards. His brain buzzed, a loud metallic hum that turned him inside out. He was a sparkler on the Fourth of July—shimmering flakes of magnesium fire shooting in all directions.

His pelvis strained upward, driven by its own powerful engine. A moist smacking sound, the luxuriant stretch of skin, the tingle of nerve endings. He thought about Salem: her long legs, the way her tight shorts molded to the outline of her crotch. Bo Franklin—*I killed a bitch with an orgasm*. China Doll and Sana and Crazy Michelle, skittering like water bugs in and out of traffic beneath the pink neon cross, everything a size too small. The brunette at the rifle range at Camp Green Mountain, the blonde behind the sand dune, a solitary bead of sweat dripping between her breasts. Sojii, so young and choice and willing, sleeping now in his basement apartment. Dulcy on their wedding night, the goddamn sparkle.

He raised the lighter again and hit the pipe. A long, slow, steady hit, not too hard, the flame whooshing, the smoke filling his lungs, the tension building, her strong lips and muscular swirling tongue . . .

And then the driver's door, against which he was leaning, suddenly gave way, and he was flying backward through space, yanked forcefully by the scruff of his sweatshirt all the way clear of the car, clear of Savannah, his black button-fly jeans bunched around his ankles, his glistening stiff penis wobbling on its root . . .

And then the landing, a violent skidding thud upon the wet and dirty antique cobblestone, the force of which literally knocked the breath from his lungs—twenty to thirty cubic feet of pristine white smoke issuing now through his ravaged nose and blistered lips.

Hands clutched and pulled and tugged at him, punching and gouging, kicking and pawing, riffling his pockets, grappling for his wedding ring, so many faces and arms and legs, set upon him like hyenas upon prey, wild-eyed, gap-toothed, the smell of shit and piss and vomit, shouting and grunting and laughing, yanking his dick, twisting sadistically . . .

And then a strong kick to his side, and then another, *oooff,* and then another, the branch-break sound of cracking ribs, and Seede crying out, a tone of utter helplessness and defeat: "Stop. *Please.*"

And then somebody yelled, "Hit em in the head!"

PART FOUR

41

Jim Freeman threw a hurried left turn across three lanes of Friday morning traffic and bounced into the rutted driveway of the Capitol City Motor Lodge, scraping the undercarriage of his Jaguar XJ6—a tax write-off, he was always quick to point out, used primarily to ferry clients.

Ever mindful of his paint job, a flawless British racing green, he pulled into a space at the far corner of the parking lot. It was just after ten A.M. For his mission he had chosen a distressed leather and shearling bomber jacket and a pair of black button-fly jeans, the same kind Seede always wore. He took the stairs two at a time, his Frye boots making a no-nonsense thunk on the metal risers. He knocked at room 215.

After an interval, the door opened partway. Salem's face could be seen in the space allowed by the chain. Her usually spiky hair, sans mousse, fell softly about her face, giving her the big-eyed, waifish look of a Keane painting.

"I'm James Freeman," he said, using his best Realtor voice, somewhat mismatched with his ensemble. "I'm good friends with Jonathan Seede—the reporter from the *Herald*?"

"I remember *you*," she said. "You was onea them protest guys on the corner the other night."

A nervous giggle, the boom restrained. "Is Jamal here?"

Jamal's head appeared above Salem's. "Go on and let him in."

The door shut, then opened again. Freeman ventured several steps into the humid room. It had a king-size bed, a mini-fridge, a breakfast nook with a yellow Formica dinette table and mismatched chair. Jamal was shirtless, wearing a shower cap, his face lined with pillow wrinkles. He did not seem pleased to be awake. "How you know where we stay at?"

Freeman smiled solicitously. "Like I said, I'm a good friend of Seede's. I was the best man at his wedding."

Grimly: "And he tole you where we stay?"

Another nervous giggle. "Let me explain. After your act of heroism the other night on the corner of Thirteenth and Corcoran—Lord knows what would have happened to our friend Wolfie had you not come along—we wanted to send you a basket, you know, some kind of thank-you gift. A token of our *appreciation*. I asked Jonathan for your address so we could have it delivered."

Jamal turned to Salem, annoyed. "Did you get a basket and not tell me about it?"

"Actually, it's in the car," Freeman clarified, gesturing in the direction of the parking lot. "I didn't know if it would be appropriate to leave it at the front desk, or if it would be better to—"

"Happy to be of help," Jamal said, pleased by the tribute, by Freeman's bended-knee approach. "A friend of Seede's is a friend of mine, know what I'm sayin? Go on now and get the basket and bring it here. And then we gotta excuse ourselves." He yawned expansively.

Freeman stood glued to the spot. He looked up at Jamal with a pregnant expression.

"Is they somethin else?" Jamal asked.

Freeman wasn't sure where to start. "Have you seen Jonathan lately, by any chance?"

Jamal thought for a moment. Living nights, sleeping days, it was hard to keep the calendar straight. He inserted a finger beneath the elastic band of his shower cap and scratched his head. "What day today?" he asked.

"Friday," Freeman said.

"Yesterday morning, I think it was." He inspected a piece of something he'd found in his hair. "Thursday. A little before noon. I hooked him up with an interview. After that, he said he was goin down to the jail. What's up? Is he missin?"

"I'm not sure," Freeman said. "It's kind of a long story. There's this girl staying in his English Basement. She's sixteen. Amazingly gorgeous. And she has this crystal skull—it's very valuable. And now I can't find her *or* Seede. The house is empty. I let myself in with my key. I have this feeling they might have been kidnapped or something—I don't know what."

"You mean, like, a human skull made of crystal?" Salem asked.

"You've seen it?"

"I seen a whole *collection*."

"Where at?" Jamal asked, indignant.

Of course Salem had not bothered to tell Jamal about the detective or the meeting with Metcalfe, and certainly not about the money, which was hidden above the acoustic tiles in the bathroom ceiling. Although Metcalfe hadn't gotten around to telling her that he was her father, he had scheduled another meeting—having broken the ice, he was ready now to break the news. Salem was planning to leave for California sometime in the next few days. She figured she'd wait around long enough for Metcalfe's next installment—by far the easiest money she'd ever made.

"I saw them at this trick's house," she explained, keeping it vague. "Rich guy. He have this big ass mansion up in Georgetown, I think it was. You know, up that hill wit all the stores?"

"Wisconsin Avenue?" Jim asked.

"Um-hmm," she confirmed. "He have this room with all these skulls—four or five of em. But they wasn't all crystal. One was a purply color. Another was green—it look like jade. Maybe one of em was crystal, I ain't sure. It was *creepy,* you know what I'm sayin?"

"Do you think you can find this house again?" Freeman asked.

42

Detective John O'Rourke stood outside the Pope's medical observation cell, speaking with an orderly in pink scrubs.

"Pancreatic," the cop repeated. He licked the end of his pencil, jotted it down on his pad.

"Advanced," the orderly pronounced gravely. His kinky topknot was secured by a purple ponytail band. He scanned the pages on a medical clipboard. "It looks like it's metastasized to the lungs and the spine. They don't know yet about the brain—ain't no money in the budget for a head CT."

"How long's he got?"

The orderly flipped a few pages. "Says here he's due to be released at five P.M."

"The judge must have just signed the order."

"*Ummm-hmm,*" the orderly said archly. "If he die in here, the city gotta pay to bury him."

"Not much of a flight risk at this point," O'Rourke chuckled. "Is he lucid?"

The orderly raised an eyebrow, carefully tweezed and sculpted. There was a hint of makeup on his lids. "With that man, it hard to tell."

O'Rourke shook his head ironically, a thread of mutual understanding between two individuals who couldn't have been more different. The orderly produced a set of keys and unlocked the door.

The Pope's head was elevated; he was wired to an array of bags and machines. A cacophonous silence filled the room—the *whoosh* of forced air from the ceiling vent; the *hissss* of oxygen running through a nasal cannula; the *beep beep beep* of the EKG.

"Michael David Rubin?"

The Pope's eyes fluttered.

"Mr. Rubin? Are you awake?"

"Howdy, honey, howdy," he said weakly.

"I'm Detective O'Rourke. From Internal Affairs? Do you remember me?"

Brightening: "Have you brought the missing sacrament?"

"No, sir, I'm afraid not." He said it politely, without hint of irony. It didn't seem to bother him at all that the Pope was here under false pretenses. In his mind the Pope of Pot was a felony-level drug dealer. What kind of drugs, how much, the details of his arrest—those were just formalities. This guy was guilty. He needed to be off the streets. Period. If anything, O'Rourke felt bad about causing the city the expense of caring for this deadbeat. "Do you mind if I ask you a few questions?"

The Pope stared off into the middle distance. "What you say and what you do are equally important," he said.

"I wanted to ask you about something that may have been stolen from your storefront."

"Be number one in a class of one."

Uncertain if he was getting through—*Is this guy delirious or just fucking with me?*—the detective pushed on. "It's a skull," he said. "Made out of crystal rock. I believe at one time it was in your possession. According to our information," consulting his pad, "it was kept behind your desk, on the credenza. Surrounded by your collection of—" he hesitated, seeking the right word. "Figurines."

"All men put on their pants one leg at a time."

"Can you tell me how you came to possess the skull? Is it possible that you might have obtained it while living in Amsterdam?"

"Respect must be earned."

"According to our investigation, the chain of custody seems to end at a pawnshop in Amsterdam—" He consulted his pad again. "On a street named"—stumbling over the pronunciation—"*Leidekkerssteeg?* Are you familiar with this pawnshop?"

"Less is more."

"I beg your pardon?"

"Win by example."

"About the skull, sir—"

"Make of your body a living sign."

O'Rourke closed the pad, replaced it in his pocket. He thought of his father some years before, full of morphine and nonsense in a similar hospital bed, his head jacked up for comfort, the conclusion foregone.

Suddenly the Pope grabbed the sleeve of O'Rourke's suede jacket—a desperate, viselike grip. He searched the detective's bland and doughy face for a hint of compassion. "Tell 'em, toots," he implored. "Tell 'em what I said. Let the world know. You *must.*"

O'Rourke peeled the Pope's fingers from his sleeve and replaced the spindly arm on the bed. "You got it, pal," the detective said, a reassuring tone. "I'll shout it from the rooftops, okay?"

"Bless you, my son," the Pope whispered. He closed his eyes. A faint smile crossed his lips.

And then the *beep beep beep* of the EKG went to flatline, the tone long and shrill and final.

43

Seede lay fetal in the alley. His skull was staved in at the left temple. His jeans were still at half-mast.

He opened his right eye, the one nearest the ground.

And there she was again.

Standing beneath the weed tree, the boy on her hip, wearing his subzero-grade snowsuit.

Seede blinked, trying to clear his vision. The image of his wife and child seemed to waver and wobble, like a faint signal from far away. He wondered if he was dreaming. He wondered if he was dead. He wondered if he'd know the difference when the time came, if it hadn't come already. He tried to move but he couldn't. He felt very heavy, yet very light—ephemeral, insubstantial, not long for this world. His mouth tasted of metal. He felt no pain.

"What do you think you're doing?" Dulcy asked.

"Research." The word came out wet and garbled. His jaw felt unhinged; he guessed it was dislocated.

"Research," she repeated.

"For my book."

"And what is this book supposed to be about, if may I ask?"

"It's kind of hard to explain."

"Give it a try."

"It's about the drug culture in the shadow of the nation's Capitol—behind the scenes of the war on drugs. It's about society and class. It's about the crack economy. Look at us: we're only a mile from the White House—the rabble in the rubble outside the castle walls."

Her lip began to tremble. Her face caved in upon itself. "Why are you doing this to me?" she sobbed.

Had his own face been functional, it would have registered utmost incredulity. "To *you*?"

She nuzzled Jake's plump cheek. "To *us*."

"I'm not doing anything to either of you."

"Then why are you doing this to yourself?"

"Because I can?" he proposed. "Because I'm not supposed to? Because everyone says it's wrong?" He thought a moment. "Because it feels good and because for so long I haven't felt good. Because *I* wanna do what *I* wanna do."

"You sound like a spoiled brat."

"What do you care, anyway?"

"I'm married to you. You're the father of my child. You're a drug addict."

"The addiction is only one small part," he said. "The book is about so much more than that." He tried again to move but couldn't. He wondered if he was paralyzed, if his condition was temporary or permanent. He wondered if he'd ever be able to type again. "As an artist, you have to see your life as a quest. You have to put yourself out there. You have to take chances. You can't be afraid to fail. You can't worry about what society expects of you, what anybody expects of you. You can't worry about anything but the process of creating your art. It's like the Pope says: You have to make your body a living sign."

"Pope John Paul said that?"

"The Pope of Pot. He has a storefront church on Fourteenth Street, near P. He's a genius. The cops are trying to kill him. I'm putting him in the book too. He's gonna be a big part, at least a whole chapter."

"What is your body supposed to be a sign of right now?"

"Make shit of me if you want, but I'm telling you—this book is gonna deal with a lot of important issues. It's about the nature of the human urge, how the whole concept of Just Say No is bad for us. How prohibition and sublimation are detrimental to a healthy life. How, if you don't satisfy your needs, if you don't do the things that are natural, that feel good, that make you distinctly human, you end up with big problems. Our culture and religion teach us to suppress our basic instincts, lest we end up consigned to hell. But guess what? It turns out that denial and suppression leads to a whole *other* kind of hell."

"And you have definitely found it, Jonathan. You are there."

"That's right," he said defiantly. "I fuckin found it. And I couldn't have done it without you."

"You are not going to blame this on *me*." Her image flickered and disappeared, then reappeared, like a neon sign on the fritz. It occurred to him that this conversation couldn't be happening, not really. Most likely, he was dreaming or hallucinating. Or maybe he'd entered purgatory, the twilight zone, wherever you actually go when you die, provided there is such a place. In real life Ducly wouldn't be by herself in this dangerous alley with Jake. And even if she really *was* here, she probably wouldn't be arguing with him like this, as they had so often during the past several months. In real life, wouldn't she be helping him at this point? Making some move to minister to his wounds, to stanch the blood flow, to cover his half-naked body?

"Who else would I blame it on?" he continued. Real or imagined, this conversation was long overdue.

"Here we go."

"Say what you want. But that was the idea, at first."

"What?"

"Seeing how far I could take this whole project before I was discovered . . . by you. Because you weren't paying attention to me—unless you needed something done, something purchased or carried or installed, some task taken care of, some errand run. It was a joke I had with myself, a little wager: *How long is it going to take her to realize what I'm doing? How far can I go? Is it really possible that she's so wrapped up in herself and the baby that she won't even notice when I become a crackhead?*"

"Of course I noticed. I left you, didn't I?"

"Yeah, but it took you nearly ten weeks."

Incredulous: "You've been smoking crack every day for ten weeks?"

"Not every day. Never on writing days. Writing is the temple."

"How could you be so selfish?"

"*Selfish?* Me? How could *you* not know what I was doing all that time?"

Her eyes fell. "I was busy. There's so much to do for Jakey. It's overwhelming."

"You act like you're the first woman who ever had a child. If women who lived in caves could do it, if women who lived in trees could do it, if pygmies in the rain forest can do it, why can't you? Why does everything have to be this huge damn drama?"

She stared at him, speechless.

"I'll make you a wager. I'll bet, if you researched the statistics—and I plan to do so before I'm done, because it's probably going to be one of the central theses of this book—I'll bet you'd discover that I'm not alone in my thinking. Maybe what I'm saying isn't popular; maybe what I'm saying is dangerous. But lemme tell you, *I am not alone*. They're out there. I've seen their faces in the malls, in the grocery stores, at Babies "R" Us, at pharmacies late at night—shoulder-slumped men, afraid to stand up and speak their minds, to demand their rights, lest their wives, to whom they've pledged eternal love (not to mention half their net worth), unleash upon their heads another hysterical tirade, another hormonal tsunami of biblical proportions. I see them everywhere, everyday, men who feel the same way I do: alienated, embattled, angry, pent-up, horny. Totally fuckin horny, ain't-been-laid-in-nine-weeks horny. Six times in twenty seven months! What the hell is that? What in the *hell* is that? Have I not brought you flowers and chocolates and jewelry? Have I not kept a roof over your head? Did I ever hit you or treat you badly? Did I ever deny you *anything*? Everybody knows that marriage is a barter system. It's give and take. I take care of your needs, you take care of mine. But then the kid comes along, and all of a sudden the whole deal is off. I'm chopped liver. Worse—I'm *rotten* chopped liver. I'm toxic spill: avoid at all costs. What about my needs, you know what I'm sayin? *What about my motherfuckin needs?* Have you ever once heard me say, 'Sorry dear, I have a headache, I don't feel like paying the mortgage this month.' Have you ever heard me say, 'Sorry dear, I have cramps, I won't be paying the phone or the cable or the electric bill.' You've *never* heard that from me. Because I hold up my end of the bargain. I do what I'm *supposed* to fuckin do.

"Check the data. I know what it's going to show. It's gonna show that a *huge* percentage of marriages break up during the first, say, eighteen months of a child's life. Sometimes the first kid is enough to do it—witness us. More often, it's the second. Because you know how people are, they have one kid in diapers, they gotta hurry up and have a second, because everybody says they have to, because everybody else does it, because the kid needs someone to play with—as if siblings ever do anything together besides fight. Think about it: how many people do we know who are divorced with two small children? Just at the *Herald* I can give you five examples."

"So what are you trying to say, Jonathan? Do you want a divorce? Is that it?"

"I'm trying to say that I'm tired of being taken for granted. Does being a father have to mean totally subverting your needs to those of everyone else? Shouldn't I be getting something out of this too? A little appreciation? A little attention? A little sex . . . at least now and then? I work my ass off to support you and Jake. I do everything anyone asks of me. And I get nothing in return. Nada. A lot of attitude. A lot of responsibilities. A lot of expenses. A *shitload* of expenses. But nobody cares about me. I am the bottom of the totem pole—least considered, holding everything up."

"What kind of person are you? You hate your son. You hate me!"

"Are you kidding? *Are you fuckin' kidding?* I love you. I want you. I *crave* you. You wanna hear something priceless? When I beat off, I fantasize about *you,* Dulcy. How pitiful is that? My own wife is my stroke fantasy. Because you are unreachable, untouchable. You are *totally* unattainable. You might as well be Halle Berry. Because I have just as much chance of getting a blow job from her as I do from you."

"If you did more for Jake and me, if you helped around the house more, maybe I'd be in the mood, maybe I'd be—"

"And for the record," he continued, "I never wanted to be a father, it wasn't in my plans for myself. I told you that up front, long before we were married. I remember the exact words: 'I don't need someone else to carry on my name.' When you're trying to be a writer, that's what you're out to do for yourself. You're out to write something memorable. Something that lasts. Something that carries on your name by its own merit. It's easy to spill sperm. It's no big accomplishment.

"I'm twenty-nine years old. For more than a third of my life, ever since high school, I've been totally dedicated to one mission. All the choices I've made, all the sacrifices—quitting law school to become a copyboy at the *Herald;* deciding to stay on graveyard shift so I could freelance during the day, coming home early one night to find my live-in girlfriend fucking the neighbor. The first two years at the *Herald,* I worked every weekend and every holiday. I never took a day off, not even a sick day. By the time I was twenty-four, I'd lost my hair. Every decision, every move, it's all been geared toward trying to write something good, something that people will remember. It's always been about one thing: putting forth my best effort, seeing how far I could go."

Dulcy shifted the boy from one hip to the other; he was restless, he wanted down. He reached out and caught hold of her necklace, an Elsa Peretti Open Heart from Tiffany, the first gift Seede had given her, its shape so artfully pulled and distorted, like love itself. "Can't you be a father *and* write something memorable at the same time?"

How many times he had asked himself the same question. It's not like he wanted to be alone. It's not like he didn't want to be loved, to have someone to love. "I just can't see how you're supposed to do both," he said, defeated. "A good father is someone who chooses his family's needs over his own. I've never read about any great artist who was known for being a great dad, have you? Can you imagine William Burroughs coaching peewee soccer? I don't think Henry Miller ever drove a minivan."

"Fine." She blew it out between her top teeth and her bottom lip, *Finnnnneeee,* a sustained note of dismissive finality that backed up abruptly into her throat and behind her nose, resonated into the frigid air, meaning: *Not fine, not fine at all, you will pay dearly for all of your sins.* Tired of struggling with the fidgety child, she lowered him to the ground.

Jake toddled toward his father, proud and purposeful, his diapered bottom twitching this way and that, like a duckling's.

He squatted beside Seede, as kids do on the playground to inspect something of fascination, his knees wide like a catcher behind home plate, only instead of dirt he was squatting in a puddle of blood. His face assumed a serious expression, brows knit. He pointed a finger at Seede's broken head. "Dada *owie,*" he declared.

Then he looked back to Dulcy. "Mama fix?"

44

Salem leaned forward from the back seat of Freeman's Jaguar. "Pull over there," she ordered, indicating the 7-Eleven.

Freeman parked at the northwest corner of Fourteenth Street and Rhode Island Avenue, careful not to scrape his fancy spoke wheel covers on the curb. Slamming the rear passenger door behind her, Salem bounded off.

The sun was in evidence; bright but not warm. The engine purred; a song by Whitney Houston played on the radio. Jamal sat in the shotgun seat, wearing a do-rag and wraparound shades. He tapped out a Newport cigarette. As was the custom among some DC natives, he'd opened the soft pack from the bottom so that it appeared unopened—local etiquette proscribed bumming from a fresh pack. "I don't see why we need *him,*" Jamal grumbled.

"Ever read the side of a squad car?" Freeman asked. "It says, 'To Protect and Serve.'"

Jamal lit the cigarette, took a deep drag. "Doesn't say that *inside* the car nowhere."

"I hear what you're sayin," Freeman assured him, drawing from his extensive experience with couple's therapy—the need to acknowledge the validity of the opinions held by the person with whom you are attempting to dialogue. "I used to teach high school in Newport News. You ever been there? Some of it's as bad as DC—worse. One thing I always noticed: We'd be on a field trip, you know, driving somewhere—the parents and I would drive because we had no budget for transportation. We'd be stopped at a light and a cop would pull up next to us, and all of the boys—I'm talking about high school boys, sixteen, seventeen, eighteen years old—all of them would go absolutely insane. They'd act all crazy and furtive and weirded out, like they were guilty of something.

"I know those kids weren't perfect. Some of them probably were guilty of something—that's the world they lived in. This one's brother was dealing crack. This one's daddy was in jail. This one's mother was violating ADC by letting her man shack up. I used to tell them, 'Acting like that draws attention to yourself. Cops are gonna think you're guilty of something because you're acting guilty.' When I see a cop, it doesn't phase me. I don't even think about the cop. I don't even notice him. Only time I think about a cop is when I need something, like if my house gets broken into, or if I get mugged, something like that."

"Obviously you ain't black."

"No, but I'm gay. And my ex-husband is black *and* gay. One thing gay people have learned: You have to assume your own innocence, despite what everybody may think. You have to stand up and demand your rights. That's the way of the world. Nobody's giving out nothin for free. And you're never gonna get nothin," his head swiveling on his neck like Rosie Perez, "if you don't ask. Not even things you think you deserve: no acres, no mules, no respect, no recognition, no thank you. With cops, you sometimes have to remind them what they're here for. Their intentions are good—they start out good anyway. They just get caught up . . . in the politics, in the quotas, in the battlefront conditions, in the trauma of it all. I used to date a cop. Believe me: it changes a person. You think those guys aren't fuckin scared? They hide behind their wall of authority. Sometimes they forget what they're really here for. Deep down, you have to believe, cops are just people who want to help. Otherwise they'd have never become cops."

Jamal grunted—*Yeah, right*. He exhaled a thick plume of smoke out the window. Freeman turned up the radio. "I Will Always Love You" was number one for the third straight week. He sang along, half under his breath, a pitchy falsetto.

A primer-gray van pulled to the curb in front of the Jag. It rolled forward a bit, taking up one space plus half of another, leaving about six feet of clearance between itself and the Jaguar's shiny hood ornament. Freeman and Jamal watched as an older white man, a chaw of tobacco bulging his cheek, stepped down from the driver's side of the van and walked around to the back. He threw open the double doors to reveal a dirty curtain, center-split, as in a theater.

After an interval, the curtain parted and a man emerged, carrying a crutch, a shopping bag, and a large, empty plastic cup. A woman followed, baby in arms. They shuffled off in a southerly direction, toward the business district.

Freeman bummed a cigarette from Jamal and poked in the lighter, which was recessed stylishly into the high-gloss, burlwood console. The song changed, an up-tempo hit from the previous summer, "Baby Got Back." Jamal's head bobbed in rhythm to the backbeat; Freeman tapped his thigh on the one.

The white guy reached inside the curtain again, rummaged around, pulled out a length of board—two by twelve, five feet long, sturdy and well worn. He angled the board to the ground, a makeshift ramp.

The curtain parted. Another man appeared. He swung his torso up and onto the ramp, a motion like a gymnast—it became immediately apparent that both of his legs had been amputated above the knees. He slid down the ramp with practiced agility, moved toward the 7-Eleven in a peculiar but powerful style: setting his gloved palms on the ground, swinging his torso forward, arm muscles rippling, and then setting his torso down again, and so on, meanwhile passing Salem, who had just emerged through the glass doors of the convenience store wearing her jeans and her comfortable sweatshirt, her usually spiky hair sans mousse, making her look very much like an ordinary girl, a college student or one of the yuppie interns who lived in group houses in the area. Her long pale fingers were wrapped possessively around the forearm of Officer Perdue Hatfield.

Salem opened the back door and slid across. Hatfield hesitated. "You didn't tell me *he* was coming," he said of Jamal.

"We don't need you no way," Jamal said, looking out the windshield, refusing to make eye contact.

For one brief second Hatfield thought about eye contact: how black men never like to make it. He'd noticed it as far back as high school, with his friends on the football team and in the morning prayer club. You could see it when you watched pro basketball too—the players were all the time hugging and patting butts, but rarely did you catch them looking one another in the eye. He wondered if it had anything to do with evolution—like the way, in the animal kingdom, that looking into the eyes can be seen as a direct challenge, an invitation to fight. On the street they called it "mad doggin." It could get you killed. *You lookin at me?* Or maybe it had to do with slavery, how the black man was trained not to look into the face of his master, how conditioned behaviors over time can become stereotypical traits, which, as everyone knows, is part of the common thinking when it comes to the existence of a permanent black underclass in America. Or maybe it's just a boundaries thing. Like people always say, the eyes are the windows of the soul. Some people like to keep their shades drawn.

Freeman leaned across Jamal and offered his hand to the cop. "Officer Hatfield? I'm James Freeman, from the Advisory Neighborhood Commission? We have a little situation in progress here, sir."

Jamal directed Freeman's arm gently but firmly out of his personal space. "Look man," the pimp said to Hatfield, still avoiding eye contact, "if you too damn busy buyin doughnuts—"

"Listen you guys," Freeman said, the high-fag sibilant at the end of the word floating through the air like a football penalty flag. "Whatever beef you have, we need to put it aside. We've got two people missing."

Salem reached for the cop's hand. "Pretty please?"

45

Still sweating from his midmorning aerobics, Bert Metcalfe entered the crystal chamber wearing a shiny red tracksuit and tiny white Reebok high-tops. He was followed by his manservant, Thornton Desmond, who was carrying what appeared to be an antique doctor's valise.

This time the retractable ceiling was closed, giving the place a dim, cavelike feel. Thornton hefted the valise onto the central pedestal, then took a step backward, allowing Metcalfe his elbow room.

Standing on his tiptoes, Metcalfe opened the clasp of the valise. The Master Skull was nestled snugly into a bed of Italian silk. "The lining was done in Savile Row," he said.

"The craftsmanship is obvious," Thornton said. "I take it the valise was among his effects?"

"In the next to last box I opened."

"Rather ironic, don't you think, sir?"

"What's that, Thornton?"

"That he lost the skull but managed to save the valise."

"The skull was stolen from him in 1924, in Amsterdam. He was there to speak before the Royal Netherlands Academy of Sciences."

Despite himself, Thornton had found himself drawn in by the tale. "How did it happen?"

"Apparently, my grandfather hadn't been totally forthcoming with his hosts at the royal academy. They thought they were getting a lecture on pre-Mayan antiquities. According to his diary, from the moment he mentioned the lost continent of Atlantis and extraterrestrials, the company started booing. In his account he mentions 'a fusillade of overripe legumes.' Fleeing into the wings of the auditorium, he escaped into an alley, apparently, and made his way eastward toward the central station, looking to get out of town. Along the route, he stopped at a bar on Zeedijk Street, not far from the red-light district. Zeedijk and Stormsteeg. It's still there. According to my woman in Amsterdam, they're still using the original beer tap, dating to 1731."

"I'm to take it he felt the need of a pint?"

"More likely scotch—his drink of choice. He woke up in an alley at dawn with a ringing headache and a big lump on the back of his head. The valise—this very valise, which he'd had custom made in 1919—was lying open on the ground beside him."

"And the skull was gone."

"For the next sixty-some years. Until that marijuana clown bought it in a pawnshop for seventy guilders."

"And now here it is," Thornton marveled.

"Here it is," Metcalfe repeated. Using both hands, he removed the skull from its bed and placed it at the center of the pedestal. The recessed light set it aglow. He pulled a chamois cloth from the zipper pocket of his tracksuit and commenced polishing.

Thornton removed the valise to the floor. "If I may ask, sir . . . ?"

Buffing intently: "Yes?"

"Have you sussed out anything further about the reasons your father never talked about your grandfather, why the facts of your background were kept secret from you for all those years?"

"My father was called Bertram Hedgewick Metcalfe II—he was not a junior. He was raised by a man named Franklin Smith, who married my grandmother when my father was two. Smith was the only father he ever knew. His birth certificate lists his father as unknown."

"Obviously there was some embarrassment."

"Metcalfe wrote nothing about it in his journals, nothing I can find, though his descriptions of my grandmother's beauty do seem a bit over the top—even for a proud adoptive papa, if you know what I mean. From what I can gather, he was still in Tumbaatum at the time of the birth. And he never met the child who bore his name—up through the time of his death at the age of seventy-eight, two years before I was born. I found this one letter, from an old friend of my grandfather's, which alludes to Stuke's 'villainous behavior.'"

"And of course there was the duel in Belize."

"Which took place the year of my father's birth."

Thornton's eyes bugged. "Are you saying that Metcalfe might not be your actual grandfather?"

"Men fought duels for many reasons in those days," said Bertram Hedgewick Metcalfe III. "And people cut off communications for many reasons, as was the case with Metcalfe and my grandmother—we called her Gram Roberta. To my knowledge, after she left Belize, they never spoke nor saw each other again. The fact is, without Metcalfe's DNA, we'll never know for certain. His body was never found. They believe his boat was struck by lightning somewhere in the Caribbean Sea—he was still searching for Atlantis."

"And what of Stuke?"

"Another riddle. I've got people on it, but so far nothing; we have no idea how or when or where he died. It's as if he just disappeared off the face of the Earth."

"A pity, sir."

"It is as it is, Thornton. Truthfully, it doesn't matter to me. I have Metcalfe's name. I have his money. And I have his thirst for discovery, for seeking, for the unknown. I am his heir in every way, DNA or not." He stepped back to admire the skull. It sparkled and gleamed, a bright thing full of promise.

"So now what?" Thornton asked.

"What do you mean?"

"You've got the Master Skull. You've got the four others. You've got this whole *chambre.*" He pronounced the word with an exaggerated French accent, making a sweeping gesture with his hand. "*Quel prochain?* What next?"

Metcalfe looked up at his butler. "To be honest," he said, "I'm not sure. To my knowledge, no one has ever gathered five skulls together in one place—at least no one we know about."

"So at this point—"

A light on the wall behind the two men began to flash, indicating the presence of visitors at the service door of the carriage house at the front of the property.

"Go see who that is, will you please?" Metcalfe requested. "And send up the detective and the girl—she was here overnight, was she not?"

"Since about midnight, sir. He brought her when he brought the skull. She stayed in the Princess Suite."

"Maybe she knows how to make this thing work."

46

Salem, Jamal, Jim Freeman, and Perdue Hatfield—who was absent from his post without permission, a potential firing offense—stood before the door of Metcalfe's carriage house in upper Georgetown.

"Ring again," Jamal ordered, annoyed.

"The main house is back there beyond the gardens," Salem explained, attempting to mollify him. "It takes a while for them to answer."

Hatfield couldn't help but notice that she'd once again dropped her black-girl accent in favor of a slight southern twang. "People of this echelon usually have a guard on duty." He unsnapped the safety strap that held his Glock in its holster. "Something here doesn't feel right."

Freeman pointed to a large ceramic gargoyle perched beneath the eaves. "That's a camera up there, isn't it?"

"I thought that was his tongue," giggled Salem.

"Girl, you mind always in the gutter," Jamal said.

"I thought that too at first," Hatfield said, coming to her defense. "It's a clever concealment—first-rate."

Salem looked up at the big cop; their eyes met. Finally it came to her—who Hatfield reminded her of. It had been bugging her since the first time she saw him, walking along Fourteenth

Street, twirling his baton: *Why does that guy look so familiar?* When she was in ninth grade, there was this boy who lived with his father a couple of spaces down from her and her mom at the Launchpad Mobile Home Park. He was two years older, played lineman on the football team. Without fail, he'd show up every morning to walk her to school. Obviously he liked her, but he was always too shy to make a move. There was something so sweet about him, so innocent and courtly. Just like Hatfield.

"There's probably a full monitoring station inside the home," Freeman opined. "It's standard these days in high-end properties."

As if on cue, Thornton's voice emanated from an unseen speaker. "Good afternoon. How may I help you?"

Salem stepped forward like Dorothy in *The Wizard of Oz*. "We'd like to see the little guy," she said.

Long pause. "Miss Clark? Is that you? I don't believe your next appointment is scheduled until Monday afternoon."

"*Appointment?*" Jamal turned angrily toward Salem, but she ignored him. She addressed the camera: "Would it be possible for me to please talk to him? Just for a minute? Tell him I remembered somethin about my father."

"I'm afraid that would be impossible, miss," Thornton intoned.

Now Hatfield stepped forward and removed his cap. He aimed his honest moon face toward the camera. "Officer Perdue Hatfield, sir, Metropolitan Police. I'm here to investigate a possible missing person. Please open the door at once."

"Do you have a warrant, officer?"

"Not at this time, sir."

"All police contacts must be made through our attorney," the butler said. "It's house policy. I'm frightfully sorry."

Hatfield pulled out a pad and pen. "Can you tell me who that is?"

"I'm afraid I'm not at liberty to divulge that information."

"Then how the *fuck* we supposed to contact him?" Salem asked, lapsing into ghetto for emphasis.

Freeman stepped forward from behind the others—a tall group, they'd kept him thus far concealed. He projected his most gracious self. "Good afternoon. I'm James Freeman, from the Advisory Neighborhood Commission? We're the group that—"

"Jim Freeman?"

"Thornton? Thornton Desmond?"

The butler hooted with laughter. "I can *not* believe this!"

"I knew that sonorous Irish tenor sounded too familiar!" Freeman enthused. "The envy in piano bars all over town."

"Aie, but ye flatter me, sir," Thornton said, laying on the brogue.

Freeman let loose a rip-roaring specimen of his trademark laugh, a booming baritone giggle that echoed off the centuries-old brick into the clean, cold air of upper Georgetown. He looked to his fellows—this unlikely confederacy—seeking his props. "It's been what . . . since the gala at the clinic?"

"I still have our photo with Liz."

"Are you kidding? I keep it on my nightstand."

"So what's up?" Thornton asked.

"We have a little problem," Freeman said. "You think you could let us in?"

Now it was Thornton's turn to laugh—a dry, wry, single malt cackle, reminiscent of the doorkeeper of the Emerald City. "Why didn't you just say so in the first place?"

47

Kwan and three of his homeboys moved along the sidewalk like a squad of marines on urban recon, the merch tags on their identical Timberland boots flapping in muffled concert. A fourth homeboy was parked around the corner in Kwan's Jeep Cherokee, engine idling. Though they were only eight blocks, as the pigeon flies, from the border of their own neighborhood, they might as well have been in Bosnia—almost every day someone in town was shot (or at least shot *at*) for no worse offense than being on the wrong block. There was a war going on in the streets of the nation's capital—a war on drugs, a war on values, a war between the haves and have nots, between different groups of have nots. Kwan and his boyz had been born and raised in this context; they thought of themselves as soldiers, they lived by their wits. Such was the fact of their lives. Deep behind enemy lines, the strain of their mission showed on their young faces.

Turning into the alley, they moved in single file past a shot-out streetlight, past an abandoned station wagon, an abandoned minivan, a blackened steel drum surrounded with milk crates and broken chairs . . .

And there he was, in a dark pool of blood beneath the weed tree.

Kwan knelt down, pulled off his right glove with his teeth, placed his fingertips on Seede's neck, looking for a pulse. His eyes narrowed with concentration.

48

Jamal stood on the roof of Metcalfe Mansion with his hands on his hips. "*Holy shit,*" he said, genuinely impressed by the view.

Salem pointed to the southeast. "There's the White House!"

"And the Washington Monument," said Freeman.

"The stone bone," Jamal laughed.

Hatfield threw him a look.

The metal catwalk led across the roof, to another door, thick and armor-plated, like a ship's hatch. Before Thornton could place his palm on the light box, the door opened.

Detective Massimo Bandini emerged from the chamber, followed by Sojii. "Where's Metcalfe?" he demanded of the butler.

"Sojii!" exclaimed Jim Freeman. Instinctively he opened his arms. The girl ran to his embrace.

Hatfield froze. He was, after all, derelict from duty. Then it occurred to him: *What the hell is IAD doing here?*

"What do you mean, 'Where's Metcalfe?'" the butler demanded. "He sent for you. He's in *there.*"

"Yeah? Then you find him," challenged Bandini.

The group followed Thornton into the crystal chamber.

The ceiling was closed, the room was dark. Sitting on their pedestals, lit from beneath, the five skulls glowed.

At the center of the room, on the floor in front of the fifth pedestal, was a puddle of red nylon—Metcalfe's tracksuit. Also in evidence were his black bikini briefs, white ankle socks, and Reebok workout shoes.

Hatfield walked over to the pile of laundry. He pulled a pen from the breast pocket of his shirt, fished out a platinum and diamond Rolex chronograph. The band was still clasped shut. He checked the time against his own watch.

"This thing stopped ten minutes ago," he said.

Epilogue

Dulcy sank, noodlelike, into the passenger seat of the four-door Saturn, a gleam of contentment in her eyes. On her feet she wore a pair of disposable rubber slippers. Little wads of cotton formed barriers between her toes, the nails of which had just been lacquered a vampish shade of red. The sun streaming through the windshield was warm on her skin; the breeze off the Pacific was cool. She stretched luxuriantly, stared into the cloudless blue sky. "There is *nothing* like a manicure/pedicure," she sighed.

Seede issued a supportive grin. "That's great, honey," he said. "Now could you please close the door?"

"Yeah, *Mom*." Jake poked his head between the sand-colored bucket seats. He was six years old, missing his two front teeth. "We've been waiting for, like, two *hours*."

"Actually, it's only been twenty minutes," Seede said, reaching into the back, giving Jake's calf a squeeze. The skin was soft and pliant; the muscle had surprising bulk. Three foot eight, fifty-two pounds, the eating-crying-shitting machine had become an ally.

It was late September 1997. They were parked on the main drag of a small coastal town in southern California. Nearly five years had passed since the Seedes left Washington, courtesy of a sizable check from Hollywood. (The movie was still "in development." It would probably never get made. No matter: the studio's drop in the bucket had been more than enough to push the reset button on their lives.) During that time, of course, history had continued its march. NASA had succeeded in putting Pathfinder on Mars. Britain had returned Hong Kong to China. A sheep named Dolly had been cloned from the udder cells of a ewe. Princess Diana of Wales had been killed in an auto accident. Conflicts raged in the Middle East, the Balkans, Chechnya, and Nepal. In Africa, hunger, AIDS, and tribal genocide ruled the day. In Indonesia a large chunk of the rain forest was on fire. Perhaps the sky *was* falling: it was certainly full of particulate matter, which made for breathtaking sunsets. The world's population had reached five and a half billion. Humankind muddled through.

On the home front, the handsome guy from Arkansas—who'd kicked off his first presidential term on a hopeful if misguided note, seeking to normalize the country's relationship with homosexuals in the military—had embarked upon his second term, promising "A New Nation for a New Century." (In the end he'd be impeached by Congress for receiving a blow job in his office—a scenario fantasized, no doubt, at one time or another, by every human male who ever had an office.) The war on drugs continued apace—the can't-miss, law-and-order platform having been co-opted by the Democrats. Jails and prisons across the nation were overflowing; more were being built. At the same time, according to the government's own figures, the use of cocaine and marijuana by teenagers was steadily rising, the use of ecstasy and crystal methamphetamine had reached "epidemic" proportions, and there was a glut on the market of cheap heroin from Afghanistan.

Shortly after Metcalfe disappeared, leaving behind a small puddle of laundry and personal effects, Thornton discovered a file of documents in the study off the master bedroom. Included was a notarized statement recognizing Salem Irene Clark as Metcalfe's legal daughter and heir, granting her a small trust fund, a healthy allowance, and a seat on the board of directors of the Metcalfe Foundation, effective immediately. Also included were the results of the DNA tests, authorized by Detective Massimo Bandini, which confirmed Metcalfe's parenthood. (After an intradepartmental hearing on charges of misconduct and abuse of police authority, Bandini and John O'Rourke were allowed to take early retirement with full pensions; they continued to be employed on a contract basis by the Metcalfe Foundation.) In return Metcalfe had asked only that Salem name her first son—if ever there was one—Bertram Hedgewick Metcalfe IV.

As it turned out, the name would go to Salem's first adopted son—the little boy from the squalid R Street rooming house. After his mother's death, Child Protective Services had never been able to locate any kin—neither could they find any record of his name. When Pastor Steinschmidt passed this information along, Perdue Hatfield knew immediately what he had to do. He married Salem, adopted the boy, and quit the police force—in that order, over the period of a year. The trio now lived in Metcalfe Mansion. Hatfield ran a company that provided security to performers and venues in the greater DC area—ushers, bouncers, bodyguards, transport, counterterrorism, full service. "You'll be safer than a pig in a blanket," he promised his prospective clients in his proud, backwoods drawl.

In granting Sojii's petition for emancipation as a minor—brought pro bono by the Pope's former *consigliore*, Waylon Weidenfeld—a DC superior court judge named Jim Freeman as Sojii's guardian and trustee. Jim died in 1995, due to complications of AIDS. He and Sojii had lived together in his Corcoran Street showplace until the day before his death. On his last morning, he awakened in his fifteen-hundred-thread-count Egyptian cotton sheets, sat bolt upright, and demanded to be removed immediately to a hospice, his entry into which had been carefully prearranged: nothing killed a property's value like a dead body in the master suite. He died that evening with his friends gathered around—a gem of a man, a pro, fabulously organized to the last. The house would eventually sell for $476,000. He and Tom paid seventy-five.

Also departed: Wayne Tony, of liver disease; Larry the Pharmacist, of an overdose; Bo Franklin, of a massive stroke suffered during a night of heavy partying with two female friends. (Seede liked to imagine the bitches killed *him* with an orgasm.) Kwan Johnston was confined to a wheelchair, paralyzed from the waist down after a shoot-out with a rival gang. Jamal Alfred was living now in Orlando, where he'd squared up with his bottom wife, Debbie. With Salem as a silent partner, he'd opened a Ford/Lincoln/Mercury dealership. Thanks to the new Mustang and the line of trucks, he was doing well. And every three months, he got a new Lincoln to drive. As for the Pope of Pot: following his death from pancreatic cancer, DCCJ officials incorrectly reported the cause to the media as lung cancer, sparking a fierce round of smoked-himself-to-the-grave happy talk by evening news anchors across the nation. It was a death, as the Pope himself had correctly predicted, that launched a thousand quips.

After Jim's death, Sojii moved into Metcalfe Mansion. Along with Thornton Desmond—who'd been granted a sizable pension but had elected to stay on to oversee the staff—she often helped care for little Bertie IV. Sojii was due to graduate in June from Georgetown University with a dual major in psychology and philosophy. Though she never met her mother again, in real time or through scrying, she did find, as the years went by, that the mysterious faux meeting in the boutique had helped to give her a sense of closure. In any case, the fact of her mother's abandonment would always be there, a part of her personal landscape.

In addition to college, Sojii was employed full-time by the Metcalfe Foundation, charged with unlocking the secrets of the Master Skull—and, ultimately, with determining the fate of Bert Metcalfe III. With no body in evidence, and no proof of his death, Metcalfe's legal status remained indeterminate. A police report had been filed; an all points bulletin had been issued through Interpol. Over the years, with the help of the budding World Wide Web, Sojii had established contact with many crystal skull groups around the globe—a staggering number of people had strong opinions and intricate beliefs. Under her direction, the foundation had summoned many of the world's brightest minds to Metcalfe Mansion. Provided a handsome stipend, they were asked to ruminate upon the tiny billionaire's disappearance. There were many hypotheses; a volume was being prepared for publication. The science guys proposed answers from the fields of biology, chemistry, and physics; the religion guys invoked their gods; the star watchers their aliens; the philosophers their philosophies; and so forth. As is the case with all of life's greatest conundrums—Is there a God? What is our purpose on Earth? What happens after we die? Why can't we all get along?—the bottom line was this: there is no good answer, you just have to live with the unknown.

Each year on Metcalfe's birthday, a large public party was held on the grounds of the mansion. As the story of his mysterious disappearance spread, the day became more widely observed. In time, a growing number of people began to think of Bertie the Hedgehog as a sort of modern Moses—a man summoned to a mountaintop by a higher power. They waited expectantly in the valley for his return.

Dulcy pulled the car door shut, a weird muffled thunk, owing to the revolutionary dent-proof material employed in the construction of the highly rated family sedan. "What we *really* need is a second car," she said.

"We have the motorcycle . . ." Seede offered.

"You haven't been on that thing in a year. You should just call the Salvation Army and take the deduction—they'll haul it away for free."

Alarmed, Jake poked his head up front again. "Daddy said *I* could have his motorcycle when I get older!"

"I said," Seede clarified, "that when you got to the NBA you could keep it for me in your garage."

"With my Humvee and my monster truck, right?"

"And one of those cute little two-door Mercedes for your dear ole dad."

"And season tickets," Jake reminded him.

"And season tickets," Seede confirmed, "so I can always watch you play."

Seede started the engine, checked the rearview mirror, pulled into traffic. It had taken time to adjust to driving. Depth perception—a critical faculty he'd definitely taken for granted. At first he'd tried a glass eye. It had to be cleaned and assiduously maintained, bathed in various solutions, sterilized. Viewed from his left side, it gave him the appearance of a wax figure at Madame Tussaud's—an uncanny likeness, not quite alive. In the end he'd elected to forgo the prosthesis in favor of a simple black patch, which served also to obscure some of the ropey scarring that radiated from his temple. It was not a pretty sight, but it was him.

Following his rescue by Kwan and his homeboys, Seede had been rushed into an operating room at George Washington University Hospital, where specialists in brain, eye, and craniofacial surgery took turns addressing his injuries—depressed skull fracture, broken orbital bone, crushed eyeball, severed optic nerve.

He awoke two days later in dim light, vaguely nauseous, feeling like he was floating on a raft in the middle of the ocean, the victim of a shipwreck. Over the next few hours, as he drifted in and out of consciousness, as the morphine in his system began to dissipate—he wasn't yet aware that he could push a button and self-administer—the details of his immediate past returned to him, first in flickering snapshots, then in longer snippets, like video clips.

With his unbandaged eye, he looked around the room, which he could see now was not a room at all, but rather an ICU bay, machines beeping and blinking, a curtain pulled around for privacy. There was no cheering public to comfort him, no blanket of accolades to keep him warm, no great American tome to hold his hand. He thought about Dulcy, playfully pinning back the curtain of her bathrobe to reveal her swelling tummy. He thought about Jake, smushing a Play-Doh man, laughing uproariously.

I could have died, he told himself.

A sinkhole opened at the center of his being; into the void flooded a molten river of panic and remorse.

He felt like someone who'd just this instant hit his head on a rock at the bottom of a murky pond and felt his neck break.

What have I done?

The Saturn labored up an incline, through a canyon, the steep slope on either side overgrown with fragrant eucalyptus and coastal sage. Cresting the hill, they went through a traffic light, then turned left into a parking lot.

A line of portable toilets stood sentry in the foreground; beyond was an immense grassy field. Here and there, knots of children were shouting and kicking balls. Parents lounged on blankets and beach chairs, whistles blew. In the distance you could see the ocean. A pair of red-tailed hawks and a lone paraglider wheeled in the thermal updrafts.

The doors opened and the Seede family emerged, reassembled itself into a tight threesome on the grass behind the car. Seede sank to his knees, a pair of size-two soccer cleats in his hand. Jake offered his right foot—for balance he rested his sticky palm atop his father's bald head. As Seede pulled the laces tight, tied a double knot, the boy plucked absently at the elastic strap of his father's eye patch. Every Halloween, Jake insisted on dressing up as a pirate. An eye patch figured prominently in his costume.

"A'ight," Seede said, finishing off the second shoe, recalling a bit of ghetto dialect lest his son forget his roots. He offered his fist for a pound, the culture's latest iteration of handshake; his son met him halfway, knuckle to knuckle, a miniature fist that very much resembled his own. The boy gamboled off to join his friends.

Retrieving a bag of soccer balls from the trunk of the Saturn, Seede took Dulcy's hand. With time, with couple's therapy, with the infusion of the new money and a chance at a new start, Seede and his wife had managed to get the wheels back onto their marriage, to set it moving forward again. Of course, as the one who'd upset the applecart in the first place, wormy though it may have been, the onus had been on Seede to repent, to renounce, to earn back trust. This he did with due diligence, becoming in time the very model of a husband and father. For her part, Dulcy never accepted any responsibily for Seede's descent into madness—at least she never said anything out loud, though certain hints and nonverbal clues (beyond the boilerplate urged by the therapist) suggested she had heard and acknowledged some of his complaints. For a while Seede resented this unfairness, the uneven standards and unspoken truths that were required to make a domestic partnership work. He couldn't help but wonder: Why should *he* have to be the big guy? Why should *he* have to be the one to suck it up? Why should *he* have to admit fault when fault was clearly shared?

As the years passed, as his experience compounded, generating as it did a few percentage points of wisdom, Seede came to realize that this was the way things were, the way they were going to be. Yes, he could have divorced her, he could have found someone else, someone with a different set of pros and cons, but the vision of the hapless weekend dad was deterrent enough. And besides: he still loved his wife; he had never stopped loving her. And he loved his son with a lightness and with a gravity that he was only beginning to understand. Together, as corny as it seemed, the three of them were truly a whole that was greater than the sum of its parts. How smug he had been in his own certainty. How little he had really known. Compromise, he now understood, doesn't always mean that everyone gets exactly what they want. It's the price you pay for being part of something bigger than yourself. It's the price you pay for not being alone.

The couple crossed the field at a comfortable pace, moving westward, toward the area reserved for Jake's team. From their vantage point on the bluff, they could see clearly the curvature of the Earth; the cerulean waters shimmered in the slanting light from the late afternoon sun. Living near the ocean, facing the limitless horizon every day, Seede had a constant reminder of his place in the order of things, small but not insignificant. He still had his lofty goals; he still wanted to make his mark; he still wanted to do what *he* wanted to do.

It just so happened that some of what he wanted to do had changed.

Acknowledgments

Special thanks to Morgan Entrekin, Jamison Stoltz, David Granger, Peter Griffin, Tyler Cabot, Mollie Glick, and Will Balliett. And to Dora Simons, John Bugge, Albert Murray, Steve Jones, Ken Ringle, Walt Harrington, Bob Love, William Greider, Kurt Andersen, Richard Ben Cramer, and Hunter S. Thompson.

And to my son, Miles, who has taught me more than any teacher.

I would also like to thank the following, who provided support, information, and inspiration, both in word and deed:

Fr. John Adams, Phil Adams, Lawrence Alfred, Ph.D., Gayla Button, James Canfield, Bob Carter, Michael Ellis Cezar, Robert E. Jones, Salem Ciuffa, Sheri and Dr. Steven R. Cohen, Marieke de Lorijn, Carole Davis-Wilson, Maureen and Geoff Diner, Desmond Gorges, Peggy and Jeff Grant, Sam Freedman, Jim Honey, James A. Johnson, Jr., O. K. Jones, Marshall Keys and Eva Hambach, Eric Konigsberg, Terrell Lamb, Edwin Lap, Ariel Levy, Andrew Mayer, Dr. Hal Meltzer, Allan Miller, Tom Morgan, Tony Morgan, Steve Mowbray, Randy Olaque, Clayton Patterson, Renay and Bill Regardie, Shiya Rebosky, Jo and Jeff Ricks, Beverly and Marvin Sager, Wendy Sager, Henry Schuster,

Susan Sharpe, Ronald K. Siegel, PhD, Col. Robert O. Sinclair, Mitch Snider, Earna and the Rev. John Steinbruck, Richard Sweren, Dr. Glenn Vanstrum, David Williams, Bill Wooby.

The following books were helpful in my research:

Danger My Ally: The True Life Adventures of F. A. Mitchell-Hedges, by F. A. Mitchell-Hedges.

The Crystal Skull, by Richard M. Garvin.

Holy Ice: Bridge to the Subconscious, by Frank Dorland.

The Skull Speaks through Carole Davis, edited by Brian Hadley-James.

Mysteries of the Crystal Skulls Revealed, by Sandra Bowen, F. R. Nocerino, and Joshua Shapiro.

The Mystery of the Crystal Skulls, by Chris Morton and Ceri Louise Thomas.